HELL'S
FURY

Copyright © 2024 by Right House

All rights reserved.

The characters and events portrayed in this ebook are fictitious. Any similarity to real persons, living or dead, is coincidental and not intended by the author.

No part of this book may be reproduced in any form or by any electronic or mechanical means, including information storage and retrieval systems, without written permission from the author, except for the use of brief quotations in a book review.

ISBN-13: 978-1-63696-407-2

ISBN-10: 1-63696-407-9

Cover design by: Damonza

Printed in the United States of America

www.righthouse.com

www.instagram.com/righthousebooks

www.facebook.com/righthousebooks

twitter.com/righthousebooks

USA TODAY **BESTSELLING** AUTHORS

BLAKE BANNER
DAVID ARCHER

HELL'S FURY

A ROGUE THRILLER

RIGHTHOUSE

But wherefore thou alone? Wherefore with thee came not all Hell broke loose?

John Milton, Paradise Lost, bk 4. 1.917

ONE

I WAS ON WEST 81ST STREET, JUST BEFORE IT MEETS Riverside Drive. I was parked outside an apartment block with a red awning, watching the elegant redbrick house across the road at number 320. I was watching it because somehow I knew it belonged to me. And though there was no one there right now, in my mind I could see a woman leaning out of the second floor bow window, waving at me and laughing.

And I knew that woman was my wife.

It was the first clear memory I'd had since I'd woken up in a RAM 1500 on South 4th Place, off Ocean Boulevard on Long Beach, and realized I had no idea who I was.[1] I should have got out of my car and gone and rung the bell. I should have spoken to the porter in the apartment block with the red awning. I should have got out and made some kind of contact to see who, if anyone, recognized me.

---

1. See *Rogue Book One, Gates of Hell*

But the thought of being recognized increased my heart rate, twisted my gut, and made me feel nauseous. So instead, I fired up the Grand Cherokee, pulled out onto the Henry Hudson Parkway, made a big twenty-minute loop around Washington Heights, and without knowing where I was going or why I was going there, I came down the Harlem River Driveway and crossed the Madison Avenue Bridge into the Bronx. On 138th, I began to slow and hustled into the center lane. I passed under the railway bridge, and when I saw Park Avenue, I knew I had to turn left. I cruised slowly through the desolation, past the hundred parked yellow cabs, past the old redbrick warehouses and the graffiti that wanted to be art but lacked soul.

And then, suddenly, it was there, on my right, the place where I was going. It was set back from the road with its red steel shutters pulled down, the Portales del Infierno Club. Two giant murals on the façade depicted cowgirls dressed in just a Stetson and a lasso, all a cowgirl needs to draw a bull through the portals of hell. One of them had wings and a halo. The other had horns.

I stopped the car and stared. I knew the place. It wasn't a clear memory, like West 81st. There I could associate a woman, the action of leaning out the window, laughter, the feeling of being welcomed home. This was different. No associated memories came with the image of the building. It was just a fact. I knew this place. The rest was blackness.

For a moment, I saw Dr. Elizabeth Grant's face in my mind, watching me carefully as she asked me, "If you could discover who you are, Rogue, who would you be?"

I had thought it was a stupid question at the time, and I had told her so. Now looking at this club, located in the darkest part of the Bronx, I began to get some idea of what she was driving at. Who was I? Upper West Side, married to a beautiful, happy wife with a happy home? Or a ruthless killer whose natural environment was a club called the Gates of Hell, opposite the railway tracks in South Bronx?

Do we get to choose who we are? Or does our inner nature decide? Or our conditioning?

A door in one of the cowgirls' calves opened, and a black guy who was six foot six barefoot and about that again from shoulder to shoulder, stepped out carrying a crate of empty Coke bottles. He dumped the crate and stood staring at me. His black T-shirt said, *Bin to Hell and Back now I Miss it*.

He was about twenty feet away. He jerked his chin at me and raised his voice.

"You want something?"

I glanced at him, then directed my attention back to the mural and smiled.

"Yeah, I used to come here. Good memories. Remind me what time you open."

He took a few steps closer and narrowed his eyes, studying my face.

"You used to come here? When was that?"

I made like I was thinking and found myself actually trying to remember.

"Must be three or four months ago at least. I went out west. Had an accident and wound up in hospital."

"You breakin' my heart."

I sighed. "Right. Nice shooting the breeze with you. What time do you open?"

"Eleven p.m. Same as we did three or four months ago."

"Right. Thanks. You have a good one."

He didn't answer, and I drove away.

I took my time. I drove slowly, scanning the shops, laundromats, parks, and lawns that lined Westchester Avenue under the railway tracks. I was searching, searching for anything familiar, for anything I knew and recognized. But I was trying too hard. There were times when everything looked familiar, but at others, it all just looked like everything else, a great miasma of maybe.

I came eventually to a large intersection, and as I looked around me, I became suddenly hyper aware. I was intensely aware of stupid things like the fish market on my right, the McDonald's on my left, the three sets of stairs rising to the railway tracks above, like a drawing by Escher. I knew the place, and I knew I had to turn right down Longwood Avenue. I glanced at the street name half concealed behind a street lamp and a telegraph pole and saw, with a hot stab in my belly, that this was Longwood Avenue.

I moved on, among old redbrick apartment blocks with their façades scarred by ancient iron fire escapes, like dark images out of Gotham City. Then there was the massive I-278 overpass. I moved through its shadows and came out in a place whose very soul was destitution, desolation, and emptiness. Here there were no apartment blocks or houses or homes. Here there were empty, overgrown lots behind broken sidewalks. Here there were ramshackle ruins overgrown with weeds. Here there were fences and walls defaced with obscene graffiti. Here there were no people. There were only cars trying to get through without being mugged or shot.

I entered this place, this ugly world, and felt the hot glow of excitement in my gut. I could sense that I was close to something, to a prey, and I was closing for the kill.

My hands, working of their own volition, turned me left onto Garrison Avenue and then right onto Burnett Place. There I pulled over and stopped. There was a corrugated steel fence over on my right. On my left a big yard with trucks in it. I pulled up to the sidewalk beside that yard and killed the engine. Maybe thirty yards away, on the far side of the road, there were three women standing talking. They were outside a small redbrick building that had green wooden shutters over the windows, and green iron bars over the shutters. The door, also green, was partly open, but inside, all you could see was darkness.

One of the girls was black. She had on a red vinyl garment that was more like a belt than a skirt. She was generously built and had on a blue halter neck that could barely contain her generosity. She was leaning against the wall beside the door talking to a second girl, who was leaning her ass against the hood of a cream '65 Mustang. That girl was white and had jeans so tight you could almost hear her legs gasping for air. She had on a purple silk blouse open and knotted at her belly. It didn't conceal much, but mainly because there wasn't much to conceal.

The third girl looked Latina. She had on denim shorts and a T-shirt that only came to her solar plexus. She was probably five foot two, but her heels gave her another four inches.

Behind her, there was a sofa on the sidewalk. There was a small dog curled up there with a tabby cat. I hit the horn, and the three girls turned and looked. The black girl shrugged and spread her hands, and mouthed, *What do you want?*

I fired up the engine again and rolled over till I was beside them. She leaned in the window and smiled, then blew a bubble with the gum she was chewing. I smiled like I thought she was cute.

"I'm looking for Sandra."

"Sandra Dee?"

I knew it meant something and I should laugh, so I did. "No, I don't know her second name. But we had a good thing, you know? Only she wouldn't give me her phone number."

She pouted and frowned and put her chin in her hand. "Oh, man. That's sad. Bad old Sandra. You're new to this whole thing, right?"

I shrugged. "I guess."

"Well, I don't know Sandra, and I know most all the girls round here, so I think maybe she moved on, lover boy. But I can introduce you to some real nice girls if you're feeling lonesome."

I gave her another smile. "That would be nice. Can you introduce me to you? I like you."

"What's your name, lover?"

"My friend told me to say my name was John. John Smith."

"Sounds like you got a friend you should listen to."

"Maybe." I laughed out loud. "I'm not sure how smart he is. I make a hell of a lot more money than he does."

Her left eyebrow arched high. "Really...?"

"Listen." I frowned. "Is there somewhere we can go, you know, for a bit of privacy?"

She looked over her shoulder at the open door. The other two girls were talking but glanced at her from time to time.

"Can you show me some cash?" She said it still looking at the door, then looked back at me.

"Sure. How much do you want to see?"

Her smile deepened. It said she was beginning to like me back. "How much you got?"

I laughed. "Don't make me go to the trunk!" I reached in my inside pocket, and from my wallet, I took two grand and showed it to her. "All I'm asking for is some privacy and some comfort. I'm not looking for champagne and oysters—not today anyhow—but I'm not looking for a five-minute fumble in a back alley either."

She pointed at me. "Don't go away!"

I watched her walk back to the old redbrick and push through the door. The girls outside grinned at me and waved. One of them called out, "You wanna party, handsome?"

I waved back and winked. "Maybe later, if you're still around."

My generous friend emerged and returned to the car. She climbed in beside me and winked. "You gonna make a right, then you gonna make another right onto Longwood and go under the freeway, then you gonna make another right onto Southern Boulevard, and you gonna stop outside eight twenty-four, and we gonna go up and have a party."

""Now you're talking my language," I said. I fired up the engine and nodded toward her friends. "Your friends said they wanted to party too."

HELL'S FURY | 7

"You want we should bring them along? I'm beginning to think you are one fun-lovin' guy!"

I laughed. "Maybe later. Let's settle in and see what kind of mood we're in. That OK with you?"

"Hey! You're payin'. I just wanna make you happy."

"Well ain't that nice!"

Eight twenty-four Southern Boulevard in the Bronx, right on the border with Hunts Point, was everything you would expect it to be. An iron gate gave access to a small courtyard, and a red fire-door gave access to a small lobby, decorated with early twenty-first century graffiti that wasn't so much erotic as disgusting. An elevator that was on the senile side of old dragged us to the sixth floor, and a soulless corridor took us to a door that had recently had the lock smashed in and replaced. She slipped in the key and pushed open the door.

I followed her through two flimsy, glass paneled doors on the left to a living room with a couple of armchairs and a sofa which looked like they'd come from the thrift shop. There was also a coffee table designed for snorting coke, a brand new giant TV bolted to the wall, and not much else.

I had grabbed my sports bag from the trunk when we'd left the Jeep, and now I dumped it on the sofa. She looked at it and came and stood close to me.

"You take that everywhere you go?"

I ignored the question and asked one of my own. "Is there anything to drink in this place?"

"Oh, now honey, you should have thought of that when we was downstairs. I can't let you drink my Charlie's liquor, can I?"

"Why not?"

"Because he'd kill me, baby!"

"That would be a shame, just when we were getting along so well."

She made a blend of a frown and a smile that suggested she didn't really get where I was coming from. "You want we should go to the bedroom, lover?"

"Charlie, huh?" That made her drop the smile and just frown. I went on. "I'm in the mood for a party. It's been a tough month, and I really need to let go. You know? What's your name?"

She arched her left eyebrow again and said, "Xena with an X."

"Xena, you're real cute, and what I really need is a few beers, some whiskey and a good snort. And some music, we could dance." She was still frowning, but the smile was touching the corners of her mouth. I cupped her face in my hands. "Money is really not a problem. You want to see something really beautiful?"

"Sure."

I took her hand and pulled her gently to the sofa. There I unzipped the sports bag and opened it. Her eyes went very wide, and the frown surrendered her whole face to the smile. She embraced my left arm with both of hers and sighed, "Oh man... Ain't that a pretty sight!"

I leaned close and whispered in her ear, "It's half a million bucks of pretty, but it's still not as pretty as you, babe. Now do you think Charlie can supply us with the essentials for a party, or not?"

"I think maybe he can, lover. I am pretty sure he can."

"Is he in the house where I picked you up?"

"Mm-hmm, but he don't like visitors."

"But he likes cash, right?"

"Let me call him, babe."

I winked at her. "Knock yourself out. But make it quick. I'm getting bored. I need a drink, and I need a rush."

She pulled her cell from a zipper in her red vinyl skirt, dialed, and put her finger to her lips telling me to be quiet. After a moment, she spoke in a husky voice all full of sugar.

"Hi, baby. Listen, I got this guy and he keeps talking about makin' a party... No, baby, he's inside, in the bedroom. I come out to the living room. He can't hear me. Listen to me. He's got a sports bag and it is full—I do mean full—of cash. There's gotta be a half a million bucks in there, babe."

She was quiet for a while, listening. Then:

"No, slow down, baby. Listen to me. First of all, he wants to buy coke and liquor and bring in a couple more girls for a party..." She sighed. "Charlie, will you just listen for a minute? Just think about it. He got that money from somewhere, right? He had that bag in his truck. How many more has he got stashed at home? Let's find out, right? Let's get him high, drunk, and happy and get him talking. We find out what he's about and how much more cash does he have. Am I wrong, Charlie?" She gave a girlie giggle and added, "I'm your baby, lover boy."

She hung up and winked at me. I said:

"You're going to get me drunk and high and make me happy?"

"You heard me."

"You are a very bad lady."

"Don't you forget it."

"Let's go and talk to Charlie."

She wagged a finger at me in the negative and brought all her generous curves over to where I was standing by the sofa.

"Not yet, lover boy. You know, cash always makes me hot. So I need to cool off just a little. You think you can cool me off a bit, Mr. Smith?"

I gave a little shrug with my eyebrows. "I guess one good turn deserves another, Xena. I think I can cool you off just a bit."

And I did.

TWO

It didn't take long to cool her off. We showered, and while I was getting dressed and she was putting her belt back on, I asked her:

"So is Charlie your boyfriend?"

She laughed a lot, high-pitched and loud. When she was done, she flapped her hand at me. "Lover, I don't know where you bin the last thirty years, or how you make your money, but you are sweet and innocent when it comes to men and women, ain't you?" She came over to me and held my face. "See, lover, I am what we call in the Bronx a whore, and Charlie, he my pimp. You know what them things are?"

"Sure. So he's your pimp. Does he live in that place with the green shutters and the sofa outside, where I picked you up?"

"No, that's like what you might call his office."

"So he lives here? He's letting us use his apartment?"

"Are you kidding? Man, you really is naïve! That boy is makin' serious *money*."

I made my laugh derisive as I pulled on my boots. "I'm not that naïve, Xena. I know how it goes. I buy my shit for five hundred grand, I sell it on the street for seven hundred and fifty grand, but two thirds of that has to go back to my supplier. And what's left I am going to blow on coke and cars and bribes, and by the end of the month I have made almost a million bucks, but I have spent almost a million bucks."

She came and stood in front of me with her hands on her hips. "Yeah?" she said and cocked a hip. "You that smart? Well let me tell you, you ain't as smart as you think you are, lover. Charlie don't touch the shit, and he don't let his boys touch it neither. That money he makes, he invest it!"

I laughed again. "He invests it? What, in the stock exchange? Does he take it down to Wall Street in a wheelbarrow?"

"No, wiseass. He invests it in money laundering. He got a restaurant on Morris Park Avenue, a nice neighborhood, he owns a bar on College Point Boulevard, and he is savin' to invest in—" She waved a dismissive hand at me. "I don't need to prove shit to you. But he don't live *here*, I can tell you that much."

I got up off the bed. "Come on, don't get mad at me. He sounds like a guy with his head screwed on. Where does he live if not here?"

She cocked her hip again, flipped her hand like she was holding Yorick's skull, and moved her head from side to side like she'd dislocated her neck. "He bought hisself a four bedroom apartment on the corner of 165th Street and the Grand Concourse, five minutes from the Yankee Stadium

HELL'S FURY | 13

and right across the road from the Bronx Museum of Fine Arts."

"Four bedrooms, huh?" I put my hand on the small of her back and eased her toward the door. "You seem awful proud of him. You going to live there too?"

"That's what he told me. And that's a thing about Charlie. He *always* does what he says he's gonna do."

"He sounds like quite a guy. I'm looking forward to meeting him."

We retraced our journey back to Burnett Place. This time I parked right outside the half open door, in front of the sofa. The girls were gone, and I followed Xena inside. The door gave directly onto a small living room where three Latino guys were sitting watching a TV that took up the entire wall. Two of the guys were on a sofa, opposite the door. They ignored me. The third was sitting in a brown vinyl armchair opposite the TV. He looked up as I came in. His expression said he was wondering if he would have to kill me.

"What do you want, gringo?"

"Coke, whores, and alcohol. I want a party."

He looked at the sports bag in my hand. "You got half a million bucks in cash in your bag? You carrying it around like it's your purse."

I shrugged. "I don't want to leave it in the truck, right?"

He grinned at his *compadres*. "You think it's safer in here than out there?"

They laughed like maybe they were going to kill me. I smiled back. "Yeah."

"You wanna tell me why I shouldn't take your money and cut your throat?"

"Sure, Xena here told me you're a smart guy. And if I walk in here, tired and frustrated from a week of hard work, with half a million bucks in my purse, willing to spend a few grand on your girls and your merchandise, maybe that's something I will do every week, or every month, and maybe, if we become friends, I can let you have some of this lucrative action. I'm guessing you are smart enough to know that a guy with half a million bucks in a sports bag is a guy worth being friends with. Now can I buy some coke and some girls, or do I have to beg?"

He sighed. "How much do you want?"

I hunched my shoulders. "We're going to use at least forty or fifty grams tonight, right? And some for breakfast. Let's play safe and go for a hundred grams. So what's that?" I looked around. Everyone was staring at me. I smiled and unzipped the bag. "Five grand? Ten grand?"

The two guys on the sofa looked at Charlie. There was an almost telepathic agreement between them. One of them said, "I don't like this guy, Jefe."

Almost simultaneously, Charlie said, "You're full of bullshit, man."

They were reaching for their weapons. I dropped the bag and had the BUL SAS II Ultralight in my hand. Xena began to scream. I gave the door a back-kick, and it slammed closed as I put a round through Charlie's head and his brains sprayed over his nearest pal on the sofa. He winced and cried out and turned away. While he was doing that, I shot his pal twice through the heart. The guy with the gore on his face was trying to stand and wipe the blood from his face while making incoherent noises. I shot him in the head, between the eyes.

I turned and put the BUL in Xena's face. I spoke quietly. "Shut up." She closed her mouth. Her eyes were bulging. "Anyone else in the house?"

She swallowed hard and gave her head a single shake.

"Ask yourself, after what you have just seen, who would you bet on, some asshole hiding in the house with a gun and pissing his pants, or me?"

She didn't say it. She mouthed it. *You...*

"You know what I'll do to you if you are lying. So I am going to ask you again. Is there anybody else in the house?"

"No."

"Good. So now we are going to collect all the money in the house and the keys to his apartment."

"*What?*"

"Now, Xena. Money and keys. Now."

She started shaking her head, like she had a bad connection in her neck. "I don't, I don't, I don't know—"

"If you don't know, Xena," I said very quietly, "you are no use to me alive."

Her skin went kind of pasty, and she started to sweat. "And after I show you...?"

I smiled. "You might still be useful. Especially if you prove you are willing to cooperate. Charlie's gone. I have arrived. Now be a smart girl and get me his cash and his keys. Now."

She was shaking badly. She went and opened a door in the wall beside the sofa. There was a narrow staircase. I followed her up, and at the top, she turned right into a bedroom with bare boards on the floor. There was a rumpled bed and a pine chest of drawers painted white. She went and pulled it away from the wall. Her legs were shaking so badly she could hardly stand, and she was beginning to weep.

Behind the chest of drawers there was a makeshift panel in the wall. She pulled it away and revealed six plastic grocery bags stuffed full of cash and what looked like ten or fifteen pounds of some kind of narcotic wrapped in plastic reinforced with packing tape.

From the drawers, she pulled out a sports bag similar to mine and stashed all the cash in it. I asked, "How much?"

"Seven hundred K."

When she was done, I got her to help me take the dope to the bathroom, cut the packets open, and dump the contents down the toilet.

When we were done, I asked her, "Whose is the Mustang outside?"

"Charlie's. Least, it was Charlie's."

"Keys?"

"In his—" Her bottom lip curled in and she started to sob. "In his pants."

I grabbed the bag with the cash and followed her back down the stairs. There I reached in Charlie's pocket and pulled out a bunch of keys. I peeled off the ones for the Mustang and handed them to her.

"Your life is a mess, Xena," I told her, "because you have made some very stupid, poor choices. Now you are one of the lucky few. Because you get a second chance. You have seen violence and murder, you have lost somebody you cared for. You have seen where this life leads. Take the car, take this money, go very far away, learn a trade, and make a useful life. Go away now, and never come back."

She stared at me for a long moment with her eyes shifting from mine to the bag and back again.

"You gonna shoot me in the back when I try to leave."

"No." I shook my head. "*You* might do that to yourself by stopping to say goodbye to your friends or phoning somebody. Dump your cell, get the hell out of here, and don't look back."

She grabbed the bag, turned, and ran. Thirty seconds later, I heard the Mustang's door slam, the big engine roar, and two seconds later, she was gone. I gave her five minutes, then slung my own bag back in the Jeep and took off for the Grand Concourse and my new temporary accommodation.

The apartments were built in the early '60s, when homes in New York were still designed for human beings to live in, rather than androids to sleep in. It was large, airy, and spacious, with a large balcony overlooking the avenue. There was also no furniture except for a sofa and a TV, and a gigantic fridge in the kitchen which contained almost exclusively beer and frozen pizza. I sighed and shook my head. Where would we be without stereotypes to tell us who we are? He had seen himself on TV a thousand times and knew exactly who he was.

The thought depressed me, and I went to explore the bedrooms. One of them had an en suite bathroom, so I dumped my bag there, had a shower, and went out with a couple of grand in my pocket to buy clothes and some food that wasn't frozen pepperoni pizza.

By eleven that night I'd had a steak and another shower, and was dressed in my new suit, and by eleven-fifteen I was in my car on the way to the Gates of Hell.

It was a short drive down the Grand Concourse as far as

144th and then a left and a right, and I pulled up outside the club. The real rush started after midnight, so there was plenty of room, and I left the Jeep beside the door. I stepped in through the cowgirl's leg and found myself in a plush lobby with red carpets and red silk on the walls. A girl behind a small desk in front of a cloakroom smiled at me, and I crossed the lobby toward two large wooden doors that stood open onto a very dark room with flashing red lights.

The big guy I'd spoken to earlier in the day was there in an evening suit with a clip-on bowtie. As I approached, he shook his head.

"I don't remember you."

I paused beside him. "I have a very forgettable face."

"No, you ain't. I never forget a face. A face like yours I would especially remember."

I smiled pleasantly. "Yeah? Why's that?"

He looked away toward the main entrance, where the door had opened and male and female voices could be heard laughing. He spoke without looking at me.

"Because your face is trouble. Go on in. If you cause any trouble I'll drag you out to the alley and break your legs."

"Thanks. I'll keep that in mind."

Inside, it was practically empty. There was a guy in a burgundy waistcoat behind the bar polishing glasses. There were four girls at the bar who looked like they were waiting for the trade to start, and there were lots of dark nooks and corners with sofas and big armchairs, but there was nobody sitting there yet. Two stages, one on the right and one on the left, had poles on them with girls doing gymnastics on them. I figured those were the portals to hell.

I approached the bar, and the guy in the waistcoat asked me, "What'll it be?"

"Bushmills, straight up."

While he was pouring it, I felt a presence beside me. I looked and it was a woman. She didn't look like she was waiting for trade. She was well dressed and attractive, with intelligent eyes. She smiled at me and narrowed those intelligent eyes.

"Don't I know you?" she said.

I was about to answer but felt suddenly embarrassed and laughed. "This is going to sound ridiculous," I said. "But I was in LA recently and had an accident, and I am now suffering from almost total amnesia."

She arched an eyebrow. "That is elaborate." She closed her eyes and opened her mouth and seemed to hesitate longer than you'd think necessary, like she was stammering. Then she drew a deep breath and said, "I *don't* know your wife, and I'm *definitely* not going to tell her I saw you here. But if I'm an unwelcome intrusion—"

She was about to move off, but I held out my hand. "Wait. It's true. What I am telling you is true. I am actually in New York trying to remember who I am." She frowned hard. I added, "It *is* actually true."

"You are trying to remember who you are in this bar?"

I shrugged. "What can I tell you? I drove past this morning and thought I recognized it. So I came back."

She was watching me hard. "You are serious, aren't you?"

"Yes. Can I buy you a drink?"

Her hard look turned to a frown of curiosity. "Vodka martini."

I told the waiter, then turned and searched her features. "Do you know my name?"

She closed her eyes for a long count of five, then slowly shook her head.

"Can you remember where you know me from?" She watched me but didn't answer. "A conference, a meeting...?"

"Maybe. Do you remember what field you are in?"

"Not really." I raised my shoulders an eighth of an inch and gave my head a small shake. "Law enforcement? Military perhaps? What about you?"

"I'm Jane, Jane Harrison." She held out her hand. "If we knew each other before, it's good to meet you again." I smiled, and she shook.

The waiter delivered her drink, and she took it from the bar. After a sip, she told me, "I was assistant district attorney in Manhattan, southern district. Now I'm in private practice. I know a lot of cops. You don't look or sound like a cop." She stared at me for a long time, then said, with a strange twist in her voice, "Ted? Ted Hansen?"

Just for a moment I thought I saw a trace of bitterness, or anger. But it passed as soon as it appeared, and I dismissed it from my mind.

THREE

The name didn't mean anything to me, but my attention was drawn over her shoulder to a group that was coming through the double doors. For some reason, the guy at the center of the group surprised me. I knew there would be some kind of 'capo' here, some kind of criminal big cheese. I knew it would probably be the owner, or at least the guy who was laundering his money through the club. Maybe I was thinking in stereotypes, but I had expected a Mexican, or maybe an Italian or a Colombian.

But this guy looked Austrian or German. He had stopped to talk to two men. One of them had the air of a manager or part owner of the club. He was in a smart, understated dinner suit with a starched front and a bow tie. He was smoking a cigar and had Mafia written all over him.

The other guy looked like Columbo. He had a dirty raincoat and an off the rack brown suit. He also had a crumpled hat in one hand and an attaché case in the other. His face was in shadow, and I couldn't make out the features, but when he spoke, the other two shut up and listened. Maybe he was what the Italians called a consigliore, the power brokers in the Mafia.

My guy was a good six foot three or four in a very expensive, very traditional evening suit. He had two gorillas with him who were also dressed by Savile Row. Then there was a woman who was as expensive and elegant as his suit and probably about as intelligent. Behind those four, there was a group of what appeared to be groupies. They seemed to have been dressed by Vulgaris, Armani's Bad Taste department, in a lot of colorful silk and satin. That was the guys. The girls had been dressed in creative spaces. Not a lot was left to the imagination, but neither was the imagination stimulated to much curiosity.

"I feel I'm talking to myself."

I looked down at her and smiled. "You're not. I can't say I know who you're talking to, but you are not talking to yourself."

"That's funny."

"Who's the guy in the Savile Row suit?"

She turned and glanced, then frowned at me. "You're interested in him?"

For some reason, the question surprised me. It was something I had taken for granted. I hadn't thought to question it.

"I'm curious. More curious than interested."

"Some time you'll have to explain the difference. That's Hans Fischer. He's a highly respectable financier nobody's ever heard of, unless your work happens to involve the investigation of white collar crime."

"And yours does?"

"Did. Now I just negotiate contracts and make a year's salary in a month. That guy—" She jerked her head in his direction. "He makes my lifetime salary in an hour."

I arched an eyebrow. "Yeah, but does his life have meaning?"

I allowed the irony to show in my voice, and she smiled. "Funny, funny boy."

"So he's a respectable pillar of society, but the Feds don't think so, and neither does the office of the DA."

"You talk like a Fed. You don't talk like a cop. You talk like a federal agent."

I scrutinized her face. "The difference being...?"

She thought about it as she sipped her drink. "This is just my personal, subjective feeling, right? A cop wants to prove you're guilty and looks for proof. A federal investigator suspects you're up to something and wants to know what, who's in it with you, what motivates you, what kind of relationship you had with your parents, and what color your shorts are."

A strange, deep silence filled my mind. I knew what she was saying. I understood it fully. I recognized that I had been like that, once. But I had to bite back the words, *I don't give a damn anymore what relationship they had with their mothers. I just want to destroy them.*

I thought it, but I didn't say it. I didn't need to. She could see it on my face. She nodded. "You went rogue, huh?"

I went cold. It was a common phrase. That was why I had chosen it as a name, but hearing her say it made my blood run cold. I hid it behind a smile and shrugged. "I don't know. I don't remember."

"Is that true? Or is it a front?"

"Is that the DA asking or the vodka martini?"

"Neither. I'm just curious. Or maybe I'm interested. It's not every day you meet a guy who doesn't remember who he is."

I watched Hans Fischer pass with his retinue. The manager, or part owner, or whatever he was led them to a dark corner, where they settled into sofas and armchairs. I watched the Columbo figure shuffle out the main door as a couple of waiters descended on their table to take their orders. I frowned down at Jane Harrison.

"So what is a nice girl like you doing in a place like this?"

"Who told you I was a nice girl? I get a lot of pressure at work. Sometimes you need a loud, bad place where you can let off steam."

"Sure. Have you let off steam yet?"

She laughed. It was nice. "I only just arrived. I haven't even started."

"Oh." I let the disappointment show. "That's a shame."

"You want to take me somewhere more quiet where you can grill me about Hans Fischer. You are very transparent for a guy with no memory."

I tried to look apologetic. "Even if Hans Fischer hadn't showed up, I would probably have wanted to take you somewhere more quiet."

"Take me?" She drained her glass. "You mean like drag me by my hair, caveman style?"

"You know? That still has its appeal, after all this time."

She put her glass on the bar. "Come on. I know a Korean place where they serve dinner all night long. You can buy me a Korean meal and we can discuss this. I have to admit I am intrigued."

I nodded. "Good. I'll be right back."

I crossed the room, making my way through the growing numbers of patrons till I reached the dark corner where Hans and his retinue were ensconced. I approached the table, smiling at him. His two gorillas stood, and one of them stepped in front of me.

I raised the smile for him to see it. "I just wanted to say something to Hans. Is that OK?"

He looked over his shoulder, and Hans gave a nod. I took a step closer. He raised his voice. "How can I help you?"

I raised my voice to answer. "Your face is real familiar. I was just wondering if we had met."

He shook his head. "Your face is not familiar to me. I think you have made a mistake." He indicated the people around him with a finger. "This is a private party, if you don't mind."

"I don't mind. Thanks for talking to me."

I returned to where Jane was waiting, and we stepped out through the lobby to the parking lot. I said, "We'll take my car and come back for yours."

She didn't say anything but gave me a look that said we'd come back to that subject in the near future.

West 32nd Street is narrow and crowded and has lots of oriental restaurants. By the time we got there, most of them were closed or closing. But Jane pointed to a neon sign halfway down which read O-Pen All Hours and had oriental characters which I guess said the same thing.

We found a space nearby, I parked and followed her inside. The place was full and noisy. She made for a table at the back like she knew her way, and as we sat, the waiter smiled at her like he knew her. As I sat, she told him, "Let's have a bottle of makgeolli while we look at the menu." He left, and she glanced over the menu. "I started coming here recently. I figure you don't remember if you are familiar with Korean food or not. So as we came in your car and will go back for mine, I get to order the food. We'll have kan poong gi."

I glanced at the menu. "Is that like, have car can travel, have chicken, can poong gi?"

"Oh, you are funny."

"Tell me about Hans Fischer."

She leaned back in her chair and studied my face for a moment. Then she gave a small shrug and said, "OK, but tell me why you're so curious. From the moment he walked into the club, he's been on your mind."

I leaned back myself while the waiter put a bottle and two glasses on the table, popped the cork, and poured the milky liquid. Jane told him we wanted kan poong gi, and he went away.

"I think I might be looking for him," I told her, choosing my words with care.

She sipped. "I think you need to explain that."

"For reasons that are too complicated to go into right now, I'm pretty sure I'm a New Yorker. I'm pretty sure. But I woke up in Los Angeles, near the beach, in a RAM 1500 which was not mine. I can't remember anything prior to that. But..." I paused, nodding down at my drink and thinking carefully about what I was going to say. "I have had the feeling, since I woke up, that some unconscious part of my mind is actively pursuing its own ends and objectives.

HELL'S FURY | 27

And one of those is to find somebody. And I think that somebody might be Hans Fischer."

"Are you aware of how weird that sounds?"

I spread my hands. "You asked. I employed a psychiatrist in LA, and she more or less agreed with that theory. Your unconscious mind can have motivations you're not aware of." I gestured at her. "Right now, your unconscious mind is making you produce acid, digest your food, beat your heart, regulate the chemistry of your brain, take in and exhale breath, all that. And you're not aware of any of it."

"And you are motivated to know about Hans Fischer, and you don't know why. What did you say to him when you went over?"

"I asked him if he knew me. I said I thought he was familiar."

She didn't look amused. Her face was hard. "That was a stupid thing to do."

I smiled. "Don't hold back. Say what you really mean."

"Those people are dangerous."

"What people?" She didn't answer. She sat and stared at my face. I asked, "Is he your client? Is he protected by privilege?"

"No." She sighed and sat forward. "I don't know how much you know about white collar crime, but essentially there are two broad areas. You have what we could call opportunist white collar crime, where a company director or an accountant, for example, embezzles money from a company or a client. They see the opportunity, and they act."

"And the other?"

"The other is a much more complex setup, the Italian

Mafia is the classic model. It is where a network of finance, banking, and ostensibly legitimate companies is built upon a foundation of violent street crime. At the bottom, you have drug trafficking, sex slavery and prostitution, and murder. At the mid-level, you have money laundering, and once the money has gone through that"—she paused, looking for a word—"filter, for want of a better word, you have that money getting fed back into the legitimate economy in the form of investments where the criminal organization effectively takes control of companies and industries through apparently legitimate means. Woven in to this process is the widespread, subtle and secret use of bribery, blackmail, and the ultimate threat of violence. And by this means, through this process, a law-abiding society can be slowly but irresistibly consumed and taken over by organized crime."

The waiter came with the chicken and placed it in front of us. When he had gone, I said, "And you are telling me that Hans Fischer is involved in that process, and I could risk getting shot by telling him his face was familiar."

She narrowed her eyes at me. "Why do I get the impression you already knew that and it almost amuses you?"

"I don't know. Maybe you're smart. I think the man my unconscious motivation is looking for is into just that kind of white collar crime."

She didn't say anything. She cut into her chicken and stuck a piece in her mouth. She spoke around it.

"OK, here's the sixty-four thousand dollar question -"

"Yeah? More questions? You were supposed to be telling me about Hans Fischer, remember?"

"Yeah, I will, but let me ask you this first. Assuming your unconscious mind recognizes Fischer and is—or was—

looking for him, what is it about..." She paused, looking at the ceiling. "It's such a great question I don't even know how to phrase it."

I supplied, "What is it about Fischer that makes my unconscious mind want to find him? Or, alternatively, what is the connection between Fischer and me?"

"Yeah, either or both of those will do."

"And I have to tell you, I don't know. I wish I did. It would make life a lot easier. But I don't know."

She gave a soft grunt and sipped her drink. As she set it down, she said, "What does it feel like? I mean, you want to run and give him a hug and thank him for something? Or is it different?"

I gave my head a small shake and smiled. "I am being tolerant because you're very cute, you're smart, I like you, and I think you might help me. But I am about to tell the waiter to take your food and drink away, after which I will take you home and spank your butt. Hans Fischer."

"You are such a damned dinosaur!"

"Yeah, that much I remember. Hans Fischer, five seconds and counting."

She counted silently to six and said, "I don't know a lot. I know the guys in Federal Plaza were looking into his connections in Poland—"

"Poland? What's he into, illegal cabbage imports?"

"Still funny, but not very. Poland is like the human trafficking hub of the world. Men, women, and children are bought and sold there, for labor and prostitution. A lot of them come from Eastern Europe: Bulgarians, Romanians, Ukrainians, but also from around the world—from Vietnam and southeastern countries like Thailand and Myanmar.

They get taken to Russia first, where the men and boys are used for forced labor and the women and girls are forced into prostitution. The more troublesome ones are forced to take addictive drugs like heroin to make them more compliant. Then they're sold into the wider world market through Poland."

"And he has connections to that industry?"

"You ask me as an assistant DA and I'd have to say it's unproven. You ask me as a person and I'd say without a shadow of a doubt."

"So what does he do, buy and sell?"

She stuffed chicken in her mouth again and shook her head, frowning. "No way. Much too risky." She swallowed. "Much too risky. He's a broker. He puts people in contact with each other and takes a commission. We've seen him do it. It might be at a glittering party in his Manhattan apartment on Central Park West, or if the guests involved are too hot and stand to get arrested, they'll meet on his yacht in international waters. A lot of the people he deals with are on the Bureau's most wanted lists, and if they step outside Mexico, Colombia, Afghanistan, or Russia, they risk being arrested. So what he does is to provide not only channels of communication but safe venues where meetings can take place."

"You're talking about drug cartels, Russian mafia, and Islamic terrorism all in one breath."

"Well—" She nodded as she laid her knife and fork down. "That *is* the way it's going. This is the crime of the future. The world is getting smaller, these people are wielding ever more huge sums of money. We are talking about budgets that run into billions of dollars—the budgets of small countries—every year that need to be laundered and reinvested through major financial institutions. It's what I was talking to you about earlier. Empires of finance and banking built on foundations of violence, drugs, and slavery. It is steadily consuming Western society."

"You're telling me that Sinaloa has ties to Russia and the Middle East?"

"Not just Sinaloa. Sinaloa are the big boys on the block, but the Gulf Cartel has had ties with West Africa, Asia, and Europe for decades, and the Zetas and the Juarez Cartel are immensely rich and well-organized. Countries like Iran and Afghanistan have a lot to offer these cartels, and the Cartels have a lot to offer in return. And then there are the mediators in the middle." She gave a small laugh. "I don't know if you are aware of this, but there are branches of the federal government involved in National Security that are outside congressional oversight. And the legislature of the European Union is unelected. That gives both of these bodies the de facto power to negotiate with Sinaloa, Hamas, and whoever the hell else they want to."

I sipped my drink and watched her over the edge of the glass. As I set it down, I said, "And Hans Fischer is the Western man in the middle. He has channels and venues where they can get together and talk."

"Yes, sir. You wanted to know. So now you know."

"You said you didn't know much about it."

She gave a small shrug. "There are people who know a lot more than I do."

I smiled. "You don't talk like an assistant DA."

She laughed. "I don't? What does an assistant DA talk like?"

I shook my head. "Good try. But that's not the question. The question is, what *do* you talk like?"

"It is? You want some dessert?"

"No, I don't want dessert. You talk like a DEA agent or a Fed. Are you a federal agent, Jane Harrison?"

She shook her head. "No, I am an attorney. I told you that. But I can't help wondering how you know what a DEA agent or a Fed talks like." She smiled suddenly and unexpectedly. "You know what? I've kind of enjoyed this. We should do it again."

I arched an eyebrow at her. "Yeah," I said. "Yeah, we should."

FOUR

I DROPPED HER IN THE PARKING LOT AT THE CLUB and leaned against the hood of my Grand Cherokee as I watched her drive away. The impulse was there to follow her, but I decided against it. It was not an imperative. Not yet, anyhow. As her red taillights faded from sight, I noticed Hans Fischer step out of the club through the cowgirl's leg. He paused in the darkness, backlit by the lobby, as his retinue followed him out and stood around him. His two gorillas stood either side and scanned the lot. One of them spotted me and stood staring. Before he could say anything to his boss, a guy in a baggy blue silk suit laughed as he lit a cigarette and pointed at me.

"Hey, Hans, isn't that the guy who thought he'd met you?"

Hans glanced in my direction but acted like he was thinking about something else. The group moved toward a Bentley and an Audi, and while they walked, he said a few words to the gorilla who'd been staring at me a moment earlier. The gorilla nodded, turned, and came walking toward me, like he was having trouble moving his legs around his thigh muscles.

He was big. He looked like he might be Samoan or from one of those islands where they play rugby with large rocks instead of leather balls. But the real treat was his face. It was the kind of face that would give you PTSD just from looking at it.

He stopped about three feet from me and jerked his chin in my direction. "What you want with Mr. Fischer?"

I smiled on the right side of my face, where the irony is slightly offensive.

"Well, shucks, Bluto. I was hoping we could be more than just friends. But if he has you, I'll just fade into the background and pray for your happiness. I know you both deserve it."

His frown said his brain was hurting. He didn't know whether to hit me or ask me what the hell I'd said. So as a compromise, he came up with "Huh?" like it was a threat.

"A good question, but one that may never get answered. After all, I mean—huh? Seriously?"

His face scrunched up like an angry fist. "Listen, pal, I ask you a question, and you gonna answer! What you want with Mr. Fischer?"

I shrugged and smiled. "Hell, I don't know. Lunch? A little light conversation. Perhaps a movie..."

He was fast. He took a fistful of my collar with his left hand and made a big ball of rock out of his right. The outlook was not good. In a fraction of a second I saw, over his right shoulder, that the group had stopped to watch.

Both his hands were occupied, so the double finger-jab

to his eyes was a cinch. Most people make the mistake of pulling back at the last moment. That's wrong. You need to follow through and go all the way, with a stiff arm and stiff fingers. It's nasty, but it can save your life.

Bluto screamed and staggered back with his hands over his eyes. I stepped forward, narrowing the gap, and smashed my right instep into his balls. He twisted and doubled up and slowly sank to his knees. I walked behind him and looked over at Fischer. I held his eye a moment, then kicked Bluto real hard in the back of the neck. He died instantly and fell forward with a heavy *whoof!*

I waited a moment to see if they were going to come for me. They didn't. They just stood and stared. It looked for a moment like Gorilla Two might come for me, but Fischer said something, and he stayed put. So I crossed the parking lot to where they were standing. When I got there, I pointed back at where Bluto lay face down in his own death and spoke to Fischer.

"He wanted to know what I want with you." I gave my head a small shake. "I just wanted an answer to a question. But now, now I have a whole raft of questions."

"What question?"

I laughed. "Oh, no, it's too late for that now. That was then. We'll talk, Hans, and next time, you won't send me away."

I walked back, climbed in the Jeep, and drove out of the parking lot. It wasn't hard to spot the tail. It was Gorilla Two in the Audi. He didn't try to be discreet, and I went too slow for him to hang back. Acting on an impulse I didn't fully understand at that time, I led him into Manhattan. It was late, and there wasn't a lot of traffic, and as we approached the park, I noticed in my rearview that Fischer's Bentley was not far behind the gorilla's Audi.

I turned right at the Duke Ellington Circle onto Central Park North and accelerated. In my mirror, I saw them follow. The gorilla I could understand, but unless Hans Fischer was crazier than I thought, his following me didn't make sense at all. Until I remembered something Jane had said.

I took the Frederick Douglass Circus and turned south down Central Park West. Four blocks down, the Bentley pulled in and stopped, but the Audi stayed on my tail. That was where Hans Fischer had his apartment. That was what she had told me.

I took the gorilla all the way down to West 81st Street, and there I parked outside the red awning opposite the house that had once been mine. I leaned my ass against the side of the Jeep and watched the Audi pull in and stop. Then I pushed off my car and walked the thirty yards to where he had stopped.

I tapped on the window, and he lowered it. "I want you to take a message to your boss. You tell him I want to know about that house." I pointed to the house where I knew I had once lived. "This time you get to go home because I need that message delivered. But next time you follow me, I will kill you. Go."

Nothing in his face showed that he had understood or registered what I had told him. But the window went up, and he drove away.

I walked back to the Jeep and sat a while looking at the crazy guy in the mirror.

"I hope to Christ you know what you're doing," I told him. "Because I haven't got a clue."

In Los Angeles, two thousand four hundred and sixty-six miles away, Special Agent Elroy Jones was staring at the Pacific. It was a thing he did regularly. He knew that some people—even some smart people—liked to meditate. They had wind chimes and water features and quiet places where they went to do it. He had no time for that, but he did like to stare at the Pacific. He was aware of its size, its immensity, its power, but above all, he was aware of its completeness. And Special Agent Elroy Jones was a man who liked things to be complete. He could not tolerate a thing half done. You start something, you finish it. It was how his father had raised him. It was how he had tried to raise his own children. You start something, you finish it.

Newton—Special Agent Cathy Newton—emerged from the bar, and he watched her approach. He enjoyed watching her. She was very small, very thin, and very pale with platinum hair, but her vitality was second to none. Her eyes were a startling deep blue, and she radiated energy. Behind her came the waiter with a tray. On it was a vodka martini and a pint of dark beer.

Newton sat down like she was getting a task done, and the waiter set their drinks before them. When he went away, she said, "OK, Elroy, spill it. You make me come out on my day off, it better be worth it."

He shifted his gaze from her back to the Pacific. "I didn't put a gun to your head. You didn't have to come."

"Don't get sensitive." She sipped her drink and set it down. "Girls get sensitive. You're not a girl. So spill. What's eating you?"

Elroy took a pull on his beer, partly to hide the smile, and as he smacked his lips and set the glass down, she said, "I knew it!"

He frowned at her. "Knew what, exactly? I haven't said anything yet."

"You didn't need to. I can see it in your face."

He made a disgusted face at the beach. "Come on! You're going to give me that feminine intuition BS now?"

She pointed at him with her small white finger like a tiny, silver Remington. "It's the Rogue case. It is eating you alive. Am I wrong? Tell me I'm wrong." She waited a moment. He ignored her. "Ha! See. I know you better than your own wife."

He let that pass, then shook his head. "That guy is a *murderer*, Newton."

"Maybe so, but the information he gave us made a measurable impact. The DEA took down *a lot* of bad guys, Elroy."[1]

"That's not the point, Cathy, and you know it. The law does not say you're not allowed to kill nice people but it's OK to kill bad guys, whatever Hollywood may tell us. That guy killed fourteen people—*that we know of*—in this country. God alone knows how many he killed in Mexico. He feeds us a line and drives away in a stolen Audi with Mexican plates. And we let him go."

She shrugged. "We take orders from upstairs, Elroy. That's what they told us to do."

He shook his head at the vast ocean, where a slight haze was beginning to rise off the water.

---

1. See *Rogue Book One, Gates of Hell*

"You know what my dad used to tell me?"

"Probably."

"Finish what you start." He emphasized the words, stabbing with his finger on the table. "*Finish* what you *start*. You do not start a new task until you have finished the last one."

She took a pull on her martini. "That's great, Elroy. But as far as the people you work for are concerned, you did finish that task." She spread her hands. "What more can you do?"

"I want to talk to New York."

She made a face like she'd bitten into a lemon. "Elroy! Come on!"

"They did not tell us not to investigate. They told us not to arrest or interrogate them. They told us to let them go on their way. But they did *not* tell us not to investigate. You do know what the I stands for in FBI, don't you?"

She leaned forward and laid her hands on the table. "Elroy, you are an intelligent man. You are not naïve. You *know* what they meant when they said, 'Do not arrest them. Let them go on their way.' Somebody is looking after this guy."

His face contracted with sudden anger. "Yeah well, you know what, Newton? That's called aiding and abetting, and it's a felony to aid and abet a felon. Whoever you are! Also it is immoral. We have such a thing as the rule of law in this country."

She sat back and sipped her drink. As she set it back on the table, she said, "But maybe they, whoever they are, are *not* aiding and abetting. Maybe it's part of an ongoing investigation. Did you think of that? How many times have you pissed off an LAPD cop by letting a felon go as part of your ongoing investigation, when he wanted to nail the son of a bitch?"

It was like he hadn't heard a word she'd said. "I'm going to go and talk to some friends in New York."

"What do you think you're going to find there?"

He held up his thumb and tapped it with his index finger. "He came from New York. That's for a start. The first guys he killed—"

"The first we know of."

"Right. The first we know of—came from New York. He followed them to Vegas and then on down to Los Angeles. And according to Dave Marshall, he went *back* to New York when he disappeared. I want to know—" He counted it out on his fingers. "One, who he has contacted in New York, two, are Federal Plaza aware of him and his return? And three, have drug dealers started dying in gruesome, ugly ways in the last few weeks? That's for starters."

She nodded and thrust out a pretty lower lip. He looked away. She said, "That would be interesting to know. I can't say it wouldn't. I'd also like to know who his guardian angel is."

"And why," he added ungrammatically.

"But suppose you can convince your New York pals to part with that kind of information." She spread her hands. "What are you going to do with it? We know he's protected."

He stared at her suddenly and intensely. "Finish the job! Prosecute this guy as a murderer."

"You're not listening. This guy is protected. You're saying you want to know who his angel is, but the point is he *has* an angel."

HELL'S FURY | 41

"Then I want to have his guardian angel explain to me on what legal grounds he should not be prosecuted for a minimum of fourteen murders."

"Elroy, they may or may not have legal grounds, but what they are going to tell you is that it's part of an ongoing investigation so go to hell and mind your own sweet goddamn business."

He was silent for a while, looking out at the vast, complete Pacific Ocean. Eventually he looked at her and said, "Are you in or not?"

"Of course I'm in. You know I'm in. What's the plan?"

"I'll make a call this afternoon. I'm due a few days. Can you get some time? We could go Thursday to Sunday."

"Fly Wednesday night?"

He nodded. "Almost four clear days. Maybe we can learn something."

"OK, let's do it. Even if it's just so you can get it off your chest and say you did all you could."

He studied her face a moment with no expression on his own. Eventually he said, "You know it's wrong. You know it's not right. People should not be allowed to get away with murder, whoever they kill. The whole of civilization rests on the principle that people are not allowed to use violence against each other."

She made a face that said she agreed up to a point. "OK." Then she drained her glass and set it down. "So are you going to buy me lunch, or do I have to get it again?"

"It's on me. Even though I got it last time."

"Oh, you mean when we had hot dogs? I was talking about *lunch*."

"Quit griping. If you wanted to be pampered, you should have gone out with your boyfriend."

"He was busy showing your wife his etchings."

"What do you want, pizza?"

"I'd settle for a big steak and a cold beer, but just seeing you put your hand in your pocket would be a treat."

He signaled the waiter. While they waited, he asked her, "Do you ever look at the ocean? I mean, really gaze at it and take it in? Don't give me a wiseass answer, Newton. I'm serious."

Her eyes shifted, and she looked at the hazy, blue water beyond the white sand. "Yeah," she said. "Sometimes."

He sighed. "Me too."

FIVE

Hans Fischer put his cell to his ear. The voice that spoke to him was sleepy and angry.

"Do you know what time it is?"

He didn't answer right away. He stood and crossed the spacious room to the sliding glass doors. Out on the terrace, he leaned on the wall and looked down at Central Park, at the small lights that moved around it like quantum particles at Christmas.

"I have no time for stupid questions," he said without feeling into the phone. There was no anger in his voice. It was a simple statement of fact. "We have a problem which is unexpected, and I don't understand it."

There was a groan and a sigh. The squeak of bed springs. When it spoke again, the voice no longer had the bedroom muffle to it. "What kind of problem?"

"What kind of problem? If I believed in a god, I would ask him for patience right now. I don't think this is a relevant question. You want to know, precisely and concretely, *what is the problem?* Not what *kind* of problem. Oh, it is an emotional problem, no it is a financial problem... Or it is a problem related to biology. Can we focus now? Are we awake? You want to make coffee?"

"Are you done?"

"I hope so. I really hope so."

"So *what is* the problem?"

Down at the corner of 108th, he saw a couple. They were drunk, and they were arguing. She turned and stormed away. The guy went after her and grabbed her arm. She yanked free and screamed at him. Her screams at that distance were silent. Unheard. Hans spoke as he watched them, wondering how far it would escalate.

"A man comes to me at the Gates of Hell, and he asks me if we know each other. He thinks he recognizes me. I tell him no and ask him to please go away. When we leave, two or three hours later, he is waiting in the parking lot, leaning against his vehicle, like he is waiting for somebody. We go to our cars, but I tell Jonah to go over and scare him a little. I don't like him. He gives me a bad feeling. So Jonah goes over. Jonah is a very frightening man. He is six foot seven and built like a bison."

"So?"

"So this guy kills Jonah with his bare hands, right there in the parking lot. It takes a few seconds. He gouges out his eyes, castrates him with a kick, walks calmly behind him, and breaks his neck with another kick. Then he walks up to me, very calm, like nothing just happened, and he tells me, 'He wanted to know what I want with you.' Then he told me, 'I just wanted an answer to a question. But now, now I have a whole lot of questions.' I asked him what question? And he laughed. He said it was too late for that. That was before, and he said we'd talk, and when the time came, I would not send him away."

"What the hell...?"

"Who is this man?"

"How the hell should I know?"

"You are supposed to guarantee my safety in this country. I could have been killed tonight."

"Did any of you do something smart like get the make, model, and registration of his car?"

"It was a silver Grand Cherokee, California registration." He gave him the number. "I can't do my job with this kind of shit going on. You need to take care of it right now."

"I'll put a man on it as soon as you hang up."

Hans shook his head and gave a small laugh. "You are not listening to me. It took him three or four seconds to kill Jonah. And we have no idea who he is or who he represents. You don't put a man on him. You put a team, and they had better be a damned good team. This is not a normal man."

The voice sighed. "OK, I'll put the best guys I have on it."

Hans turned and leaned his back against the parapet. "There was something else."

"What?"

"I had Aleki follow this guy. He followed him to a house at the end of West 81st, almost on the corner with Riverside Drive. Where the Greenway is. He parked there and waited for Aleki."

"Don't tell me he killed him too."

"No, but only because he wanted him to bring me a message. He pointed to a house, almost on the corner, and said, 'You tell your boss I want to know about that house.' It would be three eighteen or three twenty."

"West 81st?"

"That's what I said."

"You know anything about that house?"

"Not a goddamn thing."

"Keep it that way. I'll have my guys look into it."

"Scheiße! Keep it that way Scheiße! You know, and I am kept ignorant? Fick dich! Your men look into it, and I want that report! I want to know who this missgeburt is! I want to know everything about him—and about that house! You understand, you evolutionbremse?"

"Take it easy, Hans. I'll take care of it."

"Yeah, that makes me feel all warm and fuzzy. Get it sorted and *inform me!* Or I get on my Gulfstream and I am out of here. I do not need this Scheiße! Get it seen to, and inform me *in full*."

"Consider it done."

Hans Fischer hung up without answering.

SOME TWO HUNDRED MILES SOUTH, southwest of where Hans Fischer sat scowling at his cell, Staff Operations Officer Mitch Vogel sat on the suede sofa in his living room in DC, scowling at his own cell.

He dialed a number. A woman's voice said, "What?"

"You remember West 81st and Riverside Drive?"

"Yeah. Hanson."

"What happened to the guy?"

"He died."

HELL'S FURY | 47

"Is that certain?"

The woman was quiet for a long while. Then she said, "Of course it's certain. Why? What are you telling me?"

"I'm telling you we have a problem."

She sighed loudly. "Yeah, we all always have problems, Mitch. The interest on my mortgage just went up. My sister's kids play too many online games and won't study history. It's called life. Give me a break will you, at two-thirty a.m.! What are you telling me?"

"I'm telling you that a very important friend of ours, whom we have a vested interest in protecting, just had his life threatened and his Samoan bodyguard killed. Have you ever *seen* a Samoan bodyguard? But that is not the best of it. This guy gave our friend's other bodyguard—the one whose twenty-two-inch neck he didn't break—a message. He said to inform his boss that he wants to know about the house on 81st and Riverside Drive."

She was quiet for a long time before saying, "Holy shit. Who...?" She trailed off.

"That is what I would like *you* to explain to *me*. What is the status of that house right now?"

"It's empty." Another silence was followed by, "They were all dead. They *all* died. The place is in limbo. Nobody owns it right now. As far as I know, the city is trying to trace relatives. If they can't the place will escheat to the state."

"You need to find out who this guy is, and you need to neutralize him before our friend decides to go and do business somewhere else."

"I'll see to it."

"You'd better!"

There was a moment's pause. Then, "Don't threaten me, Mitch."

"Don't use my—"

"You want me to keep my mouth shut? Then keep yours shut too and don't threaten me! I'll be in touch."

She hung up, and Staff Operations Officer Mitch Vogel dropped his phone on the sofa and buried his face in his hands. Mendoza was good. She was effective. She'd take care of things. He dragged his fingers down his face, leaving ugly, bloodless streaks, and stared at his distorted reflection in the black screen of the TV.

However good Mendoza was, he told himself, it did not explain who the hell this guy was, or what his interest was—or, worst of all, how many people he had behind him. He screwed up his face and shook his head. To kill the Samoan...

Vogel had seen Jonah. To kill that man in a matter of seconds, in the middle of the parking lot, in front of everybody—that took not just extreme skill. It took the kind of cold blood seasoned professionals dream about. And a sense of invulnerability. A sense of invulnerability born of what?

He needed him found, explained, and terminated.

ON THAT LONG, dark night of the soul, it was three o'clock in the morning. Jane Harrison sat on her bed in the dark and gazed half-unseeing at the small pool of light cast by her bedside lamp on the yellow paperback on her bedside table. *The Crack Up*, F. Scott Fitzgerald. She thought about the man she had spent the evening with. He had no idea who she was, though they had slipped easily into conversation as though they had known each other for years. There was no question that his amnesia was real. She knew him well enough to know that much.

He had changed, though the change was hard to define. It was not physical or visual; he looked just the same. Yet it was impossible to miss. It was in his eyes, in his manner. It was as though she were looking at his harder, more ruthless twin brother.

So what would she tell Director Levi? What *should* she tell Director Levi? Was it him or not? It couldn't be him. Because he was dead. But it *was* him.

Her face creased. Her lower lip curled in, and she bit it trying to suppress her emotions. There was little point. They welled up like a tsunami and overwhelmed her. She fell sideways onto the bed, drew her knees up to her chest, and hugged them tightly with her arms, unconsciously moving into the fetal position. There she surrendered to the pain and the black hole of grief in her belly.

Outside her window the moon looked down over New York and cast a path of silver deception over the black waters of the East River, and smiled.

SIX

Google has been around since the summer of 1996, and with every passing decade, it has become steadily less useful. However, that early morning, having breakfast on my new terrace, it told me one useful thing: There were lots of guys called Ted Hansen in the state of New York. Some were dead, some were alive, some were doctors, others were builders, yet others still were students with Facebook profiles, and an awful lot of them were on LinkedIn. The search was, if anything, too fruitful—but none of them was me.

Eventually I tried a different approach and went online to the New York Office of the Chief Medical Examiner. There I discovered that thirteen thousand people were reported missing in New York in the previous year, and nationwide there were eighty-seven thousand active, long-term missing person cases. Among those who had gone missing in New York within the previous twelve months, there were Teds, and there were Hansens, but there were no Ted Hansens.

I went to the kitchen, made coffee, and took it out to the terrace to watch the dawn spread across the horizon. While I did that, I thought about contacting the Bureau. It made perfect sense to do so, and my gut feeling was that I trusted the Bureau as an institution. And yet that same gut told me not to contact them. Somewhere, in the dark caverns of my unconscious mind, there was a good reason not to.

Besides which, Dave Marshall, the private detective I had used in Los Angeles, had sent the Bureau my DNA and my prints, and they had not found me on any of their databases. It would be no different in New York.

Even as I thought it, I knew there was a flaw in my reasoning, but I ignored it. I ignored it partly because a sealed, classified file was a possibility I did not want to consider, but also because an alternative approach to the problem had presented itself in my mind. Instead of looking for a person, what I needed to do was look for a property. If I looked for three hundred and twenty West 81st Street and found who the owner was, I would find out who I was.

And who I was married to.

A sudden wave of anxiety washed over me at the thought and made me feel nauseous. I turned back toward the sliding glass doors, and the floor seemed to move up toward me under my feet. I steadied myself against the glass, then ran to the bathroom and vomited violently.

As I rinsed my mouth and splashed cold water on my face, I told myself I had drunk too much the night before and had a hangover. But I knew it was not true. It had been the image of that woman at the window, smiling and waving, and the knowledge that I would soon know her name, and mine. Yet there were truths, I knew in my bones, realities behind that truth, that were too terrifying to face.

I returned to the table on the terrace where I had my laptop set up. There I sat and steadied my breathing, and after a while I searched for ACRIS, the Automated City Register Information System. It took me a while, but I was aware as I navigated it that I had used the system before, and it was coming back to me. It was something I already knew how to do but, like so much else, I had forgotten.

Then, suddenly, almost out of the blue, I found myself staring at the listing. My hand was shaking badly, and with a supreme effort, I clicked on the entry and closed my eyes as the information relevant to the property displayed on the screen.

When I opened them, I saw there was no outstanding mortgage. There were no loans taken out against the property. It was free from any kind of legal claims, clogs, or fetters. It stated that the sole owner was deceased and there were no known heirs, and that after a prescribed period, if no legal heirs claimed it, the property would go to the state.

The image misted over, and I became aware that I was weeping. I wiped away the tears and forced myself to continue reading.

The property was listed as having belonged to Susan Hanson. Hanson, not Hansen. And she was listed as the sole proprietor. No husband. That didn't mean she wasn't married. It just meant she owned the house herself, outright.

But surely, if she was married, her husband would be her heir. It made no sense, and my mind struggled trying to find the logic.

What did become clear was that after Susan Hanson had died, the house had been closed up. No surviving relative had claimed it, and the state had not yet claimed it either. Why *I* had not claimed it was a fact lost in the darkness, the void that was my mind. But in theory at least, the inside of the house must be as it had been just before she died.

I grabbed my keys and my jacket, tucked the .357 under my arm, and went down to the parking garage.

When I got to the house on West 81st Street, there was a space just outside the decorative iron railings that enclosed the small front yard. I parked there and swung down from the cab, and as I approached the front door, I pulled my Swiss army knife from my pocket, just like it was a key. I selected the small screwdriver and hammered it hard into the lock. I turned and the door opened quietly inward.

It was home. Everything, from the smell of furniture polish, the Persian rug, and the mahogany staircase that led to the upper floor to the layout of the rooms and the scuff mark on the corner of the rug, was intimately familiar. The dark, double doors on my left with the authentic art deco glass panels, I knew they led into a comfortable living room with a small open fireplace, dark burgundy armchairs in leather, and a very old, very comfortable sofa in sage green. I had always complained that it did not fit, but Susan had said it was eclectic, and I was happy to go with that.

And there were books. Lots of books. There were two floor-to-ceiling bookcases in the nooks on either side of the fireplace; and then there were low bookcases taking up every bit of available wall space. I opened the double doors, and it was exactly as I had recalled it.

On the far right was the dining area. There was a long,

oval table with six chairs, and that too was dark mahogany and very old. We had found it—*Susan* had found it—in a shop in Maine. She believed it was over three hundred years old. There was a vase of dried-up, dead flowers in the middle of the table. An intolerable pain twisted my gut and my face as I realized that her hand had touched those stems, had placed those flowers in that vase. I reached out and touched them, as though I could touch her through them, but they crumbled under my fingers.

Early light filtered through the glass doors that gave onto the small lawn in the back yard, laying warped rectangles of light among shadows on the wooden floor. Beyond the table, in the right hand wall, a door stood open onto a kitchen. I moved through the door. The room was not large, but it was large enough for a round, pine breakfast table with four chairs. There was an oven in the wall, large enough for a big turkey at Christmas or Thanksgiving. There was a double sink in front of a large window that also looked out onto the green backyard. Beside it there was a dishwasher which stood slightly open. A putrid smell emanated from it.

I stood a moment staring at it, then opened it all the way and hunkered down. I reached in and extracted the items two or three at a time. There were three bowls with traces of muesli and milk in them. Then there was a small plate with traces of whole wheat toast, butter, and some dark jelly. There were three tall glasses that had contained orange juice and two cups, one large as for a cappuccino, and one small, as for an espresso. The small one had traces of black coffee; the larger one had probably held a coffee with milk. The cup had a heart on it and the legend *'the best mom*.

Some part of my mind stepped back and watched me as I

sat on the floor and wept. I wondered how it was possible to feel such pain for the loss of people you couldn't even remember. I knew she was Susan, I knew she laughed a lot, I knew she liked eclectic furniture. But ask me her birthday, her favorite color, her favorite book or song, and I had no idea. And as to the kids, I didn't know their names. I didn't even know if they were boys, girls, or one of each. And yet my heart was breaking where I sat because of their loss.

I got to my feet and splashed my face with cold water, forced myself to think. The living room and dining room were downstairs. So the bow window on the second floor, where I had seen a brass lamp and a painting on the chimneybreast, what was that? I figured it could be my den.

I walked back to the entrance hall and climbed the mahogany stairs to a broad landing. Directly ahead of me was a large, dark mahogany door with a brass handle. I turned it and pushed, stepped through, and went very cold inside.

Directly opposite me was that bow window that overlooked West 81st. There, outside, slightly to the right, was the ginkgo biloba tree which she had loved. Beside the window there was the brass lamp which I had seen from the street, and in the bow was the old, red sofa she had rescued from some shop. And there, over on the left, tucked into the corner and surrounded by bookcases, were *her* leather chair and *her* desk.

And on the desk, her computer.

The room seemed to rock under my feet. I made it to the sofa and sat.

This was *her* office. It was not my office. I did not work from home. She worked from home. I stood and moved quickly to the desk. There were four framed photographs. I grabbed the nearest and turned it with trembling hands. It was a child, a girl, perhaps eleven or twelve years old. She had fair hair and plaits. She was sitting sideways on, with her head turned to smile at the camera. I heard a strange, ugly noise in my own throat and moved around the desk to sit in the leather chair. I laid down the picture and reached for a photograph of a boy. He was younger, maybe nine or ten. His grin, affectionate but defiant, made me laugh. Though the laugh came out choked and twisted with pain.

I lay the two pictures together and knew I would never see these children again. I wanted to say goodbye to them, but an agonizing guilt inside me told me I could not, because I didn't even remember their names, let alone what they ate for breakfast, what their favorite TV shows were, what books they liked to be read at bedtime. I knew nothing about them. Yet I ached for them.

I wiped my eyes with the back of my hand and reached for the third photograph. I felt my head throb and my heart pound hard in my chest. It was the face I had been looking at in the mirror since I woke up in the Dodge RAM in Los Angeles. It was the same body, but somehow it was not the same man. It was not me. It made no sense and was not rational, but I knew that the guy in the photograph was dead.

He was fit and strong, dressed in jeans and a polo shirt. He had an easy smile and an easy manner. He looked urbane, like a guy who was an easy communicator and always had time for a chat and a laugh. He looked professional and educated. He didn't look like a guy who would cut someone open with a Samurai sword or know exactly where to kick a guy in the back of his head to break his neck. He looked like he would not invite a guy like me to one of his sparkling dinner parties.

Yet it was me. Or rather, it had been me. Or I had once been him. Then I had died and re-become as a monster, a creature less than human.

My eyes moved to the fourth picture. It was a family portrait on the beach, taken by some stranger. I had the girl on my knee. The boy was leaning against me like it was something he did a lot, and I had one arm around him. Susan was hunkered down beside me in a yellow bikini, with her head on my shoulder. It was a picture of four people who were close and enjoyed being close.

I heard the door open and close downstairs. There was no mistaking the sound of a key. Whoever it was was not breaking in. I sat and listened and heard the living room door open and close. Then there were feet on the stairs—feet that were making no effort to be quiet. The steps reached the landing. The door opened without any sign of hesitation, and a woman entered and stood looking at me. Her furrowed brows said she was mad.

She was mad in a blue business suit. Her dark hair was neatly collected in a bun at the back of her neck, and she was frowning at me like it was her business to frown at people. She said, "Who are you? What are you doing in this house?"

I was about to tell her I was John Rogue, I didn't have to explain a goddamn thing to her, and who the hell was she anyway? But I looked down at the pictures again and spoke quietly instead.

"Who am I? Who are *you*? FBI?" I looked up at her. "CIA? You're definitely not NYPD in that suit, and you're sure as hell not from City Hall Land Registry and Records. So who are you, and what are *you* doing in this house?"

She narrowed her eyes and took a step closer. "The owner of this house is deceased."

"Yeah, I know that. I asked you who you are."

Her face contracted with anger. "I asked you first, mister. And if I don't get an answer pretty soon—"

I tossed the picture of Ted Hanson across the desk for her to see. She picked it up slow, still frowning. I smiled without much humor.

"What? If you don't get an answer pretty soon you'll what? Are you going to shoot me in the head or spank my ass? Or are you going to call for backup from the Records Office at City Hall?" I stood as she looked up from the picture. Her face said she was having real trouble believing what she was seeing. That made me laugh a small laugh. "It seems I am Ted Hanson," I said. "Now it's your turn. Who the hell are you, and what the hell are you doing in my house?"

SEVEN

She shook her head and scoured my face with her eyes, then looked back at the photograph.

"You can't—" She cut herself short and shook her head again. "What is this? Ted Hanson is dead. How did you get in here?"

"I don't have to answer your questions. And right now"—I pointed at the photograph—"on the balance of probabilities, you are in my house, and I am asking you for the last time, who are you and what are you doing here?" I arched a hostile eyebrow and added, "I won't shoot you in the head, and I have nobody to call for backup, but I might just tan your hide."

She looked up from the photograph again. Her frown turned to an alarmed scowl, and her right hand moved a couple of inches toward her pancake behind her back. "Don't even think about it, mister."

"That's Mr. Hanson to you. And to the best of my knowledge, employees at the New York City Records

Office don't carry semi-automatics in pancakes under their jackets. Which kind of narrows this down some. You are either a Fed or CIA. If you were a Fed, you would have identified yourself by now. Which makes you either a CIA officer or an impostor. I think it's time you sat down and told me what you're doing in my house. And that's the last time I'm going to tell you before I start defending my property."

You could almost hear the cogs and wheels spinning in her head. Her eyes were darting over my face and my body. Her hand was still poised for a quick draw.

I said, "I am unarmed, and on the available evidence"—I pointed at the picture—"I am who I say I am. It would not be the first time the Agency's intelligence was wrong. So why don't you relax your right hand, take a seat, and tell me what is going on."

She moved around a chair on her side of the desk and sat. I sat in what had been Susan's chair and studied the woman's face. She was attractive in a dark, sultry way. She was probably Mexican, with very dark eyes, very black hair, and olive skin. There was no accent, so she was at least second generation, more like third or fourth. "Who are you?"

"I told you. I am Ted Hanson. Who are you?"

"Ted Hanson is dead."

"OK, first you are going to tell me who you are, and then you are going to tell me why you're so sure I'm dead."

She took a moment to answer, like she was finishing reading my face before talking to me. Finally she said, "I was there. I saw it happen."

"You saw what happen?"

"I saw Ted Hanson get shot multiple times, and I saw him die."

"Who shot him?"

"If you're him, you should know. It's not the kind of thing you forget."

I grunted, thinking she didn't know just how wrong she could be.

"I am going to ask you for the last, last time. Who are you? And while you're at it, how did you come to see me getting shot? Did you shoot me?"

She narrowed her eyes and said suddenly, "Take off your shirt."

"Seriously?"

"Take off your shirt. If you are Ted Hanson, you'll have bullet wounds, and I know exactly where they'll be."

I was suddenly curious. Aside from the few times when I had stared at my face in search of recognition, I had avoided looking in mirrors. They depressed and frustrated me. But now I was searching my memory. Were there scars I had simply taken for granted? I got to my feet, unbuttoned my shirt, and pulled it off. She stood and came around the desk, staring at my chest. She reached out with her finger and touched just below my left shoulder, then traced down to my floating ribs. Then she moved across my chest to my right side, below the collarbone, and again down six inches.

"This one." She looked into my eyes and pointed below the collarbone again. "That was through and through. Turn around."

I turned and heard her breathe and whisper, "*Son of a bitch!*"

I turned back to her. My belly was on fire. She held my

eye, and a smile played at the corner of her mouth. "You are one tough customer. But you don't remember a goddamn thing, do you?"

The admission was on my lips. Instead I said, "Who are you and who do you work for?"

She turned and went back to her seat. She remained silent, thinking, while I put my shirt back on and buttoned it up. She watched me sit and said, "My name is Carmen Mendoza. I work for the Central Intelligence Agency."

"This house"—I said it and tapped the desk with my finger—"is on US soil. You want to explain to me what you are doing walking into this house, with a key, and trying to interrogate me? You have no jurisdiction here. In fact, you are prohibited from collecting information on US persons."

She arched an eyebrow. "I guess you remember some things, huh?"

"Are you going to give me some answers, or do I have to take that pancake, smother it in maple syrup, and shove it—"

"OK!" She raised both hands like I had a gun on her. "OK, let's dial it down a notch."

"Start talking."

"You know so much, you should know that the CIA would be completely hamstrung if it couldn't operate at home. The idea is we share intelligence with the Feds, the NSA, and with the Five Eyes, but intelligence agencies tend to be more interested in secrecy than in sharing. So they tell each other what they think the other needs to know rather than letting each other decide what they need. You following me?"

"Yeah. Intelligence agencies don't share unless they have to, and then they share the minimum."

"Right, so the CIA runs operations at home as well as abroad, because if we didn't, not only would our foreign operations collapse, the USA would be run by Mexican organized crime and Islamic jihadists."

"OK, so now explain to me what the hell that has to do with my getting shot."

She sat staring at me for a long time. Eventually she took a deep breath and said, "You really don't remember, do you? How much do you remember?"

"Go to hell. Answer the question."

She smiled. "I could tell you, but then I'd have to kill you."

"You want to give it a try?"

"Not really, but I don't see you torturing a government officer to get information. We can do this a better way. I talk to my operations officer, I tell him you are still alive, but you don't remember much. We arrange a meeting, and we see how we can help."

I tried to read her face, but there wasn't much written there. I ran over her words a moment.

"Are you telling me I worked for Central Intelligence?"

"No. I'm not telling you anything, Ted. I'm offering you the chance to talk to my staff operations officer. He can make decisions about what to tell you."

I thought about it. "My wife and my kids. Were they murdered? Was their killing connected to my shooting?"

"I can't talk to you about that."

"Why did you come to this house today?"

"Ted, we have reached a point where the only way forward is for me to talk to my head of operations."

"Call him."

She didn't call him. She asked me, "Where are you staying?"

"Here."

She gave her head a couple of short shakes. "You can't prove this is your house. You haven't even applied for probate."

"Is that your problem?"

"Fine!"

"Call him. Here. Now."

"You're one pushy son of a bitch, Hanson!"

"You have no idea. You don't leave this house till you have called your boss." I stood, and as I stood, I had the BUL in my hand. "And let me clarify something for you, Mendoza. Maybe you're right and I would not shoot or torture a federal officer. But I only have your word you are one. For all I know, you are just a well-trained Sinaloa operative. So make the arrangement where I can hear you before I lose my patience."

Her face said if she'd been feeling cocky earlier, she wasn't feeling so cocky now. She pulled her phone from her pocket, dialed, and put it on speaker. A man's voice said, "Yeah."

She said, "I am sitting here, at 320 West 81st with a man who claims to be Ted Hanson. I have the phone on speaker."

There was a long silence. Then, "You want to run that by me again?"

"Not really. It's exactly as I said. I checked his wounds. They are all there. The son of a bitch survived the shooting at the terminal. He's sitting here with me now and listening to our conversation. He wants answers to questions. I told him I can't answer them, but we should arrange a meeting where you can explain to him as much as we are free to explain."

Another long silence. Then a careful, "OK... Give me a minute to think about this—"

"There is nothing to think about." I snarled it. "If you're who you say you are, we drive down to Virginia, we meet in your office, you tell me, I tell you, and we're all happy Americans together."

Another silence. Then, "Who am I talking to?"

"Ted Hanson, who the hell do you think you're talking to, the Tooth Fairy? Quit playing games. Are we going to do this, or are we going to start shooting each other?"

"Take it easy, Ted—"

"You tell me to take it easy when I know your name and we're sitting in your office at Langley. Till then, be nervous because I am unpredictable. Now for the last time, are we doing this or not?"

"OK, we'll meet here in DC—"

"Why not Langley?"

"Man! Give me a chance will you, Ted! Langley is out of bounds right now, and I will explain why, to your satisfaction, right here in DC. You're not the only one adjusting, Ted. This is real unexpected. Trust... Did you give him your name?"

She said, "Yes, I had to."

"OK, so trust Carmen, she'll make sure you're OK. I'll see you here in about four hours. We'll have lunch, and I'll explain everything I can."

I said, very slowly and deliberately, "What is your name?"

This guy liked his silences, either that or he had a problem with being decisive. Eventually he said, "Mitch, Mitch Vogel." Before I could answer, he said, "Carmen, we'll meet at the Stone House, OK? Then we'll come in to DC together."

"Gotcha."

He hung up. She looked at me and shrugged. "OK? You know my name, you know his name, everything is going to be explained." She reached in her jacket, and my finger slipped from the guard onto the trigger, but she pulled out a leather wallet and tossed it across the desk to me. "Can we start to relax a little now?"

I looked at her ID card and tossed it back.

"We take my car. You drive, and I shoot you if you do anything stupid." I pointed at her card. "They make those by the million in China, and Kellogg's gives them out with their Cornflakes. You and I both know the purpose of ID cards is not to prove who you are but to carry information about who you are so the powers that be can control you. When we are in your friend Mitch's office in Langley, I might start to take you seriously. Right now all I have is questions which you don't want to answer."

I took the photographs from their frames, found a manilla envelope, and slipped them in. She stood, but instead of joining her, I went and opened the bow window. I looked out and figured it was a twelve to fifteen foot drop. Her voice came to me from inside the room.

"What are you doing?"

I turned and went to stand a couple of feet from her. "That is a fifteen foot drop. If it doesn't kill you, it will break bits of you you don't want broken. Give me the keys to my

HELL'S FURY | 67

house or I will take them from you and throw you out the window."

Her face flushed with anger. Her hand flashed under her jacket behind her back to her pancake. I slapped my left hand against her elbow, put the heel of my right hand against her forehead and hooked my right heel behind her ankle. It took a fraction of a second, and she went down painfully on her back, pinning her right arm under her. She cried out and tried to pull out her arm. By that time, I was kneeling on her solar plexus with the BUL in her face.

"See? That was a stupid thing to do. This is my house. The keys to my house are mine. I don't care if you're CIA or the ASS. You have keys to my house that belong to me, and you either give them to me or you go out the window. And while you're at it, you can hand me the Glock 17 you have in your pancake."

She scowled at me, and her cheeks flushed red. "I will need my right hand to give you your damned keys, you damned animal!"

"Then you'd better make sure you keep it. Now nice and slow, pull out the Glock."

She frowned in spite of herself. "How did you know it was a Glock 17?"

"You're small, and it's in a pancake, so it has to be light. But you're smart and ambitious, so it's going to be a Glock or a Sig. Sig's too heavy. Glock is light and reliable."

She pulled out the Glock and handed it to me. "You're a real asshole, you know that?"

"My keys."

She pulled them out of her pocket and handed them to me too. I stood, and she scrambled to her feet. I jerked my head toward the door as I pulled my cell from my pocket. I said, "Car" as I dialed Jane Harrison's number. She answered as we were going down the stairs to the front door. She sounded both pleased and surprised.

"Hi, how are you?"

"Good. Right now I am in a situation. I am on my way to DC, but I need to see you, late tonight or early tomorrow. I am Ted Hanson—"

"Shit..." She didn't sound real pleased. "You remembered that? Then—"

"No. I went to the house and I saw the photographs in my wife's office." Mendoza had stopped with the front door open and was watching me. "You're an attorney. I need you to take my case, claim the house, and help me prove who I am."

"Jesus, Ted! That's not easy."

"If you don't want to do it, I'll find somebody else."

"No! No, call me as soon as you get back, and we'll talk."

"I am going in my Jeep. I am with someone who claims to be CIA, and she might try to kill me on the way."

"Christ, Ted! Are you serious?"

I looked Carmen straight in the eye. "Yes. Her car is parked in my street. I'll send you a picture. The woman's name is Carmen Mendoza, and her prints are all over my wife's office. I'll call you before eleven. If you haven't heard from me by then, you'll know this woman has killed me."

I hung up. Mendoza was shaking her head. "I thought you were an asshole. I have changed my mind. I now know you are a real big asshole on steroids. You didn't need to do that."

HELL'S FURY | 69

"Yeah? Am I supposed to take your word for that? Get out and get in the Jeep."

Out on the sidewalk as I pressed the fob to open the doors, I glanced up and down the road. I spoke conversationally as she reached for the driver's door. "The white Honda Accord is yours, right?"

Her face registered astonishment, and by then it was too late to deny it. "How did you know?"

I smiled and opened my Whatsapp. I sent Jane a couple of photographs of the Honda and climbed into the passenger seat. She got behind the wheel, and we slammed the doors.

"It's the only car that was here when I arrived and is still here now, after everybody has gone to work. You were waiting for me. I can wait for the explanation, but be sure, Carmen, there will be an explanation."

She put the car in Drive, and we moved off.

EIGHT

She took the Lincoln Tunnel and turned south onto I-95 at Penhorn Marsh. The next one hundred and twenty-five miles were a straight run on the interstate as far as Newark. In those two hours, she didn't say a word. At the Yorkshire interchange, she came off I-95 and joined State Route 896, headed north.

"Where are we going?"

She didn't look at me. She spoke like an automaton. "Stone House."

"What's Stone House?"

"A small restaurant. You'll love it. Good honest American fare."

She said it like she was dictating numbers into her cell phone.

"Wow, I can't wait."

"You heard him. We meet there. It's quiet and we can talk. Then he'll take us to DC."

At Main Street, she turned west, and I watched through

the windshield as the landscape grew steadily more rural. After twenty miles, I was seeing a lot of grass and a lot of trees and the odd roof and chimney stack poking through, set back from the road. We were getting remote. I studied her face a moment.

"If we are ambushed, you know what I'm going to do, don't you?"

She sighed and rolled her eyes. "Catch the bullets in your teeth and spit them back?"

"I'm going to grab you and use you as a shield. They might kill me, but they'll have to go through you to do it."

She studied me back for a moment. "You're not just an asshole, Hanson. You're a paranoid asshole. We thought you were dead. You became involved in an investigation, and you were murdered. I watched you gunned down. Now you show up alive. We are not planning to ambush or kill you. Just relax a little, will you?"

"If that's true, how come you didn't recognize me?"

"We never met face to face. I watched it from a distance."

She looked back at the road, slowed, and turned right onto Rock Springs Road. As she turned, she muttered, "This is not the Bay of Pigs or MK Ultra. That was a different CIA and a long time ago."

Stone House was in fact a one-story clapboard building set back from the road in a large parking lot. There were a few houses nearby, largely hidden among abundant foliage. If somebody had told me I was in Maine or Vermont, I would have believed them.

She pulled into the lot and parked beside a cream Dodge Charger. She killed the engine and sat looking at me. Finally she pointed to the BUL in my lap. "You going to point that at me through the parking lot and the restaurant until we sit down?"

I shrugged with my eyebrows. "I don't know. I'll have to check with my gut and see how I feel about you."

Her expression said she was somewhere between bored and irritated. "Just dial it down a bit, will you, Hanson?"

She opened the door and got out. I swung down, put the BUL in my waistband behind my back, and followed her into the restaurant. It was half full. Mainly families getting their kids obese on simple carbohydrates and processed protein while they connected to the Hive through their phones.

Mendoza didn't look for him. She knew where he would be sitting and crossed the dining room to the windowless corner where he was largely out of sight. He watched me carefully as I followed her. He was in his sixties. His hair had turned white, and he had the kind of scrawniness you get from worrying compulsively about things you can't fix. He stood as we approached. Aside from glancing at her, he ignored Mendoza and offered me his hand. His eyes were warm.

"Ted," he said. "I can hardly believe it's you."

I took the hand with not much enthusiasm and agreed with him. "Yeah, me too."

It took him a moment, but he laughed like I'd said something funny. "Sit," he said. "Sit, sit."

It was directed at me, but Mendoza sat too. A waitress appeared with menus. I handed mine back and told her, "I want a New York strip, medium rare, and a beer. No sides, no salad. You can take the salad home for your pet bunnies."

She didn't know whether to laugh, so she just looked

queasy. Mendoza ordered a special burger with fries, and Mitch Vogel said he'd have the same as me. Maybe he thought he was doing NLP mirroring.

When the waitress had gone he stared at me across the table. He didn't look happy, but he said, "Ted, you have no idea how happy I am to see you."

"You're right. I have no idea. Maybe you can explain it to me."

He narrowed his eyes. "You don't remember me, do you?"

"What makes you say that, Mitch?"

"We were friends. We were close friends."

I nodded for a bit, studying his face. "How about you start by telling me how and why I got shot and Miss Mendoza here left me for dead? No." I shook my head. "Better than that, start by telling my how the hell I am involved with the CIA. Then you can tell me how and why I got shot, and why this alleged CIA officer left me for dead."

He looked sad. He even looked contrite and leaned back in his chair like he was hurt by my rebuff but figured he, the CIA, and America had earned it.

"It sounds like a couple of simple questions, Ted, but there is a hell of a lot of explaining that goes into those questions."

"I'm not in a hurry."

He sighed heavily and glanced at Mendoza. She shrugged. He said to me, "How much do you remember, Ted? What happened to you after the shooting?"

"Do you guys always answer a question with a question? What's it to you how much I remember or what happened?"

He gave a short laugh and nodded. "I'm telling you it's complex. How much knowledge can I assume?"

"None. Your genius Mendoza here thought I was an impostor using plastic surgery. Assume she was right."

He spread his hands. "OK, if that's how you want to play it, I'll assume you remember practically nothing. But..." He paused and looked at me from under his eyebrows. "Do you remember what your wife was working on, just before..."

He trailed off, and I leaned forward with my elbows on the table.

"Here's what *I* am going to assume. I am going to assume that you both work for a Mexican cartel and you are trying to pump me for information. So the next time you ask me a question instead of answering mine, I am going to blow your brains and hers all over the wall. Then I am going to take the keys to your Dodge, and I am going to disappear into the sunset. My advice to you, Mitch, my old friend, is don't bore me. I bore very easily, and you would really not like me, as a human being, when I am bored." "That was unnecessary." He looked wounded.

"Maybe you're right, Mitch. But until you stop hedging and start answering my questions, I am going to be getting more bored, more pissed..." I leaned across the table and stared hard into his eyes. "And more dangerous."

He closed his eyes and took a deep breath. "Your wife was engaged in a very sensitive investigation into the growing ties between Middle Eastern terrorists and the Mexican cartels."

I felt a hot rage in my belly but spoke quietly. "Bullshit."

He frowned. "Excuse me?"

"She was not in law enforcement…"

I realized too late I had given away too much. How much I could remember, and how much I had forgotten, was something they were keen to find out. And I had just given them a clear insight into just how little I remembered.

A small smile touched the corner of his mouth. Mendoza said, "You don't remember anything about her, do you?"

"I remember she was not in law enforcement. So she was not engaged in any kind of investigation into ties between drug cartels and terrorism. That is bullshit and you know it."

He glanced at Mendoza. The smile was still lingering on his face, though she remained expressionless. She said, "What was your wife's job, Ted?"

I stared at her. My breathing was shallow and my heart was pounding hard. I said, "Go to hell," but it came out as a barely audible rasp.

"You don't know, do you? You were in her office today. It didn't occur to you to wonder? A big house on the Upper West Side, right by Riverside Drive? The biggest room on the second floor is devoted entirely to her office? You never stopped to ask where was this money coming from? Because, let's see, what do you do for a living, big guy?"

"Cut it out, Mendoza." It was Vogel. "He can't remember." He turned to me. "Susan, your wife, was a highly intelligent woman and a very talented researcher, on many levels. On the face of it, she was an anthropologist at Columbia, but her doctorate had been in how violent crime shaped social order. Her thesis was that all social establishments are founded on early violent crime. Her continuing research in that area brought her to the attention of the Federal Bureau of Investigation and also to the CIA. Over the years, her studies were invaluable in helping us understand how organized crime worked in Mexico and how terrorist groups shaped society in the Middle East." He gave a small laugh and shook his head. "She was tireless and brilliant. She somehow found time to write a series of fictional thrillers too. They became *New York Times* bestsellers, and she became a very wealthy woman."

I stared at him while they both studied my face. Finally Mendoza said, "You don't remember a goddamn thing. How bad is it, Hanson?"

I gave my head a small shake. "I am not saying another word until you take me to an office in Langley where the people know who you are."

The food and our drinks arrived, and while the waitress delivered them, Vogel pulled his cell and made a call, keeping eye contact with me throughout.

"Sir, I'm here at the Stone House with Carmen and Ted Hanson... Yeah, it's really him. He doesn't remember much, and we are having trouble gaining his trust. What he wants is to see us, as it were, in context at Langley. In his words, if he sees us there and people recognize us, he'll believe us."

He waited, listening, still keeping eye contact with me. After a moment, he gave me a small nod and said, "Thank you sir. I'll do that."

He waited. I didn't say anything. Finally he shrugged. "OK, let's eat, and then I'll take you to Virginia. There you can meet all the guys. See if you remember anything."

They started eating.

"Are you telling me I worked for the CIA?"

He spoke with his mouth full, looking into his plate.

"I'm not telling you anything, Hanson." He looked up and shrugged. "What's the point? You won't believe me anyway. When we get to the office, we can sit down and talk, and maybe then you'll drop the damned attitude."

I pulled off half my beer, set it down, and picked up my knife and fork. "Yeah, maybe," I said, half to myself, and cut into the bloody meat.

We ate in silence, and when we were done, he ordered coffee. When the waitress had taken our plates, I said, "Are we waiting for something?"

He nodded. "An escort."

"An escort?"

He leaned on the table with one elbow and pointed at me. "Yeah, partly to protect you because my gut tells me there is a growing number of people who would like to attend your *real* funeral. And partly to protect us. Because wherever you go, dead people seem to show up."

I narrowed my eyes, suddenly alarmed. "How would you know that?"

"Yeah, well, that's why they call us Central Intelligence."

"Who have you been talking to?"

It was Mendoza who answered. "Oh, yeah, what was his name? I remember! He was called mind your own goddamn business. You remember him, Vogel?"

Vogel smiled as the waitress set down the coffee and the check. He said:

"Trust is a two-way street, Hanson."

As if on cue, four guys walked into the restaurant and stood looking around. They weren't wearing suits, wires in their ears, and heavy shades, but they might as well have been. Instead they were all wearing jeans, Doc Martens-style boots, and brown leather jackets, the uniform of the special operative under cover. They saw us and came over.

They didn't speak to us, and we didn't speak to them. Vogel paid cash, we stood, and all seven of us trooped out together. It was as subtle and inconspicuous as a fluorescent yellow condom inflated with helium and set loose at a vicar's tea party.

Vogel got behind the wheel, and Mendoza and one of the special operatives got in the rear passenger seats. I got in next to Vogel, and as I went to slam the door, I got a flash of a memory of a conversation I'd had with some guy. I could hear his voice as clear as if he was talking to me right there and then. He was in his fifties, in an expensive Italian suit, and he had that unmistakable New Jersey Italian accent. He would have said he was from Noo Joisey. He said, "We all knew that. It's like a thing, right? If they come and say, 'Let's go for a ride,' and they put you in the front passenger seat, you know it's over. The game's over for you. All you can hope is they do it quick. Not a rope, you know? Maybe a gun."

I stopped with the door open. Vogel looked at me. I said, "Front passenger seat with these two characters in the back?"

He made the face of tedium. "Come on, will you, Hanson! This is not the Mafia. We have other, more efficient ways of doing things. Just close the damned door and let's get you in an office in Langley and get this goddamn thing over with. You want to know who you are and what happened, we want to debrief you. We want to know what happened too. We are the good guys, Hanson. Close the damned door!"

It wasn't so much that I believed him as I felt I had no

choices left and in the end it was like what that guy had said, you just hope they make it quick. After that, at least you can rest.

I slammed the door. On my left, I saw the other three guys get in a truck, and we pulled out of the parking lot. I had expected us to turn left to pick up Route 1 through Baltimore to DC. Instead we turned right. I raised an eyebrow at Vogel.

"North?"

"For crying out loud! Relax, will you? We take the back roads, cross over the Susquehanna at Lock Twelve. We take a little detour and come in to DC via Westminster on Route 97." He looked at me with sudden bile and viciousness in his face. "Is that OK with you, Mr. Hanson?"

I nodded slowly, holding his eye. "Yeah, that suits me just fine."

NINE

WE DROVE NORTH FOR ABOUT SEVEN MILES, AND IN the quiet, pretty village of Wakefield, we turned left onto Furniss Road. Furniss Road was a narrow blacktop that wound its way through green, rolling fields and woodlands. It connected, after many bucolic twists and turns, with River Road, which took us to the Kelly's Run Nature Reserve and the Holtwood Bridge that crossed the railway tracks and the Susquehanna River.

And it was as we came off the bridge and began to climb into the forest that I knew, as a certainty, that they planned to kill me. There was a gentle curve to the right as the road climbed, but just before the bend a smaller road crossed our path, and to the left it plunged into deep shadows where the canopy of the trees formed a roof, turning the road into a dark tunnel. Here Vogel spun the wheel, and we went in among the shadows.

"Is this another shortcut to Langley?"

He ignored me and drove on. After about one hundred

yards, he came off the road and nosed his way in among ferns and undergrowth until we were no longer visible from the road. There he killed the engine and turned to look at me. There was an unpleasant smile playing on his lips. I said, "Is this where you plan to kill me?"

He didn't answer. Instead there was a flash of movement, and suddenly I had what felt like a mountaineer's bootlace around my neck. I knew it was Mendoza sitting behind me, and I knew she was getting a kick out of showing me how damned strong she was.

There is a simple rule when you're getting strangled: If you think about trying to breathe, your throat, or the hands of your killer, you will die. If you are being strangled, there is just one thing you need to think about—your available weapons.

I had the BUL under my arm, but I knew I had no time to reach for it, and even if I got a hold of it, I had no way of getting a bead on Mendoza. I acted without thinking. I made an iron rod of my left index and middle fingers and rammed it into Vogel's eye. I felt the eye pop, and he screamed a high, shrill scream. I felt the string loosen around my neck, and I knew the special operative was reaching for his piece. I also knew he couldn't use it. The last thing they needed was a shot-up car full of blood.

I didn't have that problem.

Vogel was screaming, "*My eye! My eye!*" I lunged toward him, pulling the string from Mendoza's hand as she clawed at my arm. At the same time, I hauled Vogel toward me, my right hand went inside his jacket and came out with his Glock 17. I put two rounds over my left arm, and the special operative's brains sprayed over the window.

Mendoza was in my blind spot. In a split second I knew one of two things was going to happen. Either she was going to jump out and run, or she was going to shoot me in the back. Whichever one she went for, I knew I had to get out. She was panicking and went for the former, and we both jumped at the same time. As her door flew open, I slammed it closed in her face. She staggered back, and I went after her as their backup car turned into the forest behind us.

The kicks came as a surprise. She was good. She threw a front kick and a side kick at my knees, forcing me to back up, and followed with a viper-fast high roundhouse kick at my head. I managed to weave back, and it grazed my chin just as the three guys jumped from their truck.

Tae kwon do is a fearsome art, and I have a lot of respect for it. It just has one big drawback. To do it well, you need to be Korean and start practicing when you're four. Mendoza wasn't Korean, and she hadn't started when she was four. She followed her spinning roundhouse to my head with a spinning back kick—or tried to. But by the time she had her second leg in the air, I was at her back with my right arm around her throat and my left forearm at the back of her neck. The three special operatives had their weapons trained on me. I spoke into her ear, loud enough for them to hear.

"I squeeze, you die."

One of the operatives, Midwest with blue eyes and very short platinum hair, said, "You kill her and you're a colander, mister."

I gave him the kind of smile you have nightmares about.

"And what if I don't kill her, son? What if I just make her pass out through lack of oxygen? Will we both be colanders together? Drop your weapon and lie on the ground."

HELL'S FURY | 83

He hesitated and glanced at his buddies. I began to squeeze, and Mendoza began to make ugly guttural noises, clawing at my arm and kicking her feet.

The guy dropped his weapon and got face down on the forest floor. The other two did a little dance, shifting their feet. One of them said, "Take it easy, mister."

I snapped, "What's your name?"

He glanced at his buddy but got no help there. So he licked his lips and said, "Gutmeyer. Don't do anything crazy. Nobody needs to get hurt, sir."

"Shut up." I said it quietly, then addressed his pal, who was still standing and looked real nervous. "You. Drop your weapon and get on your belly, hands behind your head." I didn't give him a chance to argue. I started squeezing and leered at him. "Do I have to kill her just so you can make a colander out of us?"

He glanced at Gutmeyer, and they both nodded at each other. He dropped his weapon and got on his face.

"Now you listen to me, Gutmeyer. You are going to take their bootlaces and you are going to tie their ankles nice and tight and their wrists behind their backs. You should see this as a good thing, because it would be easier for me to shoot them where they lie. But I am not in the business of killing federal officers. However, I will check the bonds, and if they are loose, I will make an exception with you and with Mendoza. Do it."

He went about the task with the energy and commitment of a man who does not want to become an exception to a rule. While he did it, I was aware that I had left Vogel eyeless in the car. I edged over toward the vehicle, and through the open door, I could see him with both hands cupped over his right eye socket. Whether his eye was in there I had no idea, and right then, I didn't care much.

Gutmeyer said, "OK. I've done what you asked, what now?"

I looked over and saw he had his weapon in his holster under his arm.

"Drop your weapon." He dropped it. "Come over here. And relax. I don't aim to kill anybody today unless you force me to."

He wasn't convinced, and I can't say I blamed him. But he came over on hesitant feet and stood in front of me. I made it quick. I slipped my left arm, which had been behind Mendoza's neck, across her throat, and smacked him hard with my right fist in a straight jab to the tip of his chin. You could hit King Kong like that and he'd go down. Gutmeyer was not King Kong. He keeled over like a felled tree.

I gave Mendoza another little squeeze, and her legs went spaghetti. I dragged her to the special ops guys' truck and shoved her in the back. Then I went and dragged Vogel out of his vehicle. He'd gone into shock and was shivering and sobbing. I put him on his knees and shot him in the back of the head. Then I took his shoelaces and his socks and went back to Mendoza. I tied her ankles tight and her wrists behind her back. Then I shoved Vogel's socks in her mouth.

The last thing I did before I drove away was to take Vogel's Glock over and shoot the two guys who were tied up. Then I went to where Gutmeyer was lying unconscious. I wrapped his right hand around the weapon and pulled off a couple of shots up into the dense foliage overhead. I kept the casings so the only ones forensics would find would be the ones in the car, the ones beside Vogel's body, and the ones beside the dead guys.

Then I went back to the truck, dragged Mendoza onto the floor behind the driver's seat, got behind the wheel, and took off, with no idea where in hell I was going. I drove around for maybe an hour with no fixed direction, making a mental note of all the densely forested areas. After a quarter of an hour, I heard Mendoza begin to thrash and try and kick and shout. I ignored her until shortly after three o'clock, when I came to Bridgeton, where Piney Hill Road borders Muddy Creek deep into an exceptionally dense, sprawling forest.

I followed the road beside the creek for a little over a mile until I found a suitable place to come off the road and tuck the truck in among the thick foliage and ferns. There I opened the rear door and heaved Mendoza out onto her feet. Her eyes were wide with fear, but her pupils were black pinpricks. Her skin looked pasty, and for a moment I felt something like compassion for her.

"This can go one of three ways," I told her. "You can walk on your own two feet. I can knock you unconscious and carry you, or I can call it a day and kill you right here. Nod if you understand."

She nodded.

"I'm going to take the socks out of your mouth. If you scream, I'll knock you unconscious. If you keep giving me trouble, I'll break your neck. Nod if you understand."

She nodded again, and I removed the socks. She took a deep breath and hissed savagely, "You said you'd never kill a federal officer."

I nodded. "Yeah, and it's true, but using the title of

federal officer as a cover so you can commit murder and traffic in drugs, sex slaves, and prostitution puts you outside that category, whatever your ID card says."

She swallowed hard. "I don't know anything about that."

"Right. You trying to strangle me just now was just a misunderstanding. So maybe we can get along and be friends after all."

"I can explain if you'll let me."

"Save it for later. Right now I am going to untie your feet, and we are going to take a walk. I have just killed Vogel and four CIA special operatives. And the deck was kind of stacked against me, Mendoza. I hope you understand that I will kill you stone dead without hesitation if you become an inconvenience."

She nodded and spoke quietly. "I understand that."

"Good. Be smart and you might even become useful. That means you get to live. Be smart."

I untied her ankles and led her through the dense, aromatic green undergrowth and the mottled green light, toward the sigh and the splash of the creek. We walked in silence for maybe a hundred and fifty yards and finally broke out of the trees onto the banks of the river. I stopped her, held her shoulder from behind, and rammed my knee into the back of hers so she collapsed forward. She expostulated, "*Mother f—*"

I nodded and sat on a rock, facing her with my BUL in my hand.

"That's good," I said. "Self-control is what it's all about, and it might just get you out of here alive. Let me tell you what I am going to do, Mendoza, and then I'll tell you how you can stop me." I pointed at the slow-moving brown water in the stream. "I am going to drag you over there and stick your head in the water. I'll do it three times, and on the fourth time I'll hold you down till you drown. Do you believe me? Do I need to prove I am serious?"

She spoke very quietly. "I believe you completely. You don't need to prove anything."

"Good."

"How can I stop you?"

"By answering all my questions, truthfully and without hesitation and without trying to mislead me." I pointed at her. "You are a pro, Mendoza. You know that I will know if you lie." I shook my head. "And in any case, I will check up, follow up, and investigate. And if you have lied to me…" I trailed off and left the words hanging. "Are we on the same page?"

"Yes."

I studied her carefully for a few seconds where she knelt, just a few feet from where I had told her I would drown her, holding her head face down under the water. I wondered if I would be capable of doing it. I didn't think so, even though she had been willing to strangle me with a nylon bootlace.

"What benefit would you and Vogel have got from my death?"

She closed her eyes and sighed. "You have amnesia. As it turns out, you seem to have almost total amnesia. But if your memory comes back…" She paused. "If your memory comes back, you could cause an awful lot of damage to some very powerful people. We couldn't allow that to happen."

"Is one of those people Hans Fischer?"

"Jesus Christ…" She said it without emphasis. It was

more like a statement of helplessness. She shook her head, her mouth worked but no words came out. Finally she said, "Yes, Hans Fischer is one of those people."

"But he's a fixer, a middle man. He arranges things and brings people together, right?"

She screwed up her face and stared at me. "And this is total amnesia?"

I almost smiled. "I don't remember this. I have found this out in the last couple of days. I want you to confirm it."

"Yes! I confirm it!"

"So what we are looking at here is that there are people within the CIA who are dealing illegally with a second party via Fischer, using him as their agent. Is that correct?"

"Yes. More or less."

"You and Vogel were the front men. But you are covering for somebody."

"Yes. Well, he was the front man. I was his assistant. But we took orders from somebody else."

"Who?"

"I don't know."

"I warned you."

"Come on, Hanson! Get real! You seriously think they would let me know who they were? Not even Vogel knew. You want me to give you a name? Fine! I can give you a dozen names. But they won't be worth shit." She sighed, then said more quietly, "I can help you find out. But you have to see that I can't possibly know!"

It made sense. I wondered for a moment if I would have thought it made sense if she'd been a man. Was my judgment skewed when it came to vulnerable women? I changed tack slightly.

HELL'S FURY | 89

"So my wife knew."

"Your wife, Susan Hanson." She nodded and looked down at the damp grass. "She knew. She found out."

I felt a hot burn in my belly. "Did you order her murder?"

She looked surprised. "No. It wasn't us."

"Who was it?"

"We all assumed the order came from Mexico. The hit men were Mexican. They left town and wound up dead in Los Angeles."

I didn't answer for a while. Then I nodded and said, "Yeah, I know. I killed them." I got to my feet, looked deep into her eyes. There was real fear there. I said, "Stand up."

TEN

It was a three and a half hour drive back to New York. I took it slow and made it in a little over four because I wanted to get back as late as possible. I had Mendoza sitting in the front passenger seat with her hands still tied behind her back.

For the first half hour, we drove in silence. At Quarryville, I told her, "I am going to take you home with me. Be smart and you might not only get out of this alive, you might even avoid spending the rest of your life behind bars."

She didn't say anything. She just glanced at me, and her expression was rich with contempt, then shifted her gaze back to the road ahead.

I returned her glance. We were doing a steady, monotonous fifty miles an hour along the long, straight 372 toward Atglen.

"I don't need you, Mendoza," I said. "You can be useful if you play your cards right, and if you're useful, you can come out of this relatively unharmed. But act stupid and you've seen how quickly things can change."

"Yes, I have seen that, and you've told me all this already. I get it." She sounded like a spoiled kid who's been told she can't go out Friday night.

"So why do I get the feeling I'm not getting through to you? Why do I have the feeling you are playing me along?"

"I don't know. Maybe I'm playing you along. Maybe I have a bad reaction to bossy, authoritarian men. Maybe I just don't like you. Stop repeating yourself already. OK, you're a big, tough dangerous guy, and you'll kill me without batting an eyelid. I get it."

"I don't think you do. You see, I have nothing left to lose. You do. You could still have a life ahead of you." I fixed my eyes on the road. "You're young, you're attractive, you're smart. It is still worth your while to try and make it work."

Her face looked like she'd just stepped in something the dog left behind. "Cut it out, will you! What the hell! You're going to get paternal on me now? Screw you!"

For a moment, I was confused, and the words came out in a savage burst. "I'm telling you this so you understand! I am quite happy to open that damned door, here and now, and kick you out of this moving truck into the traffic. I'm quite happy to shoot you in the head crossing the sidewalk on West 81st Street. I have nothing to lose! You get it? I have nothing to lose! So if I am telling you it's in your interest to be smart, I mean it. Be smart!"

She looked out the window like the view bored her. "Thanks, Pop."

At King of Prussia, we picked up I-276. I said, "You will be a prisoner in my house. You will tell me everything you know, and you will help me to acquire more intelligence as well as material, forensic evidence. In exchange, I will help negotiate a bargain with the district attorney. You get to live and you get to walk free, and I get to take down the people who killed my wife."

"That simple, huh? And you can guarantee that?"

"I can't guarantee it, Mendoza, no. Because there are too many stupid people involved, and you are the first among them. But I can guarantee two things. First I can guarantee I'll give it my best shot, and my best shot seems to be a pretty good one. The second thing I can guarantee is that if you don't play ball, I will kill you without hesitation. Now maybe you'd like to tell me which option you prefer." She didn't answer, so I went on. "Another thing I can guarantee is this. If I pull over on West 41st and let you out, your pals in Central Intelligence will have you skin diving in the East River before the end of the week. That crime scene in the forest by the Susquehanna river? It says loud and clear that you and Gutmeyer killed Vogel and the boys. How long do you think it will be before this reaches Director Burns' desk? How long before an inquiry is set up? You and your cabal are finished whichever way you look at it. And your smart move is to jump ship and join the winning side before it's too late. And you know it."

Again she didn't answer, and we lapsed into silence. I knew she was thinking through all the angles, and I knew also that she would have to come to the realization sooner or later that she was as screwed as a two-dollar whore during shore leave. And what she needed was a way out where she could save face—at least to some extent—and also make it credible for the DA and her own top brass that she genuinely regretted what she had been involved in and wanted to reform.

So I let her think, but at Bristol, as I merged onto I-95, I told her, "I get to avenge my family and the people I loved, I get closure, and, with your help, I get to discover who I am. You get to start over and put all this behind you."

I kept my eyes on the road, but in my peripheral vision, I was aware of her staring at me for a long while.

By the time I eventually pulled up outside my house on West 81st. It was gone seven p.m. The rush-hour traffic and my own efforts to go slow had worked together. I killed the engine and sat looking at her for a moment, trying to assess what she was going to do.

"I am going to untie you. I am going to go around and open the door for you, and we are both going to enter the house like normal people. Make a bolt for it, run, scream, do anything to attract attention to yourself, and I will kill you without hesitation. Do you believe me?"

She nodded. "You have told me enough times. I believe you. You are a very scary bad man, and I will obey your every command, sir."

I pulled my Swiss Army knife from my pocket and cut her bonds. She sat motionless, staring at the windshield. I climbed out and walked around to her door. I pulled it open, and she climbed out. She stared up into my face and for a few seconds tried out several different smiles, like she was trying to find one that worked. In the end, she gave up, and we walked together to the door. I unlocked it, and we went inside.

I showed her into the living room and stood in the doorway while she sat.

"You hungry?"

She shook her head.

"You want a drink?"

"Do you remember where they are?" She stood. "I'll get them. I'm figuring you're a whiskey guy. Bourbon?"

"Irish."

She went to the dresser, found a bottle of Bushmills, and poured a couple of inches into two tumblers. She handed me one. I sipped and said, "I'm going to show you to your room. I am going to give you pen and paper, and you are going to write down a detailed statement of everything you and Vogel were involved in. You will name names, and you will detail everything you have stolen from my wife's office—"

"You don't —"

I raised a finger. "Let's be smart. Susan was killed because of the research she was doing. You had a key to our house. Logic dictates that you took all her files and her hard drives. Anything that is left upstairs was of no interest to you. So you will list everything you took and state where it is now being held. And keep remembering, Mendoza, you are fighting to save your life. Every corner you cut, every lie you tell, brings you a little bit closer to not leaving this house alive."

She made a face of disbelief. She closed her eyes, opened her mouth, and shook her head. "You are one holy son of a bitch."

I nodded. "You'd do well to keep that in mind too. Come on, upstairs."

I took her upstairs to a room that looked like a guest room. There was no escape through the window. It was a sheer drop to a stone-flagged yard. There was no bedding with which to improvise a rope, but there was a small, roll-top desk where she could sit and write. I had picked up a couple of large notepads from the office on the way up, and I now dropped them on the desk along with a pen.

I held her eye a moment and said, "Take your clothes off."

Her jaw actually sagged open. "You are kidding me. You are not serious."

"Strip or I'll take them off for you."

She was laughing. It was an incredulous laugh, but she was laughing. "Are you...? You're not. I don't believe..."

"Take your clothes off, Mendoza."

She pulled off her jacket and was about to drop it on the bed. I said, "Hand it to me."

She handed it over, and I felt through the pockets. I took her wallet and her cell. There was nothing else, so I threw it on the bed. She had removed her pancake where she'd had the Glock and was now unbuttoning her blouse, holding my eye. She was looking to see if she was turning me on. It dawned on me that in fact, watching the way she was taking her time over each button, she was actually, deliberately trying to turn me on.

She handed over her blouse. It held nothing, and I tossed that on the bed too. She kicked off her shoes, which I picked up and examined, and then she slipped off her skirt, making something of an elaborate show of it. She smiled at me, and I smiled back.

"This is kind of weird," she said. "What about my bra and panties? Do I have to remove them too?"

"Yes."

"You're a very bad man, Ted Hanson."

She handed them to me, and I checked them for wires. There was nothing, and I handed them back. "Make a start on that statement."

"That's it? You don't want to check anywhere else?"

I shook my head. "I guess I'll die someday, probably sooner than later, but when I do, it won't be having meaningless sex with a CIA killer."

I held up her phone so it saw her face and unlocked.

"You son of a bitch."

"Get that statement written. I need it tonight."

I closed the door. It was solid mahogany and had an old-fashioned chub lock. I locked it and left the key half-turned. Then I reset her phone to open on seeing my face and went down to the next floor, into what had been my wife's office, and sat on the sofa in the bow window, staring at the desk with the computer on it. A writer, an anthropologist, a researcher...

I took out my own cell and called Jane Harrison. She answered on the first ring. There was a moment's silence, then, "Ted?"

"I'm back home. Can you come over?"

"Sure, I'll be there in fifteen minutes. Are you OK?"

"I'm fine. I need to talk to you."

There was a moment's silence, then, "OK, I'm on my way."

I had time to crack a beer and eat a ham sandwich, then there was a ring at the bell. I opened the door, and she stood staring at me like she was trying to make sure it was really my face.

"Come on in."

She crossed the threshold, and I led her into the living room. She sat on the sofa, and I stood by the fireplace, looking down at her. She frowned. "What's going on? What's this about, Ted?"

"You're an FBI agent." She drew breath to answer, but I cut her short. "So am I."

She sagged back a bit. "You remembered."

"No. But you've just confirmed what I suspected." She closed her eyes and swore under her breath. I said, "Why the charade? Why didn't you just tell me?"

"Because you're supposed to be dead."

I narrowed my eyes at her. "Call me crazy but 'My God, you're alive! It's great to see you!' might have been more helpful than 'Don't I know you?'"

"It's not that simple. Have you got something to drink that isn't water?"

"Sure."

I poured us both an inch of whiskey and handed her a glass. I sat in one of the armchairs and sipped. "You want to tell me why it's not that simple?"

"You are officially dead. You and…" She hesitated. "You and Susan and the children were gunned down. There were witnesses, and a couple of those witnesses were CIA officers."

"That much I have managed to find out. And I've been told I have all the right wounds, even the through and through. Where is my body supposed to be?"

"Incinerated."

"Who incinerated it"?"

She puffed out her cheeks. "Again, it's not that simple."

A wave of frustration made me raise my voice. "Why

not, Jane? Stop bullshitting me and be straight with me. Who incinerated my body?"

"Susan and the kids were gunned down by four men in a car. You were at the Cruise Terminal. A car pulled up. Four men got out and started shooting. You charged them and got shot several times. Everyone assumed you were dead. But they got back in their vehicle and turned it around. Meanwhile, somehow, you got up and got into your car and went after them. They fired an assault rifle into your gas tank, and your truck exploded." She gave a small shrug. "It exploded and burned."

"My family were all dead. So the Bureau took care of the funeral."

"What was left of you was incinerated."

I smiled without much humor. "I became a biscuit, twice cooked."

She shook her head. "That's not funny."

I ignored her and spoke half to myself. "And yet here I am. I've seen the photograph of myself upstairs in Susan's office. I have all the right scars. It's me." She didn't say anything. I frowned at her. "I have to ask again, if I was shot multiple times and then *incinerated*—twice!—how come you were so cool in the club? 'Hi, don't I know you?' Wouldn't 'What the hell! You're supposed to be dead and incinerated!' have been more to the point? I don't get it, Jane. You're explaining it, and it isn't making sense."

She took a deep breath and let it out through puffed cheeks. "I told you it wasn't simple. A couple of weeks back, the Los Angeles field office ran your prints and your DNA. For some reason I am not privy to, your DNA and prints are sealed and classified and not available on the database. So

HELL'S FURY | 99

they drew a negative result. But we were alerted to the search."

"Who's 'we'?"

"Your director, Paul Levi, and me."

"Why? Why you? If you're not privy to the reasons for my prints and DNA being classified, why were you alerted?"

She took a long, deep breath. "Because you and I worked together. We were friends. We were very close friends. When Director Levi was alerted to the search, he called me and told me."

"That can't be protocol."

"It's not." She fixed me with her eye. "But protocol is not always right."

I frowned, wondering where this was going. "...OK."

"Special Agents Elroy Jones and Cathy Newton contacted us from the Wilshire Boulevard office in LA and said they were involved in the investigation of an amnesiac whom they suspected of killing several men, among them Nestor Gavilan, Felipe Ochoa, Oliver Peralta, and Eulogio Borja. These were the four men who gunned down Susan and the kids and, supposedly, killed you. It was one hell of a coincidence."

"So Levi told you to meet me and test me. How did you know I would be at the club?"

She gave me one of those 'Really?' looks and arched an eyebrow. It was familiar and made me smile.

"Duh! The first thing we did was stake out this house. When you showed up, I tailed you. When you went to the club, I joined you and had a closer look. It was you." She sighed and shrugged. "It was incredible, impossible to explain, but it was you."

"So back to my initial question. Why not tell me? Why not pull me in and debrief me? Why the charade?"

She stared at me for a long time before answering, and I saw she had tears in her eyes. Finally she said, "Because, like I said, it is impossible to explain. It *can't* be you. How has this happened? How come you have the same DNA? How come you have the same prints? We even checked to see if you had a twin we didn't know about. You haven't. We can't explain how this has happened. But one thing we are absolutely sure about is that you died that day in that burning truck. You are dead."

"But I'm not!" I exploded. "Clearly I am not. I'm here! Breathing! Talking! It is me, Jane. I can't be anybody else."

"It is"—she took a deep breath—"and it isn't. You look like you, you sound like you, apparently you have all the right scars; and yet there is something different. You were always good at martial arts, but you were also the sweetest, kindest, most gentle man I had ever..." She shook her head. "...you could imagine. I've seen you in difficult and dangerous situations, but I never saw you act out of rage or aggression. Yet from what the LA field office have reported..." She trailed off and shook her head again. "*Fourteen men*, and in brutal ways. And who knows what you did in Mexico? The reports we have from the Mexican authorities talk of a massacre. That's not the man I knew."

I was quiet for a long time, trying to search inside the darkness that was my own mind. In the end, I said simply, "They killed my wife and my kids. You said yourself I charged them, and after they shot me, I got in my car and went after them. Maybe you didn't know me that well. Maybe you only knew the Ted Hanson at the office."

She smiled. It was a sad smile, and I saw tears in her eyes again.

"No," she said. "I knew you about as well as anybody did. Even…" She didn't finish but changed tack. "I knew you, believe me. Not just the you at the office. We were close. We were very close friends."

So many questions crowded my mind. In the end, the one I asked was simply "Am I? Do you think I am? Ted Hanson?"

She gave her head a small shake. "I don't know who you are."

ELEVEN

I ROSE AND WALKED TO THE WINDOW AND GAZED out at the street as it sank slowly into grainy dusk. Street lamps winked on, windows became suddenly warm and illuminated before heavy drapes were drawn across them. The few cars that passed, passed with their headlamps on, though darkness had not yet closed in. I spoke, still staring at the street.

"What do you know about the CIA's involvement in Susan and the kids' murder?"

She was quiet so long I turned to look at her. She was watching me, motionless.

"Nothing." It was a lie. Her face said it was a lie, and she knew that I could see it.

"Were you investigating them?"

She closed her eyes. "Don't go there."

"Was the FBI investigating the CIA?"

"We don't do that. It's an unwritten law."

"Like not prosecuting or indicting presidents? The CIA

was involved in an illegal operation on American soil. Somehow Susan found out about it. Did she inform you?"

She opened her mouth to answer, but nothing came out.

"Why did she go to you and not me?"

"Stop. You are jumping to conclusions. You don't remember any of this."

"So help me. Why are you hiding this from me?"

"Because—" She stopped dead and closed her eyes again.

"You don't trust me."

She opened her eyes, and her stare was direct. She didn't deny it. Instead she said, "I *don't know who you are anymore.* This isn't science fiction. I know that physically, your body—you! You are the same man. I don't know how the hell you survived what happened to you, but physically, genetically, you are the same man..."

She trailed off. I said, "But...?"

"But inside *you*—your mind, your *soul!*—I don't recognize you. I don't know you anymore. I don't know what is going on in your mind, in your..." She shrugged and shook her head. "In your heart."

I frowned. One word she had used had stirred something in me. "My soul?"

There was bitterness in her face when she answered. "Do you still have one?"

"I don't know." I approached her and sat down again. "Is that something we used to talk about, you and me?"

She almost smiled. The glimmer was in her eyes and at the corners of her mouth, like early sunshine on a clear pool, just before the sky clouds over.

"Yeah, it's something we used to talk about."

"Someday, not today, we need to talk about that again."

She nodded. I went on, "Before I die. I don't know how long I have. It feels sometimes like I'm overdue."

She smiled a smile that had little amusement in it. "Either that or you reincarnated into the same body you had before."

Again the tug at my mind, like the darkness was stretching and about to snap. Without thinking, I asked her, "Are you a Buddhist?"

"No." She looked like she was going to say something else but stopped herself.

"I was abducted this morning by CIA officers, Jane."

"Is that true? When you called me this morning—"

"Her name is Carmen Mendoza. She took me to a place called Stone House in Maryland, north of Baltimore, just over the border. It's a kind of diner. We met a guy there called Mitch Vogel, a staff operations officer. He had four special operatives join us. He said he was going to take me to DC and tell me all about what happened to Susan. Instead they took me to a forest on the Susquehanna River. There Mendoza tried to strangle me with a nylon bootlace."

She covered her face with her hands, rubbed it a couple of times, and looked at me with sagging shoulders. "I'm guessing," she said with weary irony, "that she didn't have a sudden change of heart and let you go."

"No," I said. "She didn't have a sudden change of heart."

"And yet"—she gestured at me with an upturned palm—"here you are." She gave a small, weary sigh. "You said there was Mendoza, Vogel, and four other guys, special operatives. How many did you kill?"

"Vogel and three of the guys. I framed the fourth one so it looked like he had done most of the killing."

"And what about Mendoza?"

"She's locked in a room upstairs, writing a statement. I said I would get her immunity if she disclosed the nature of the operation she and Vogel were involved in. It was that operation that got Susan and my kids killed."

"Jesus Christ!"

"Were you investigating them, Jane?"

"I can't have this conversation with you. I don't even know who you are! You go around killing people as though that didn't mean anything. You're like a law unto yourself. Now you tell me you have murdered four CIA officers—"

"It wasn't murder. It was self-defense."

"Is that why you framed one of them to take the fall?"

"No, that was just a precaution. Jane, these people discovered somehow that my wife was researching the spread of corruption within the establishment and how organized crime was taking control of the organs of government. They learned somehow that she was going to publish what she knew, and it would implicate them and bring them down. I don't know these things for facts, but I am not far from the truth. And she and my kids were killed because of it. I need to know if you—if we, the FBI, were investigating this."

"I need to discuss this with Director Levi."

"I want to talk to him."

"I'll arrange it, but you should know you might well get arrested."

"I don't care about that. Tell him I'll have information for him, evidence, proof, but Jane, I need to ask you, and whether you answer me or not, you really need to think about this question—"

Her eyes searched my face. "What?"

"Can you trust Levi? I don't remember him. I don't remember anything about him. Can he be trusted? And more to the point, is there anyone close to him or to you, that cannot be trusted? That might be in—" I was about to say the CIA but stopped, and my mouth seemed to speak of its own volition. I said, "Is there anyone who might be in Sinaloa's pocket or who might be owned by organized crime? Think about it. Susan and my children were killed for a reason."

She sighed. "I have to go. Please, Ted, don't do anything until you hear from me."

I smiled. "Do nothin' till you hear from me. Duke Ellington and, uh..." My gaze drifted toward the cold fireplace. "Ella?" I looked at Jane. "Ella Fitzgerald?"

"You remember that? Is that something you remember?"

"It came to me just now when you said that. Does it mean something?"

For a moment, her face went rigid. "That's something only you can answer. I have to go."

She stood. I stood and faced her.

"You have to help me, Jane. You have to stop avoiding answering me and playing games. We were friends." I frowned. "We were more than friends. We were partners."

"Were we?"

"Why are you doing this? Why won't you help me?"

She looked into my eyes, but there was no expression that I could recognize or interpret. She placed her index finger in the middle of my chest and shifted her eyes to where my heart would be.

"You need to remember. You don't need to be reminded. You need to remember. For yourself."

HELL'S FURY | 107

She walked out of the room, and after a few seconds, I heard the front door open and close. A couple of minutes after that, I heard the hum of an engine, and the glow of headlamps filled the bow window, then passed.

I stood for a long while with her words ringing and echoing in my head. I had to remember; not be reminded. I had to remember.

For myself.

I climbed the stairs to the guest room. When I opened the door, Mendoza was sitting at the small desk writing. She looked up and after a moment asked, "What?"

"I've just been speaking to a special agent."

"FBI?"

"Yes."

"So?"

"I'm negotiating your immunity from prosecution. I said I want you to be completely free from any threat. In exchange I said you'd give them everything."

"Wow," she said with bored eyes. "You're my hero."

"Did you know they were investigating you?"

"Is that what they told you?"

"Don't answer my questions with questions of your own. Did you know?"

She turned back to her notebook. "It's all in my report."

"This is the last time I'll warn you, Mendoza. Next time you give me an evasive answer, I will throw you out of the window. Did you know the FBI were investigating you?"

"I don't know what you're talking about. Investigating who? The CIA? Me as a person? Me and Vogel?"

I took a step toward her, and she went to stand, holding her pen like a knife. It was at that moment that the doorbell chimed. Our eyes locked for a few seconds. I stepped back, left the room, and locked her in.

Downstairs, I opened the door and saw two people I recognized from the Mexican border.

"Special Agents Elroy Jones and Cathy Newton. You're a long way from California.[1]"

It was Newton who answered. "May we come in? We would like to have a chat with you."

"You mean you'd like to waterboard me?"

"No." She shook her head. "The CIA do that kind of thing. We use methods that actually work. May we come in or not?"

"Sure." I stood back and held the door open for them, then gestured to the living room. Newton sat in an armchair, but Jones stood in the middle of the floor, staring past the dining table at the lawn beyond the French doors. I spoke to his back.

"Can I offer you a drink? As far as I know, I have only Irish whiskey."

Newton looked like she was about to say she would, but Jones' voice drowned her out.

"This house," he said. "It belonged to Susan Hanson, the academic and novelist."

"Thanks. I didn't know that."

He turned to face me. "So what are you doing here?"

"Gee, Special Agent Jones, I don't know. Let me check with my spirit guide. Huh! He says I should ask you, what damned business is it of yours?"

"Susan Hanson was murdered."

---

1. See *Rogue Book One, Gates of Hell*

"No shit, Sherlock."

Special Agent Newton stepped in. "We are investigating Susan Hanson's death, Mr. Rogue. We last saw you at the Mexican border, and you were on your way to New York. When we spoke to Mike Marshall, he said you'd come from New York. Now we find you seem to be living in Susan Hanson's house—in New York."

I listened till she'd finished, then gave my head a little shake. "You are trying to make this sound like a series of unexplained coincidences. I was returning *to* New York, so it is no surprise I came originally *from* New York, and if you are investigating my wife's murder, it should be no surprise to find me living in the house I shared with her. In New York."

Jones went up on his toes. When he came down again, he rubbed his jaw with the palm of his hand.

"Your wife," he said.

"Was there anything else?"

His forehead contracted like he had brain-ache. Newton stepped in again.

"When we spoke to you in California, the story was you had total amnesia."

"That was not a story, Agent Newton. I had, and have, almost total amnesia."

"But you suddenly remember being married to a very successful academic and writer with a house on the Upper West Side of Manhattan."

"No."

She sighed. "You want to explain?"

"Not really. Can you think of any reason why I should?"

"Yeah." It was Jones. "Susan Hanson was gunned down

here in New York by four Mexicans wanted by the FBI in connection with crimes of drug trafficking, murder, extortion, and prostitution. Those same four men showed up brutally murdered in Los Angeles in the same street on the same day and at the same time that you claim you woke up with total amnesia."

"What's your point, Agent Jones? Every day, all over America, people wake up next door to people who have died. It doesn't mean they killed them, and it doesn't mean they owe the FBI an explanation about where they live or who they are married to." I looked at Agent Newton. "Am I wrong?"

"No, you're not wrong, Mr. Rogue"—she stressed the name—"but you could cooperate with us. It never hurts to assist the Bureau in its investigations."

"Even when they are trying to frame you for murder?"

"We are not trying to frame you—"

"Oh, we just got off to a bad start? Is that it? While I was offering you a drink in my living room, you accidentally accused me of murder and attempted theft."

She nodded like she got my point. Then she asked me, "What's your name?"

"I don't remember, but from what I can ascertain, I was Ted Hanson."

She arched an eyebrow. "You *were* Ted Hanson? Now you're somebody else?"

I raised my shoulders an eighth of an inch and gave my head a small twitch. "Apparently I was murdered at the same time as my wife and children. I was shot several times but made it to a car. They fired into the gas tank, and the car exploded. I remember nothing of that, but I seem to bear the scars, both mental and physical. As an aside, I can say that I find it a crying shame that the Bureau has decided to investigate and frame the victim of this brutal massacre of a family instead of hunting down the organization that perpetrated it.

"However, that all happened to Ted Hanson, and his photograph was on Susan's desk. The photograph is of me. Now, agents, I have been more than patient. I have taken your bad manners, your innuendo, and your insults. I have explained more than I needed to explain, and I would now like you to leave my house."

Newton nodded and moved toward the door, but she stopped when she saw that Jones wasn't following her. Jones was standing with his head on one side, staring at me.

I said, "Do I need to call the cops and have you removed?"

He gave his head a slow shake. "No, I am leaving. I was just thinking, assuming that your story is true, it would give you one hell of a motive to go after those SOBs and their boss in Sinaloa. What was his name?"

I said, "Jesus Sanchez."

"That's the one. That guy was murdered while you were in Mexico. Did you know that?"

I smiled. "Having a motive is not a crime, Agent Jones. Right now I have a very strong motive for kicking your ass out of my house. But that does not make me guilty of physical violence. Now I am going to tell you very clearly for the last time: Get out of my house."

He moved to the door and opened it. This time it was Newton who paused.

"We may want to talk to you again. If we call to make an appointment, will you talk to us?"

I was about to tell her to go to hell; she might find my soul down there. But she was smart and subtle and cute, so instead I said, "Sure." To Jones I said, "See? That's how it's done."

He grunted and turned away, and they both made their way out to the street. I watched them through the bow window climb into a nondescript car and drive away. It didn't make a lot of sense. If the Feds were investigating Susan's death, why was it in the hands of the LA office instead of Federal Plaza? And even if there was a legitimate reason for LA to be investigating instead of New York, why send two agents all the way across the continent instead of reaching out to the field office and getting some local agents to... I trailed off in my thoughts. To do what? What had they asked me, after all? What was I doing in this house? It made no sense.

Just as it made no sense that Jane had not mentioned the investigation into Susan's death. If the Los Angeles field office were investigating her death, surely New York would have known about it. Certainly Director Levi would have, and by extension Jane, and she would have told me about it. It seemed there were two independent FBI investigations, one into Susan's murder and one into me. The investigation into me came from a tip-off from Los Angeles, probably directly from Jones and Newton themselves. Yet those same two agents hadn't mentioned in that tip-off their own investigation into Susan's murder. It wasn't credible.

It could only mean one thing. It was not an official investigation. This was Jones' pet project. Which meant I had a damned, obsessive crusader on my back.

TWELVE

Hans Fischer put down the phone for the sixth time. Vogel was not answering. He ran his fingertips over the leather blotter on his vast oak desk and controlled his breathing to keep his anger in check. He toyed with the idea of phoning Vogel's office and asking for him, but he knew that would be rash and could have repercussions. Especially now, so close to the meeting.

Was he avoiding him? Could he be that stupid? It seemed unlikely; with a deal about to go down between Yahya Sanjar of Hamas and Oscar Guzman, the de facto new leader of the Sinaloa Cartel, Vogel stood to make a great deal of money. So why the silence?

His mind went back to the parking lot at the Gates of Hell and the ruthless, brutal speed of the man's attack on his bodyguard. He calculated it in his mind. It was no more than five seconds, and that included the time it took him to walk behind Jonah and kick him in the neck.

He picked up the phone on his desk. "Send me Alex."

Ten minutes later, there was a knock on the door, and a well-dressed young man in his thirties entered. He was slim but athletic and muscular, and his deep-set blue eyes and platinum hair marked him as of Germanic origin. He was in fact Austrian.

"Herr Fischer?"

"Come, Alex, sit." As the man took the chair across the desk, Fischer rubbed his chin and spoke. "I have a complex problem. I need to find Mitch Vogel. He is not answering his telephone, and going to seek him at the CIA headquarters would be indiscreet, you understand."

"Yes, Herr Fischer."

"You remember the incident at the Gates of Hell parking lot the other night?"

"I was in the car with Aleki, sir, when we followed the man to West 81st Street."

"Good. I need you to stake out this house. See who lives there and who comes in and out. I want to know about that house. And if you see that man from the Gates of Hell, inform me immediately."

"You want me to take some action, sir?"

"If you see him going in, call for backup. Then go in on some pretext, and when backup arrives, subdue him and make him tell you where Vogel is. Then kill him."

"Yes, sir."

If you see him leaving the house, follow him and see where he goes. When he gets there, if you have the opportunity, subdue him and interrogate him."

"Then kill him?"

"Then kill him. That is all."

"Yes, Herr Fischer."

He stood and gave a small bow, then went to the door. Fischer's voice stopped him.

"Alex." Alex stopped and looked back at his master. "Do not underestimate this man. He is very, very dangerous."

"Yes, Herr Fischer."

The door closed behind him, and Fischer sat staring at his telephone again. He had been putting off the call because he had no idea what to say. Finally he snatched up the instrument and dialed.

"I have been waiting for your call, Mr. Fischer. I was expecting your call yesterday, in fact. I was surprised, a little bit worried."

"The important thing, Yahya, is that we are talking now. Where are you now?"

"We passed Ilha das Flores a couple of hours ago, making good time for Bermuda. My cousin has leant me his yacht, Mr. Fischer. It is like a small city. We are now traveling at sixty miles per hour. Can you believe it? We will be off the coast of Bermuda in maybe a day and half. Perhaps less."

"Mr. Guzman will be there, and we shall meet on my yacht for lunch and discuss the details of the agreement."

"Your yacht. Why not my yacht, Mr. Fischer? You cannot imagine the technology. I think maybe this yacht can fly to the moon!"

He had a loud, raucous laugh that was unpleasant to listen to, but Fischer forced himself to laugh along with him.

"It probably can, Yahya, but until the formal trading and negotiating is finished, we will stay on neutral ground."

"You are neutral ground." It was said with no particular emphasis or stress.

"I am neutral ground, Yahya, or at least my yacht is. Once the formal negotiations are finished, I am sure Mr. Guzman would love to be a guest on your cousin's ship. I know I certainly would."

"Yes, yes, we shall drink water in the name of Allah." Again the shrill laugh.

"I look forward to it. Have you given any further thought to Mr. Guzman's comments? We want this first encounter to be as harmonious as possible, Yahya."

"I have thought about it, Hans, and we can supply opium, unprocessed, from Afghanistan. We must discuss the price, but I am sure we can reach an arrangement."

"As I said to you, payment can be made in weapons and explosives aboard ships sailing from Mexico and the northeastern coast of Colombia."

"I am not hostile to the possibility, Hans. We shall talk. Please extend my compliments to Mr. Vogel. I am looking forward very much to meeting and discussing future ventures. I will see you in a few hours."

He hung up without waiting for a reply. Fischer ran his hands through his hair. Vogel. What was he playing at? Was this a show of force—a 'look how much you need me'? If it was, he would have to be punished. He could not allow his associates to jeopardize his operations like this. Bringing Yahya Sanjar and Vogel together was an essential part of the deal. With Vogel missing from the package, there was no telling what Yahya might do.

He picked up the phone again and called the only other number on that cell. It rang three or four times before a lazy voice said, "Hans, viejo amigo, que paso? You askin' yourself, 'Is this son of a bitch in his boat sailin' for Bermuda, or is this son of a bitch lyin' by his pool drinkin' tequila and havin' a liddle party with some fine girls?' Eh?" he laughed like he'd said something hilarious. "You was! Huh? Huh? You was thinkin' 'What is this hijo de puta doin'?,' right?"

"It never crossed my mind, Oscar. But as you mention it, where are you?"

"I am lyin' by my pool drinkin' tequila and havin' a liddle party with some *fine* girls!" He roared with laughter again. Hans struggled to keep the smile in his voice. He said simply, "Seriously." It wasn't a question. It was a courteous demand for a serious answer.

"*Seriously!* Bot relax compa, I am doin' all that *on my yacht!*"

Hans pinched the bridge of his nose and closed his eyes while he listened to the uproar at the other end of the phone. When it had died down, he forced a smile onto his face.

"Aah, you rascal, you really had me going there. So what is your ETA for Bermuda?"

"If we don't get lost in the Triangle—eh? Eh?" More laughter. Hans rolled his eyes and sank back in his chair. "If the ET don't come down an' take us away, one day, day and a half. No ET, tha's the ETA!"

Hans waited again for the laughter to subside. "Good, that's great to hear. Listen, Yahya has been thinking about your proposal."

"What proposal, compa? I don't remember no proposal. So much goin' on in my life, you know? Did I tell you it was my boy's birthday? Sixteen, man! How did that happen? I'm tellin' you, one minute he's just bin born, and then wham! He's a man!"

"You're not interested in crude opium anymore then?"

"Oh, that, yeah, well, you know, like I say, so much goin' on. What did he say?"

"He said it can be done, provided the price is right. But he's more interested in guns and explosives than in cash."

"Yeah, OK, that's cool."

"Oscar, I am here as intermediary. I understand your way of negotiating, like I understand his. Don't make him think you're not interested or he'll walk away and we all lose. I have my commission riding on this deal. Let's help each other out, OK?"

Oscar Guzman chuckled quietly. "Don't worry, my friend. You get your commission. Ey, more than crude opium I am interested in your man from the CIA. Bogel, yeah?"

"Vogel."

"Yeah, Bogel, this guy I wanna talk to."

"Any deal you do with Vogel or via Vogel, Oscar, goes through me. Let's be clear about that."

"You got it, compa. Tranquilo. Hey, I got a lady who wants to give me a special, southern massage. I'll talk to you soon."

He hung up.

Hans set down the phone with care, as though if he aligned it wrong by a fraction of an inch, everything might go disastrously wrong. Then he covered his face with his hands and tried hard not to think.

He needed a solution. He knew—or at least he told himself he knew—that Mitch Vogel would show up at the last minute. He told himself Mitch was just making him aware of how much he needed him and the vast power of the CIA that came with him.

But what if? It was unthinkable, yet he needed a solution in case the unthinkable had happened. He reached for his cell again, and again he called Vogel. It rang and rang, but there was no answer.

THIRTEEN

I sat looking at Vogel's cell. The caller was listed as *Coordinator*. He had called seven times. I stood and climbed the stairs to where Mendoza was locked in. When I opened the door, she was still sitting at the desk. I said:

"Who is coordinator?"

She didn't look up. She just kept writing. I closed the door and went and opened the window. Then I grabbed her by the scruff of her neck and yanked her from the chair, which clattered to the floor. She was wearing a skirt instead of trousers, so I couldn't grab her by the seat of her pants. Instead I hooked my arm between her legs and heaved her out of the window. She screamed. Just as she was about to drop, I gripped her right leg and let go of her collar. She was thrashing like crazy, trying to get a grip on anything from the windowsill to the wall, and the few glimpses I got of her face showed real terror.

I didn't pull her in. I spoke calmly and quietly.

"Think very carefully about your answer to my next

question, Mendoza. Procrastinate, prevaricate, obfuscate, dodge, avoid, answer my question with a question of your own, anything of that sort, and I will decide you are of no use to me and you go down head first." I let her slip an inch, and she squealed. Her face showed real panic. "Show me you are serious about cooperating, and I will give you one last and final chance. So are we ready? You're getting heavy, and you have nice, smooth, slippery legs."

I let her slip another inch, and she started to weep and claw at the wall.

"Who is coordinator?"

"Hans! Hans Fischer! Hans Fischer! Pull me in! For Christ's sake!"

I heaved her in and turned her around. I shoved her against the wall beside the open window and leaned against her, with my face just a couple of inches from hers.

"Now I asked you once before, and you said no. So I am going to ask you again, do I need to prove to you that I am serious? Since I asked you last time, you have done nothing but obstruct me and give me a hard time. So I am asking you, do I need to go and get some pliers and take a finger or a toe? Do I need to shoot out a kneecap? Because the next time you bullshit me, that is what we are talking about. Or do I need to do it now so you'll believe me? Do I need to go downstairs and get the pliers? Is that what I need to do to get your cooperation, Mendoza?"

She was sickly and pasty, the color of a church candle, and she was sweating and trembling. She didn't answer.

"You are alive and in one peace because things work more efficiently if everyone is on the same page and cooperating. We do this right and you live and I get what I want.

HELL'S FURY

But I am beginning to believe that in your case, you are too damned stupid to understand that your side lost already, and the chance to join the winning side is slipping through your fingers. My advice to you, Mendoza, is prove to me that I am wrong. Your life depends on it. And you are running out of time."

She nodded a lot and very fast. "OK, OK, OK..." She bent down, picked up the chair, and sat in it. "Vogel," she said and took a couple of deep breaths. "Vogel had Hans Fischer listed as Coordinator."

"Why?"

"Because Fischer coordinates meetings between people and organizations who would otherwise probably never meet and do business." She raised her eyes to look at me. She was on the verge of tears but fighting hard to hide it. If she was playacting, she was damned good. "A person like that is really useful to the CIA in the kind of operations we do."

"Operations like murder and kidnapping?"

"I'm guessing that's rhetorical and you won't throw me out of the window if I don't answer."

"Yeah, it's rhetorical, but don't be too sure I won't throw you out the window anyway. You're still on probation."

She gave a weary nod and took a moment to steady her breathing. "In any case, that wasn't the CIA. That was Vogel and me. We have—had—a group set up to deal with Fischer. They are all dead now, except me and Gutmeyer. He can corroborate everything I tell you."

I jerked my chin at the desk. "What about the report? Is it finished?"

Her eyes dropped. "I'm nearly finished." She paused and

raised her eyes to look at me again. "And I want to revise it, to make sure everything is clear and correct."

I arched an eyebrow at her. "That sounds like a smart idea." Downstairs, the doorbell rang. I said, "Finish it and let's get this thing done."

"How do I know you won't kill me when it's done?"

"Because I need your oral testimony."

I stepped out of the room and turned the key. Downstairs, I peered through the spy hole in the door and saw a man in his thirties with fair hair and a well cut suit. I opened the door.

"Yes?"

"Oh, I am looking for a Mrs. Susan Hanson." He glanced above my head at the number above the door. "I understand she lives at three-twenty..."

"She's my wife. What do you want her for?"

He looked surprised but tried to hide it. "Oh, Mr. Hanson, then? Your wife had very kindly answered a brief survey on line regarding projected voting trends regarding Democrats and Republicans in New York's Five Boroughs, and the class implications of those trends..."

"She's dead."

His mouth sagged, and his eyebrows went in the opposite direction. "I'm so sorry," he said. "I had no idea."

"No reason why you should have known. Was there anything else?"

"No, no, not at all. Thank you for your time, and I am sorry for your loss."

"Thanks." I closed the door and went into the living room, keeping back and in the shadows to watch what he did and where he went. He crossed the road and climbed into a gray Audi, then took off at a moderate pace without giving the house another look.

He wasn't a Fed because they already knew from Jane and from Newton and Jones that I was here. He wasn't CIA because a Company man would not have given up so fast and so easily. Which made him a potential hit man scoping out the territory.

That was if he wasn't doing a political survey, which seemed the least likely of the four options.

I climbed the stairs again, unlocked the door, and pushed in. The stupidest mistakes are the ones even smart people can make. They are things that are so elementary and obvious you forget to be aware of them. My mistake was a double one. The first part was working on the premise that Mendoza worked for the CIA, when it was patently obvious that she worked first and foremost for Hans Fischer within the CIA. My second mistake, which was a knock-on from the first, was assuming she gave a damn about immunity from prosecution.

As I stepped through the door, the heavy mahogany bed knob she had unscrewed from the bedpost hit me in the head like a cannonball, the room lurched in a sickening diagonal shift, and the floor rushed up to smack me in the face.

I could hear my groaning as though it was somebody else's, and beyond it, I could hear the hammering of feet racing down the stairs, receding, growing farther away.

Time passed. It may have been minutes or it may have been seconds. I had no sense of time. I gripped the foot of the bed and dragged myself to my feet, but when I tried to walk, my legs didn't get the memo, and I sprawled on the floor. My second attempt was more successful, but I had to stagger for the bathroom and retch into the sink.

As I rinsed my mouth and stuck my head under the cold shower, I told myself Mendoza was either freakishly strong or was driven by an intense passion for revenge. The latter seemed more likely and, I thought, something I could identify with.

After a couple of minutes, I grabbed a towel and made my way to the small desk, drying my head and face as I went. The notepad and the pen were there. The pad contained four hand-written pages, and every page had scrawled on it, over and over again, *All work and no play makes Carmen a dull girl.*

Funny girl.

I swore quietly but abundantly and made my way downstairs again in search of a couple of aspirins and a glass of whiskey.

I stood in the kitchen, leaning on the work surface beside the sink. I put two aspirins in my mouth and drained an inch of whiskey from a tumbler. Then I stood looking at the lawn in the back yard. In my mind I could see Jane with her finger on my chest, staring at my shirt button. No, not my shirt button. I had thought it was the place where my heart should be.

You need to remember. You don't need to be reminded. You need to remember. For yourself.

I poured another shot of whiskey into the glass and stared at it, thinking of Ernestina in Los Angeles. I had said, *Information is power, but the wrong information can be a death sentence*, and Ernestina had asked, *Who said that?*

Susan had said it. I could see her on a TV. The colors

were bright and intense. She was in a violet dress, looking beautiful, sitting talking to a man in a suit behind a desk. They were both very serious. He asked her, "Do the people have a right to know?"

"Information is power." She had answered that. "Information is power, but the wrong information can be a death sentence."

Her death sentence.

And some mechanism in my own mind had deleted practically all my information.

You need to remember. You don't need to be reminded. You need to remember. For yourself.

Remember what? "*God damn it!*" I slammed my fist down hard on the work surface. "*Why the hell did she have to go now when I most need her!*"

I climbed the stairs, stripped, and stood under the cold shower for fifteen minutes, waiting for the pain to ease in my head and my body and brain to start functioning again. By the time I climbed out and started toweling myself dry, I had understood that there was no way I could now track down Mendoza. The most likely thing was that she would be executed by her partners, if she had any left, or by order of Hans Fischer. Why? Because if they hadn't yet found Vogel's and the others' bodies, they soon would, and when they did, she would become a seriously unknown quantity. Why had *she* not been killed? Why did she and I disappear together? Why was she unhurt? Where had she been all this time?

As a potential threat, the simple solution would be to eliminate her. Which left me three areas where I could look for answers. One, Jane Harrison, and through her Director Paul Levi and whatever intelligence the Bureau had on me and Susan which had, since her death, become classified. But with her words still playing on a loop in my mind, *You need to remember. You don't need to be reminded. You need to remember. For yourself.* I set her aside, at least for the present. There was too much about Jane I did not understand.

Two was to set about a systematic, documentary investigation of Ted Hanson. He must have had credit cards, a driver's license, a bank account, a birth certificate, and a marriage certificate. Hell! He even had a death certificate.

And as an extension of that research, the same was true of Susan, with the added fact that she had a public profile. If she was interviewed on TV, there might be newspaper articles, magazine features. Her murder was probably covered by the press and television, plus she'd probably also had a presence on social media. All of that would probably provide a very fruitful area of research. But it would also be limited. Because any information about her research and about the motive for her killing would not be in the public domain.

And then, finally, there was three: stake out Hans Fischer. Follow him, and he might just lead me to Mendoza and a full confession about what happened to Susan, what information she'd had which had turned out to be her death sentence, who ordered her killing and... I trailed off and smiled to myself. I already knew who executed her, and they had been dealt with appropriately.

Now I wanted the people behind the sentence, the people who ordered it, and the reason why. And it seemed to me that, interesting as documentary research might be, the shortest path to what I wanted to know, and achieve, was through Hans Fischer and Carmen Mendoza.

I finished dressing, slipped the BUL SAS into the

pancake behind my back, and pulled on my jacket. I took the Smith and Wesson 29 too. I'd have that in the glove compartment just in case I needed to blow down a door.

Ten minutes later, I stepped out into the late afternoon sun, slipped on some very black shades to protect my aching head from the glare, and headed for my Jeep.

My Jeep and Hans Fischer.

FOURTEEN

Mendoza clattered down the stairs and ran across the hall, reaching for the door, feeling death closing in just behind her, stabbing at her back and reaching for her neck. She stifled the scream in her throat as she forced herself to stop and grab the door to wrench it open. Then she was out on the street, in the air and the sun, racing for her car.

She clambered behind the wheel, slammed the door, and fired up the engine, did a U-turn and hurtled the wrong way down West 81st, making the tires complain as she fishtailed onto West End Avenue and then again onto West 82nd, where she broke the speed limit for half a mile as far as Central Park West.

At the Park West Hotel, she skidded to a halt and left her car across the bike lane. She crossed the road at a run, dodging the traffic among honks and horns and bellowed abuse and ran into the apartment block, where she crossed the lobby and stabbed savagely at the buttons at the bank of elevators.

She waited an eternity staring across the shady lobby at the luminous oblong of bright sunlight where her car stood. Behind her, an elevator pinged and the doors hissed opened. A handful of people emerged, and she shouldered past them, ignoring their glares.

At the top floor, she hammered on the door of the penthouse and leaned on the bell. After twenty seconds, the door opened, and a guy who looked like King Kong on steroids looked down at her with all the expressiveness of a cast iron frying pan. She showed him her CIA ID card and said, "I need to talk to Hans Fischer, *now*."

"You wait."

He closed the door, and she started hammering and leaning on the bell again. Nothing happened for a full minute and a half. Then Inscrutable Kong opened the door and said, "Stop."

"I *need*—"

"Come."

He turned and walked away. She followed. The door closed behind her, and he led her down a long passage and through a tall, walnut door into a large, airy room with sliding glass doors onto a large terrace. The walls were lined with low bookcases above which hung abstract and impressionist paintings. There was a large oak desk, and behind it sat the man she knew was Hans Fischer. Even if she hadn't seen numerous photos and videos, there would have been no doubt. His pale, Germanic eyes, his wispy platinum hair, and the aura of unemotional, ruthless authority which permeated the air about him made it clear that this was Hans Fischer. He didn't say anything; he just watched her and waited.

"My name is Carmen Mendoza. I am a staff operations officer with the CIA. I worked with Mitch Vogel. I need to talk to you."

He took a moment, like there was a delay in the transmission. Then, with no change in expression, he pointed to the chair opposite him. When she sat, he said, "You are here, I am here. Talk."

"Vogel is dead."

"Who is Vogel?"

"Come on. You know what I am talking about. I was on Vogel's team. You told him about a guy at the Gates of Hell who killed your bodyguard, Jonah. We picked him up and took him to some remote woodland in Pennsylvania. There was me and Vogel and four guys, professionals. He blinded Vogel, then killed him. He killed three of the four guys, framed the fourth, and abducted me. This guy is very dangerous."

Fischer sighed, took a deep breath, and drummed his fingers on his desk. Without looking at her, he gestured at her with his open palm.

"Carmen Mendoza. You come in here with your toy ID card, spouting some incredible story about a man called Vogel and some dangerous character who can kill four or five highly trained government agents with his bare hands. It is clear that either you want something from me or you are insane. However, you are an attractive woman, and I am a red-blooded man. Let us say that I humor you and I invite you to a drink. Tell me, what has all this story to do with me?"

She closed her eyes and gritted her teeth. Then she

snapped, "Yeah, I'll have that drink. Vodka martini and don't go crazy on the martini."

She said it as she stood and started unbuttoning her blouse. He watched her as he pressed a button on his desk and said, "Vodka martini, strong. I'll have the same."

She threw her blouse on the desk. She snapped, "Check it!" She slipped her skirt over her hips and threw that on his desk too, along with her shoes. "You want me to take my bra and panties off too? There is no wire, Hans!"

He checked her clothes with care, then stood and examined her hair, her ears, and her underwear. Then he smiled into her face and returned to his desk.

"Get dressed," he said, tossing her skirt to her. As he watched her putting her clothes back on, he said, "So Vogel is dead, and this man killed him."

"That's what I am telling you. He believes he is Susan Hanson's husband, and he is out for revenge. He has total amnesia, but he is obsessed with finding his wife's killer—or killers."

There was no doubt in his mind who the man was. "And Susan Hanson lived at 320 West 81st. Where he is now."

"Yeah."

There was a knock at the door. It opened, and Aleki Expressionless Kong came in with a silver tray, a shaker, and two martinis. He set it down and left. When the door had closed, Hans said, "Sinaloa killed this woman and her children?"

"Yeah, but who cares? What actually happened, in *all* of its complexity, is irrelevant. What is relevant is what this animal believes. And what he believes is that Susan Hanson, his wife, was uncovering something about organized crime cozying up with Mexican cartels, Islamic terrorists, and elements within the CIA. And he has the idea that you gave the order for her to be executed. You being Organized Crime."

"Where did he get this idea? You told him this?"

"I told him sweet Fanny Adams, Fischer. And I still have the damned bruises to prove it. He had me locked in a room writing down a statement for the FBI and the district attorney and told me he'd throw me out of the damned window if I didn't do it."

"What did you write?"

"*All work and no play makes Carmen a dull girl* five hundred times. When he came up to collect it, I smashed a solid mahogany bed knob into his head and ran."

"What do you want from me?"

"Three things. I want protection, I want Vogel's place in your setup, and I want you to pull strings when I walk into Langley and tell them my story. I *do not* need to be investigated. And *you* do not need two CIA murders to dodge if the Feds or the CIA's inspector general starts getting curious. We need to bury this and get back to normal before it gets out of hand."

He studied his fingertips spread out along the edge of his desk and nodded slowly.

"What about this man?"

"Kill him. He's living at Susan Hanson's old house. He needs to die. Hell, we thought he *was* dead! He was shot like four or five times, and his car exploded. Yet here he is."

"All right. I will have him eliminated. You will come to Bermuda in Vogel's place. Are you familiar with the brief?"

"Intimately."

"Good. Do you need to make any arrangements? Aleki will take you to pack a bag. We will fly tonight and pick up the yacht at Hamilton. You had better contact your superiors."

She went out on the terrace and called Kathleen Harragan, who had been Vogel's superior. She told her that Vogel and a number of his men had been murdered, that Gutmeyer had been framed, and that she was in the field and could not come in.

"Where are you, Carmen?"

"I am on my way to Bermuda. I can't talk now, but it is the case that Mitch was working on, and it's coming to a head."

"You should be debriefed. The Office of the Inspector General is opening an investigation into what happened at Susquehanna. I need a report from you."

"I'll get one to you as soon as I can. Right now it is impossible. I'll call you."

She returned to Fischer's office and stood framed in the sliding door.

"There is no way I am going back to my apartment, even with King Kong in tow. Have him take me shopping and I'll get some luggage together. I'll be back before two hours. You got a credit card I can borrow?"

A LITTLE OVER six miles to the south as the crow flies, Special Agent Jane Harrison sat in a windowless room, surrounded by gray, steel shelves that contained cartons of various sizes filled with every imaginable type of article, from knives and guns, to samurai swords, frilly panties, passionate letters of love, equally passionate letters of hatred, shirts stained with blood and whiskey, drawings, photographs, and video recordings, not to mention a million other things that in some bizarre way had become evidence pointing to somebody's guilty involvement in a crime.

She sat at a small table made of steel tubing, composite wood, and Formica. Something somebody back in the '60s had thought was a good idea and in the intervening sixty years nobody had thought to throw in the trash. On that table was a computer, and plugged into the computer was a flash drive containing footage from security cameras showing, in grainy gray and white, the moment Susan Hanson and her children were murdered. She had watched it five times and had gone back to the beginning again to watch it once more in slow motion, frame by frame. Something was nagging at her mind as she watched it. Something was wrong.

She inched forward and watched Susan Hanson and the two kids emerge in jerky, indistinct images from the ferry terminal. She held their hands and took a couple of steps forward. The girl had her right hand and the boy her left. The girl was looking back, over her shoulder.

Jane paused and went back to the point where the door started to open. There she stopped and scrutinized the fore ground. The gunmen's car was in the parking lot, opposite the entrance. Inching forward, she saw the door open and Susan and the kids move through. She could just make out the figure of a man behind them holding the door. At that same instant, the doors of the gunmen's car opened. The girl looked back over her shoulder at the man emerging now from the terminal. Harrison inched forward a fraction more and was struck by the man's posture.

He was leaning forward. His right leg was stretched out in front of him. He was lunging through the door, running. At the car, the gunmen were out of the vehicle. The two on the near side holding weapons. The two on the far side running, one around the hood, the other around the trunk.

Moving on a little further, she saw now not just the girl but Susan looking over her shoulder at the man who was now clearly running toward the gunmen. She expanded the image and saw that he now had a weapon in his hand. The four men were lined up by their truck and were holding out their weapons. She froze and again expanded the image. They were, all four of them, aiming at Susan and the kids, even though he was closer to the gunmen than she was.

She inched forward a little further and was able to see small clouds of smoke emerging from the guns. The little girl had fallen to the ground. Susan had stopped and turned. The man had stopped running, holding his weapon in both hands, his right foot slightly forward.

Moving on a fraction, she saw Susan bending to her daughter. The boy was frozen, looking at the men shooting. Two had now turned their guns on the man. Very slowly, she moved the video forward fraction by fraction. Three of the gunmen were now shooting at the man. The one remaining gunman aimed toward the woman and the boy. The woman was hunkered down with her daughter. The boy was clearly hit and fell to his knees as his mother stood.

She froze.

It was there. She expanded the image to its full extent, and it was there, at the bottom edge of the frame, a tiny puff of smoke. She took a piece of paper from her notepad and folded it into a makeshift ruler to lay it across the screen. If the grainy haziness was, as she suspected, gun smoke, it lined up directly with Susan, who stood frozen and, as Jane inched forward, immediately began to collapse.

Jane swore softly under her breath. There had been a fifth gunman.

She watched it again a dozen times, and each time she was more convinced of what she saw. A fifth gunman, off screen, had been observing the hit, and when the man had charged out shooting, drawing the fire of the four shooters, the fifth gunman had shot Susan.

She reached in her bag and pulled out a flask of coffee. She poured a measure into the lid and sat sipping it, staring at the frozen scene. She ate a chicken and lettuce sandwich still staring at that scene, thinking. Then she sat forward and shifted her focus to the man. Painfully slowly. Jerky image by image, she saw him hit once, twice and three times. He remained upright and returning fire. The fourth shot, which she knew narrowly missed his heart, knocked him to the ground.

The shooters scrambled in slow, jerky movements to get back in their truck. Meanwhile, the man struggled to his feet and made for a Jeep parked behind him. She fought to ignore the impossibility of what she was seeing and focus simply on what happened. Moments after he had climbed in, with the door still open, the Jeep lurched forward and crossed the parking lot toward the gunmen's truck. She saw the windshield of the Jeep shatter and the gunmen's truck reverse out of the screen. The Jeep went after it and suddenly erupted in flames.

She reversed and played it again. It was barely visible with the smoke and flames, but the third time she played it, there was no doubt in her mind. The Jeep erupted with the passenger door open. With the damn door open.

She spent the next hour making copies of all the essential details and saving them onto a separate flash drive. Then she collected her stuff and went upstairs and knocked on Director Paul Levi's door.

He watched her enter with eyes that said he knew she was going to try and complicate his life for him. He leaned back and laced his fingers over a belly that had grown not wisely but too well.

"Agent Harrison. What can I do for you?" He pointed to the chair across his desk. "Sit down."

She sat and placed the flash drive on his desk.

"It's the Susan Hanson case, sir."

"That's not a case, Agent Harrison. We know who murdered her, and we know they were later killed in Los Angeles."

"Yes, but there are loose ends, things that remained unexplained."

"Such as?"

"Well, for a start, the fact that a man with total amnesia showed up on the very street where those very four gunmen were killed, and his DNA was a perfect match for—"

"Stop." He held up his hand. "That information is classified, and it is not open for discussion."

"OK, but he left the door open."

He screwed up his face. "*What?*"

"When he climbed in the Jeep, he left the passenger door open. They shoot out the windshield, and by the time the

Jeep bursts into flames, they are off screen, but you can clearly see through the smoke that his passenger door is open."

He closed his eyes and rubbed his face. "Jane, I thought I had made it clear that that case was closed *and* classified and not to be discussed."

She raised her shoulders a quarter of an inch. "You asked me. Besides, I haven't discussed it with anyone, I just re-ran the film. A guy turns up with the DNA of a dead man..."

He interrupted her with a sigh. "Agent Harrison, Jane, I understand what this means to you, but his body was found in the Jeep—"

"Charred beyond recognition."

"Officially it was him. And more to the point, once again, the data you are referring to is *classified,* and I cannot discuss it with you."

"OK, sir, without referring to any classified data: He is alive, he is in New York, and he is going after Hans Fischer. What is more, he has a growing interest in the CIA and what they had to do with Susan Hanson's death."

He took a long, deep breath and let it out as a heartfelt groan. "This," he said. "This is what you get for indulging in professional courtesy." He leveled his eyes at her and shook his head. "You didn't need to follow him to the club. I should not have assigned you to it."

"Why did you?"

He glanced at her then gazed out the window for a while before answering. His voice became sullen. "Probably because I knew you'd be a pain in the ass and start digging where you weren't supposed to. That and because I miss him and feel guilty about his death."

She suppressed a sad smile. "I think we should bring him in and you should talk to him. Since they shot him and set fire to him, the man seems have become some kind of a killing machine. So far he's only killed narcos and people involved in the sex slave trade. That's not anything I am going to lose any sleep over, but I think it's only a matter of time before something really bad happens."

Director Levi groaned softly. "Where is he now?"

"Last time I saw him, he was at what he now says is his home, on 81st Avenue. Susan's house. But I know him, and from the way he was talking, he is lining up Hans Fischer and the CIA."

"OK, you'd better go get him. But what the hell do I tell him, Jane?"

She arched an eyebrow at him. "What about the truth?"

"The truth?" He said it and rolled his eyes and shook his head. "The truth, she says! What truth?"

FIFTEEN

I opened the door as she was about to ring, and we stood staring at each other.

"I was on my way out," I said.

"I'll come with you."

"No, you can't."

Special Agent Jane Harrison narrowed her eyes. "Why not?"

"Because I am going to stake out Hans Fischer, and you can't be any part of that. Why are you here? The way you left, I thought I was never going to see you again."

"I need to talk to you. It's very important."

I frowned and sighed. "How important is very important? I can't let this guy get away."

"Life and death."

"Whose?"

"For crying out loud! It's important. I am an intelligent, responsible investigator, and I am telling you it's important!"

"Let's go walk in the park."

"Sweet mother of God!"

I stepped out and closed the door behind me. "Are you Irish?"

She looked at me a moment with hooded eyes. "No. I am not Irish."

"Walk and talk. That's a very Irish thing to say, sweet mother of God. Catholic."

She followed me out onto the sidewalk. I said, "We'll take your car. Park as close as you can to West 107th, and we'll walk in the park for a while."

We found a space on 107th, left her car there, jumped the wall into the park, and found a space in the shade of some trees, up an easy slope directly opposite Fischer's block. A little to our left, I could see Mendoza's car parked at an angle across the cycle path. That made me smile. She had come to Fischer, then.

In the car, we hadn't spoken, but when we were sitting by the trees, I pointed at the terrace of the penthouse. "That's where he lives, in the penthouse."

"I think I knew that."

"I think my CIA informant has come to see him. That's her car down there." She made a *What?* face. I said, "She hit me with a solid mahogany bed knob and escaped. She couldn't go back to the Company. Things have got far too hot for her there. Besides, her true employer was always either Fischer or Sinaloa. So I imagine she has come here to Fischer to inform him about me and for security."

"You should not be telling me this kind of thing. Listen to me, I have some information for you that I think could be important."

"What is it?" I asked it with my eyes on the main entrance to the apartment block.

"There was a fifth shooter."

I froze. I felt the coldness in my skin, in my brain, and in my heart.

"A fifth shooter?"

"Do you remember that day?"

"No."

"But you know what I am talking about."

"Yes."

"You can explain that to me some other time. Right now I have to tell you, there were the four shooters in the truck, directly in front of you—"

"Felipe Ochoa, Nestor Gavilan, Oliver Peralta, and Eulogio Borja."

"That's the guys. The official view was they had targeted Susan Hanson for reasons that were not specifically known but could be guessed at."

"Her investigation into high-level corruption and organized crime."

"Correct. Those four guys were then killed in Los Angeles."

"I killed them just before I lost my memory."

"I didn't hear that. But reviewing the tapes a while back, I found something."

I glanced at her. "What?"

"First of all, if it was you back there, you got shot four times. Then you got up, climbed into your Jeep, and charged these guys. They shot out your windscreen. The action moves largely off screen, and your Jeep erupts in flames. All that we already knew, except that three things stood out for me this time that I had not seen before. One, when you got in the Jeep and charged them, you left your passenger door open. Second, the angle they were shooting at you from, they could not have hit your gas tank. So I don't know why your Jeep caught fire."

"What about this fifth shooter?"

"I am coming to that. Three, they gun down Susan's daughter while you are advancing on them shooting. While she's tending to her, they shoot the boy. Now all four guns are turned on you, and just off screen there is a minute puff of smoke and Susan is shot while they are trying to shoot you. There is a fifth gunman, behind the four men, and to their right. I think he is the guy who put an incendiary round into your gas tank."

I took my eyes off the building across the road and stared at her for a moment. "Why are you telling me this?"

Her gaze shifted from me to the building. "That is not the issue. You need to be asking yourself—" She paused and took a flash drive from her purse and handed it to me. As she did so, she muttered, "If anyone ever finds out you have that, you stole it from me." Then she started over. "What you need to be asking yourself is, why did you come out of the building running? Why does the girl look over her shoulder at you? Are you shouting something? What have you seen or recognized before anybody else?"

"That's what I need to be asking? Do you know the answers to those questions?"

"You also need to be asking what Sinaloa had against Susan, and, much, much more important, who is the fifth shooter? Or, perhaps more to the point—"

I cut her short because I knew what she was going to say. "Who did the fifth shooter work for?"

She looked at me and nodded. "Yeah, that is what you need to be asking."

We were silent for a bit watching the building. After a time, I saw a dark Audi pull up, and Mendoza climbed out. The hulk named Aleki heaved himself from behind the wheel and opened the trunk. Mendoza took a bunch of bags and a suitcase from the trunk, and the doorman hurried to help her. They went inside, and the driver took the car away, presumably to park it.

Special Agent Jane Harrison said quietly, "That guy, the driver, he was with Hans Fischer the other night." I nodded. She asked, "Who's the girl?"

"She is a CIA officer named Carmen Mendoza." I decided to change the subject before she enquired any further and asked her, "Will Director Levi see me?"

"Yeah. He's thinking about it. It would probably help if you stopped killing people."

I was going to tell her it would probably help if people stopped trying to kill me. Instead I said, "I don't remember, but I'd say it's a fair guess that the reason I came through the door shouting is because I gave a damn. There is an infestation in our world, Jane. It's a spreading infestation of evil. And if we stand back and wait for our political leaders to clean up that infestation, it will spread so far it will engulf everything. For the simple reason that our political leaders are the most badly infected. Each one of us has to take responsibility, and my way of doing that right now is hunting them down and killing them."

She took a deep breath and let it out as a sigh.

HELL'S FURY | 147

"I guess it might be a while then before you see Director Levi."

I studied her face a moment. "Maybe it's time," I told her, "that somebody reminded him he is sworn to protect the people of this country from the likes of Hans Fischer and Carmen Mendoza."

Her nod was reluctant. "Yeah, maybe you're right at that. I need to go. What are you going to do? You need me to drive you back?"

I thought about it for a moment, then asked, "Are you in a hurry?"

She gave a noncommittal shrug. "What's on your mind?"

"Drive me home, wait for me to pack a bag, then take me to Teterboro Airport."

Her forehead clenched. "The airport?" She looked over at the building. "Mendoza had a suitcase."

"And a bunch of new clothes."

"She's a CIA officer, she obviously doesn't live with Fischer…"

"So they are going on a trip together. To me, a new suitcase suggests something more than going upstate or visiting friends. A boat or a plane is involved."

She nodded. "And Fischer is not going to waste time at JFK. So he'll fly in a private jet from Teterboro. You want to be there before they arrive to see where they go."

"That's how I figure it."

She creased her brow again. "How did you know she'd be here?"

I stared into her face for a moment. I decided it was a

face I liked and trusted. "She was cornered," I said. "She had nowhere else left to go."

She returned the stare, then gave another small sigh. "Come on, Sherlock. Let's get you packed."

She dropped me at home and left me to pack, which took five minutes as most of what I packed was cash. She told me she had something to collect from home. It didn't take her long. She was back within fifteen minutes, and I carried my bag out. Harrison smiled and nodded at a woman I assumed was my neighbor. She stood in her doorway watching us but didn't respond to Harrison's greeting.

At the car, as I slung my bag in the trunk, I attempted a smile. "Like the song says, I'm going to Bermuda. Let's go."

I opened the passenger door, and as she climbed in behind the wheel, she said, "Keep me in the loop, please. You call me when you get there."

The drive to the airport took all of twenty minutes, which meant we arrived there a little less than an hour after Mendoza had returned from shopping. We sat in her car in the parking lot and watched the passengers arrive and leave through the gate onto Industrial Avenue. Jane stayed with me for the time it took for Fischer and Mendoza to show up, and most of that time, we sat in silence. It was a comfortable silence that had all the benefits of familiarity and none of the drawbacks. Eventually I gave her what you'd call a lopsided smile and said, "We've done this before, haven't we?"

She arched an eyebrow at the windshield. The eyebrow said she wasn't as amused as I was. "Have we?"

"You've got an issue with me. Why don't you tell me what it is?"

"Because *you* need to remember."

"So you *have* got an issue with me."

She turned to face me. Her expression was hard to read. She was mad at me, that much was clear, but there was more to it than that. All she said was, "Yes."

I sighed and shifted my attention back to the gate. My mind drifted for the hundredth time to what she had told me about the day Susan and the kids were killed. They had emerged through the door. The child had looked back at me as I came out running behind them…

"I was expecting the hit."

She glanced at me and studied my face for a second. "You remember that?"

I gave my head a small shake. "No, but why else would I come out running at the very moment the gunmen were getting out of the truck? I must have recognized them or the vehicle."

She turned back to watch a small, dark bus with tinted windows that was exiting the gate. "Makes sense."

"The guys in the truck were hit men for Sinaloa. I followed them to Vegas and then to Los Angeles. I caught up with them on Ocean Boulevard and killed them there. I must have returned to my truck and passed out. When I woke up, I had no idea who I was or how I got there."

She glanced at me but didn't say anything. I went on.

"That tells me Sinaloa had a grudge against Susan. They wanted to remove her, punish her, and send a warning to the people she was associated with, but from what you are telling me today, there was somebody else at the ferry terminal. Someone who was keeping out of the way and watching but who was prepared enough to bring incendiary rounds with him."

She nodded. "Yes."

"That is not..." I paused, searching for the right words. "That is not how Sinaloa operate. They are big and bold, and they defy authority by murdering people on the street and declaring war on the government. It would make no sense for them to send a truck full of gunmen to murder a woman and two children in broad daylight at a busy terminal and have one guy watching in secret in case it didn't work out."

"I agree," she told the windscreen.

"So who was the fifth gunman? Who did he work for?"

She looked at me and shook her head. "I don't know."

Before I could answer, she said, "There!"

A dark blue Bentley had rolled into the parking lot. The driver and another guy climbed out and opened the rear doors while scanning the surrounding area with their eyes. Hans Fischer and Carmen Mendoza climbed out and were escorted to the departure lounge by one of the hulks while the other pulled out their luggage and followed after them.

When the door closed behind them, she asked me, "Have you given any thought to how you are going to follow them if you have no passport and no ID?"

I frowned. A cold wave of anger and frustration made my belly burn. I took a deep breath. "No, I guess not. I'm kind of crossing each bridge as I come to it."

"Well, this is a bridge you are not going to cross without the right documents."

She reached in her purse and pulled out a passport and a driver's license. She handed them to me. They had photographs of me and named me as Mark Connors.

HELL'S FURY

I screwed up my brow and shook my head at her. "What the hell? Where did you get these, from a slot machine?"

"You're welcome."

I felt my face flush. "No, I'm sorry. Thank you and I am grateful. But you can't just nip into Federal Plaza and get a set of these in ten minutes. There have to be official requests through the appropriate channels…" I trailed off. "How did you get them, Jane?"

She looked sad. "I kept it as a souvenir some time back. When you said you were going to follow them to the airport, I thought they might be useful…" She shrugged. "I'm afraid there's no wallet or credit card to go with them."

"You kept them as a souvenir?"

"From another life." She jerked her chin past me toward the tarmac. "They're headed for the plane. It's that Gulfstream. Give me the passport." She took it from my fingers and climbed out. "Wait here."

I watched her cross the parking lot and push into the departure lounge. A mild feeling of nausea invaded my belly, followed by a rage of frustration that was hard to control. For a moment, I considered going after her, though that minute part of my brain that remained rational told me not to. After fifteen minutes that, to quote Led Zeppelin, seemed to slip into days, she reemerged and climbed in beside me. She handed me the passport and a small, crimson folder. Inside it was a ticket to Bermuda, along with a hotel reservation and a car rental which you pick up at the hotel.

"What is this, Jane?"

"You owe me fifteen grand. I just maxed out two credit cards. That's what it is. According to you, that should not be a problem because you have sports bags full of millions of bucks, right? So your flight departs in an hour, and the details of your hotel are in there. What are you going to do for money when you get there?"

"That won't be a problem." I frowned hard at her. "You did this for me?"

"Yeah, I'm stupid that way."

I handed her the key to my house. "In the wardrobe in my room. There are two sports bags."

I saw her bite back words before she had uttered them. Then she snatched the key from my fingers. "You have my number. Keep me posted."

"Thanks."

"You got it. Try to come back alive."

I got out and made my way to the departure lounge.

SIXTEEN

We touched down at L. F. Wade International on St. David's Island as the sun was turning to copper and the shadows were stretching long toward evening. I had no luggage other than my sports bag, so I moved quickly through customs and passport control and caught a cab outside. I told him to take me to the Sandyman Boutique Hotel overlooking Bailey's Bay and the vast dark expanse of the North Atlantic.

We crossed the Causeway, a long, narrow piece of remarkable British engineering from the days of empire, across half a mile of crystal clear turquoise waters to the island of Bermuda itself. There the narrow roads wound and twisted through the kind of lush, green woodland you might associate with Vermont, only it lay under a blue sky and was peppered by a startling variety of tall palm trees.

It was a short drive, and once out of the woodlands, we came to North Shore Road, where we followed the transparent, turquoise coastline for a quarter of a mile before turning in through the large, wrought iron gates to the Sandyman Hotel.

The Sandyman was not a hotel in the traditional sense of the word. It was not a single building with the reception, restaurant, and cocktail bar on the ground floor and rooms and suites up above. Reception was a circular, single-story building with a thatched, conical roof and a shaded veranda which encircled the structure. The bar and restaurant sprawled out across a couple of terraces on the north side, shaded by large parasols and tall, sighing trees with unobstructed views of the North Atlantic.

From the reception, a number of paths twisted and wended away into the grounds, bordered by parks and gardens, dotted with pools and groves containing artificial waterfalls and statues of the Buddha. Located apparently randomly along these paths and among the grottos and gardens were cabins and cottages of varying sizes. Some were little more than a room with a bed and a bathroom, others were to all intents and purposes houses with several bedrooms, a kitchen, and bathrooms.

Jane had secured me a two-bedroom cabin with a comfortable living room and a perfect view of the ocean. Once in, I tipped the bellboy generously, stored my cash in the safe, had a shower and shaved, went to collect my car from reception, and took a slow drive across town to Hamilton Harbor. According to the receptionist, that was pretty much where all the shops were. I told him I needed clothes, and he told me Front Street had clothes shops, bars, restaurants—anything and everything I needed.

In Bermuda, shops close early, about five-thirty or six. So I had just enough time to grab the most expensive designer pants, shirts, socks, and shoes I could find and a couple of jackets that would probably do for a down payment on a small house. I stuck it all in the trunk of my rental along with a handsome leather bag and made my way back, driving slowly along North Shore Road, enjoying the slightly bizarre landscapes and the vast sweep of the ocean on my left. And it was as I arrived at Bailey's Bay, almost a mile from the hotel, that I noticed the white gleam of a couple of yachts maybe a mile off shore.

It was as I looked at them that I had a flash of realization which I half dismissed because it was too simplistic. But the more I thought about it, the more logic it seemed to have. Bermuda had a population of maybe sixty thousand people. It was basically a town sprawled across an island. It would be only a slight exaggeration to say that everybody here knew everybody else. But if that was a slightly exaggerated generalization when talking about the island as a whole, when talking about the billionaire elite who inhabited the island, it was no more than the truth. They were a handful, and they all knew each other—and you could be sure the Bermuda Police Service knew all of them, their cars and their yachts. Your well-behaved American or Anglo-Saxon billionaire would be acknowledged and not disturbed. However, your Russian Mafioso, your jihadist, or your Sinaloa billionaire might attract some unwanted attention.

So if you wanted to have a cozy meeting with disreputable business associates, Bermuda was not a bad place to do it, but a superyacht one or two miles off Bermuda was even better.

I filed the thought away for future reference and pulled in to the Sandyman. There I had another shower, changed into my new, very expensive clothes, and took a stroll to the bar for a martini before dinner.

I sat outside. The sun was setting in the west and streaking the northern horizon with red and orange, and making the two yachts glint amber against the dark sea. A young waiter with a bowtie arrived and gave a little bow.

"I'll have a vodka martini." I pointed at the yachts. "Who comes to Bermuda to anchor a mile off shore?"

He gave a small laugh. "They don't know what they're missing. They've been there a couple of days. I had a look through my friend's telescope. They are fabulous. Real superyachts."

"Any idea who they belong to?"

"None, I'm afraid, sir. But I can ask around if you're interested."

As an invitation to give him a fat tip, it was subtle. I smiled like I'd got the hint and told him, "More curious than interested, but if you find out I'd be grateful."

"Of course, sir." and he went away to get my martini.

The martini arrived, the colors faded from the sky, and the yachts became a couple of lights glimmering in the gathering dusk. Pretty soon, the flames from the barbeque griddle were sending dancing shadows around the terrace, and the smell of expertly singed seafood was wafting on the cool Atlantic breeze.

I drained my drink and was about to call the waiter to bring me a menu when I noticed a tall, elegant woman emerge onto the terrace. She looked around, frowning, and spoke to a waiter, who indicated a table close to mine. The table was set for two, but there was nobody sitting there. The waiter pulled out her chair. She hesitated a moment and sat. It wasn't hard to see she was getting mad. Women don't like to arrive at restaurants alone, period. But arriving and finding your date isn't there and you have to sit alone at the table is a hanging offense.

She pulled her cell from her bag and made a call. I signaled the waiter, tried not to listen to her conversation, and failed. Her accent was what the English call cut glass.

"I am here at the Sandyman, sitting *alone* at a table set for two. Where are you?"

My waiter handed me a menu. I slipped him twenty bucks and told him, "Bring me another martini, will you?"

The woman was trying to control her voice but not doing a great job. "Well, couldn't you have *called* me?" She listened for a moment with her eyebrows halfway to her hairline. "It's quite simple, Adrian, you say, 'Excuse me a moment, I must make a telephone call'! Do you realize how *humiliating* this is?"

Her eyes became hooded and her face flushed. "Oh, well, I would not want you to make a poor impression on your managing director, Adrian. We couldn't have that, could we! Far better that you make a poor impression on me." There was enough acid in her tone to dissolve granite. She listened for a couple of seconds, and you just knew she was going to cut him short, and she did. "No, Adrian, please don't bother. You continue making a good impression on your MD."

She didn't wait for an answer. She hung up, put her cell back in her purse, and flashed me a 'What the hell are *you* looking at?' look, plus everything was probably my fault anyway because I was a man. I offered her the ghost of a smile. She ignored it and looked around for a waiter, like she needed a drink. There wasn't one handy, so she sighed and went to stand.

Something made me raise my voice just enough for her to hear me. I gave some life to my smile and said, "We seem to be in the same boat."

She looked at me with no detectable expression, looked at the empty chair opposite me, and sagged back in her own chair.

"Don't say that," she said. "Now I can't blame men."

I laughed. "That is one privilege I would be glad to deprive you of. May I offer you a drink and try to redeem the male of the species, even if just a little?"

A smile touched the corner of her mouth. "I *should* say no, but you offered so nicely it would seem churlish. Thank you." She stood. I stood and held her chair for her. She gave a small giggle as she sat.

"Good heavens, a gentleman! Are you the one that got away?"

I sat, and we smiled at each other. "I'm Mark Connors, nicknamed Rogue by my friends, last of a dying breed and grateful to Adrian for being such a cad."

He cheeks flushed, and her eyes looked mildly outraged.

"Cheeky!" she said.

I ignored her and saw the waiter approaching with my drink. I said, "The lady will have…?" I made a question of my face and showed it to her.

She saw my glass and said, "One of those."

I told him, "Another vodka martini."

"Rogue? Are you some kind of wild maverick or something?"

"Not really. I'm not great at following other people's rules, but you'd hardly notice. What about you? Do I get to learn your name?"

"Caroline Gordon." She reached in her purse and pulled out an embossed business card. I glanced at it and put it in my wallet while she said, "I'm an investment consultant, and the only rule I have is that I refuse to invest less than ten million dollars."

I gave an appreciative nod. "With that kind of positive attitude, you're bound to make the big time before you're thirty."

It took her a moment, but she threw back her head and laughed out loud. "Do you know," she said, "I think *you* are the cad! Adrian is just a sad little man, but you? You are naughty. And I'm beginning to think I am grateful he didn't show up."

Her drink arrived. I said, "That makes two of us. I was going to eat. Will you join me?" She almost hesitated. I ignored her and told the waiter, "Bring another menu, will you?"

He went away. She said, "You are bossy."

I gave my head a small shake. "Having a menu to look at does not oblige you to dine. But I'd be very disappointed if you didn't. You live on Bermuda?"

Her face said she was aware I had changed the subject and closed the issue of whether she would stay or not. She thought about it for a moment and decided she didn't mind being bossed around a little.

"I live on Bermuda. You?"

"New York."

"Don't tell me. I am good at guessing. The bossiness pegs you as a lawyer or the CEO of a large company, but there's that anarchic streak, the rule breaker, so you could be a dotcom billionaire. Are you building hotels on Mars?"

I shook my head. "Way off, I'm afraid, Caroline. I made a fortune hunting down high-level drug dealers, mainly Sinaloa, but not exclusively. If I had been DEA, they would have paid me a hundred grand a year and given me a Rolex on retirement, if I survived that long. But I did it as..." I looked up at the translucent sky with its scattering of stars, then down at the lights twinkling on the horizon. "I was more of a private contractor, which meant I could charge more and also derive collateral benefits—spoils of war, if you like. I made a lot and invested it wisely, and now I live on the interest and do whatever takes my fancy."

Her eyes flitted over my face. She looked serious. "Are you pulling my leg?"

"No." I shook my head. "It's absolutely true. If I was going to pull your leg, I'd say I was CIA. But I am not. That's how I made my money, as a kind of mercenary consultant."

"That's quite a story."

"You don't have to believe it."

"I do. I won't ask you how you got into it. Instead I'll ask you, if you have retired, what takes your fancy now?"

I made a show of frowning and studied my drink. "I think getting to know a fascinating English woman who lives on Bermuda and invests hundreds of millions of dollars and makes awful choices about whom to get invited to dinner by."

She arched an eyebrow. "You don't waste time, do you?"

I sipped my drink and allowed myself to become serious. "We each of us have a limited number of heartbeats that we can use up. We are not aware of that when we are kids, or teenagers, even into our twenties. But sometimes an event happens in your life, and you become aware that your time in this world is limited and precious." I studied her face. She was frowning at me. "I'm not an existentialist," I said and smiled. "I don't think everything is pointless, and I am open to the possibility that life goes on. But we are here, now, in this life, and we shouldn't waste it."

"Boy, you're pretty intense, mister."

I raised my shoulders an eighth of an inch. "You asked, kiddo. I can also be light and fluffy if you prefer."

"I'll stick with intense for now, thanks."

I nodded once and signaled the waiter. As he approached, I said, "I could get pretty intense over a dozen oysters followed by a leg of lamb broiled in honey and eucalyptus."

I made a question of my face and showed it to Caroline.

"I'll join you in the oysters, but I'll have a sirloin steak. Broiled lamb might be a little heavy."

I glanced at the wine menu and told the waiter, "Blanc de Blancs, Laurent-Perrier, brute with the oysters. Then a Marques de Murieta Gran Reserva, 2012 with the meat."

He went away, and she sat watching me with a funny smile on her face. "Maybe," she said, "I don't like brute champagne, and maybe I don't like red wine from Rioja."

I shook my head. "No."

"No?"

"No, because then I would be completely wrong about you, and I'm not."

She laughed again. "You are impossible! I'm not sure how long I could put up with you, Mr. Rogue, but for now I am finding you rather refreshing."

"I'll drink to that."

And we toasted.

SEVENTEEN

It was two a.m. by the time we rose from the table after a shared pudding involving five different types of chocolate and whipped cream, followed by two generous cognacs for Caroline and two large Bushmills for me.

We stepped out under the stars and half a silver moon, and she turned to face me. She placed her hand on my chest and looked up into my eyes. It might have been what you'd call a mixed message, but there was no force in her hand at all, against a strong magnetic pull in her eyes. I smiled at her. She returned the smile but shifted her gaze to a button on my shirt.

"You're a very unusual man, Rogue. It's been quite an evening."

"Would you like me to drive you home?"

Her smile, directed at my button, deepened. "I'm not sure if you're a gentlemanly cad or a caddish gentleman." Now she looked up at me. "Whichever one it is, I think I had better drive myself home."

"Sure?"

"It's all been very sudden and intense." She laughed and rested her forehead on my chest. "I shall have to talk to Adrian in the morning." She took a deep breath and raised her eyes to meet mine. "And that's a conversation I would like to keep as uncomplicated as possible."

I let a smile tug at my right cheek. "My driving you home would complicate that conversation?"

"You *know* it would, Mr. Cad."

"Can I call you a cab?"

"I am not drunk. I can drive perfectly well. Thank you all the same."

She stood on tiptoes and gave me a lingering kiss on the cheek, then turned swiftly and trotted to a silver Mercedes. The lights flashed, then bleeped, and a few moments later, I saw her rear lights, like two red eyes, fade into the darkness toward Hamilton.

I turned away, shoved my hands in my pockets, and strolled down the winding path toward my cabin. Halfway there, I pulled my cell from my pocket and called Jane Harrison. It rang twice, and when she spoke, she sounded like she'd just woken up.

"You OK?"

I smiled to myself but didn't let it show in my voice. "Fine. Did I wake you?"

"It's past midnight. I work."

"I need to ask you a question."

"Shoot."

"On a scale of one to ten, how attractive am I?"

"*What?*" I heard her sit up. "*Are you serious? Screw you, Mark!*"

"Hey, don't get mad. It's a serious question."

"Ask the damned woman you're interested in!"

"Will you relax! I am not interested in any woman. It's a serious question. Will you tell me, please, objectively?"

There was a loud sigh. "A six! If you had asked me under different circumstances, maybe a seven. Now can I get some sleep, asshole?"

"Yeah, nice to hear from you, too."

She was quiet for a moment, and I didn't hang up. Then, "Everything OK?"

"Yeah, I've only been here a few hours, but I noticed there were a couple of superyachts anchored a mile or so off the north coast, and I have a hunch Fischer might know I'm here."

"How come?"

"I'm not sure. A gut feeling. Get some sleep, I'll call you tomorrow."

"OK, be careful, will you?"

"You too."

I slipped the phone in my back pocket and frowned at my feet the rest of the way back to my cabin.

I slept fitfully with troubled dreams I didn't remember in the morning. I rose at six and walked down to a small, sandy cove a short distance from my cabin. The swim helped clear my mind and get things in perspective, and by twenty to eight, I was showered, shaved, and dressed and making my way to the bar for breakfast.

My waiter from the night before saw me coming, greeted me, and offered me a table on the terrace, overlooking the ocean. He gestured at the gleaming superyachts and said, "They have become three."

I studied them a moment and sat. "Maybe they were breeding overnight. Did you learn anything?"

"Yes, sir. The first two yachts to arrive were the *Alsafinat Alumcadasa*, from Saudi Arabia, and the *Dama de Blanco* from Colombia. My brother's girlfriend is in the police, and she says that the rumor going around BPS—that's the Bermuda Police Service—is that there is not a Saudi prince aboard the *Alsafinat Alumcadasa*. It is really a terrorist leader."

I managed to frown and arch an eyebrow at the same time. "How would they know that?"

"Because her cousin is an inspector, and he told her that MI6 had asked them to keep a close eye on the ship because they believed a man called…" He trailed off and narrowed his eyes at the sea, like his memory had gone blank.

I smiled, took out twenty bucks, and gave them to him. He gave a big smile. "Oh! Thank you sir!" He snapped his fingers. "Yahya Sanjar! Who is some kind of terrorist, he said."

I frowned. "That's pretty interesting. So what is an Arab terrorist doing in Bermuda? Did he say?"

He shook his head. "No, he just said the BPS keeps an eye on them. The other yacht, the *Dama de Blanco*, is well known here. It comes pretty regularly, though usually it comes in to port or anchors close by."

"And who does that belong to?"

I asked, but I was pretty sure I knew the answer, and I wasn't wrong.

"That belongs to Oscar Guzman, who's like a narco trafficker. He has friends here. He doesn't always come in person, but his yacht stops here several times each year."

"Is he on it this time?"

"According to my sister-in-law's cousin, they have footage from a drone of Yahya Sanjar and Oscar Guzman."

I gave a short laugh. "OK, for another fifty bucks, who showed up this morning?"

"I don't know who's on board yet, but Sharon, that's my sister-in-law, says the yacht is the *Eden Dawn* and is registered to the Universal Trading Corporation."

I gave him a hundred bucks because his sister-in-law was a cop, and her cousin was in touch with the British Secret Intelligence Service. I told him I wanted two croissants and a pot of strong black coffee but stopped him as he was about to leave.

"Listen, does Guzman come ashore?" One thing I know about Mexican narcos is they love to party. "Does he have a place where he hangs out, a night club or something?"

He hunched his shoulders. "Sure. It's the only place on the Island. The Dharma Night Club, on Front Street." He grinned. "Where you went to buy your clothes."

When he'd gone, I called Jane.

"It's seven in the morning here."

"Congratulations. That's a great time. Do me a favor. Find out who's on the board of directors of the Universal Trading Corporation."

"Would you like me to bathe your feet and massage aromatic oils into them too?"

"Yeah, but that can wait till I get back."

"Funny. When is that likely to be?"

I gazed out at the three gleaming yachts and spoke absently. "Two or three days. No more."

"OK, Mark, I'll get back to you as soon as I know something."

"Jane? Why do you call me Mark?"

She was silent for a while. "I... It just came out without thinking." She gave a small laugh. "Keeping the cover. What do you want me to call you?"

"Rogue."

"Is that who you are now?"

"Like you said, until I remember."

"I'll call you later."

My breakfast arrived, and I spent a long while sipping coffee and tearing off small bits of croissant to chew on while I stared at the three huge luxury yachts on the horizon. It was everything Jane had told me about Hans Fischer on the first night we'd met at the club played out before my very eyes. Yahya Sanjar, a senior leader in Hamas, whose stated objective was to completely eliminate Israel, and Oscar Guzman, the most senior leader of the Sinaloa Cartel, now that Jesus Sanchez was dead. Two groups with absolutely nothing in common except a sworn hatred of the United States, anchored within a quarter of a mile of each other off the coast of Bermuda.

And then along comes Hans Fischer to bridge the gap. To bridge the gap and, while he was at it, identify more things that the two groups might have in common. Hamas, for example, though a Sunni organization, had overcome their hatred of the Shiite faction of Islam under the guidance of Ismail Haniyeh to become close allies of Iran, a Shiite regime. With Haniyeh dead, Yahya Sanjar had taken over and reaffirmed Hamas' deep friendship with Iran. This was a friendship which gave them almost unlimited access to weaponry from Iran itself and more indirectly from Russia and even China.

But where they had ready access to weapons, cash was not so easy for Hamas to come by. Rooted as they were in a zone crippled by centuries of conflict and relying for cash on Iran, itself crippled by economic sanctions and trade sanctions, money was a scarce commodity.

Sinaloa, on the other hand, had a superabundance of money and the financial expertise and political contacts to allow them to move that money around the globe at the touch of a key. What was harder for Sinaloa was to get free access to large amounts of modern armament. And there, right there, Hans Fischer, like a satanic Cupid, could bring these strange bedfellows together to make not love, but war.

This was what Susan had seen, and it had cost her her life. But she had seen more than that. Hans Fischer had arranged this meeting, that much seemed obvious, but he had arranged it well away from United States jurisdiction, on the high seas, where they could not be interfered with, bugged, or spied upon. The reason was obvious: The United States would view a close relationship between Sinaloa and Hamas—or Iran—as a dangerous threat and would act to stop it.

But that being the case, why did Fischer have a penthouse on Central Park West? Why was he based there, and why had he had Mitch Vogel and Carmen Mendoza on his payroll? The answer was clear, and this was the crucial thing Susan had seen. The cancer that was Sinaloa, Hamas, and Hans Fischer had metastasized within the CIA and from there into the United States government. But where I and a thousand conspiracy theorists might make that statement in general terms, Susan had the facts and could state the names, the departments, and the offices.

She was that kind of researcher. She was passionate and relentless.

The thought made me smile. I knew that about her. It reminded me of what Dr. Elizabeth Grant had said to me: Feeling was just one way of thinking. You could think and remember in pictures and movies, you could think or remember in sounds and dialogues, or you could think and remember in feelings. And right then I was remembering the feeling of certainty—the *knowledge*—that Susan was a thorough, meticulous researcher.

She knew who Sinaloa owned in local and federal government, and if Iran owned anyone in the United States government, she knew who that was too.

That was the kind of information that was a death sentence, and that was why they had had to kill her. So if the four guys in the car were Felipe Ochoa, Nestor Gavilan, Oliver Peralta, and Eulogio Borja, hit men from the cartel, it was not an insane step to speculate that the fifth gunman, who'd kept hidden in the shadows, was CIA.

Vogel or Mendoza? It was possible. If it was not one of them, it might have been Gutmeyer or one of the other guys I'd killed. The fact was, who actually pulled the trigger was much less important than the person who formed the idea and took the decision—whoever was giving Vogel and Mendoza their orders. It might be someone sitting out there on one of those yachts, but I didn't think so.

Why?

Because Hans Fischer was not forming a bridge between Yahya Sanjar, Oscar Guzman, and a CIA middle manager.

That was too easy and had been done before. He was forming a bridge between these bastards and somebody in DC who could make things happen. Vogel and Mendoza were low profile representatives that nobody would notice. Somebody back home was giving them orders, and I wanted to know who. There was a third element in this equation. There were weapons, there was drugs money—and there was oil. Iran's big asset, and an asset that that was capable of turning heads in DC. Heads that were well above Mendoza's and Vogel's.

I drained my coffee and reached for my cell. It rang as I picked it up, and I saw it was Jane.

"Did you phone to make me happy?"

"I guess that depends on what makes you happy. The board of directors of the Universal Trading Corporation is composed of three men and a woman. Camilla Johnston, Rude Van Dreiver, William Cawdrey, and the man you knew all along would be there, Hans Fischer."

"Do any of those other names mean anything to you?"

"Not a thing, but we are looking into it."

"Has Levi decided to see me yet?"

"He's reluctant, Ma—sorry. Rogue. But I figure he hasn't actually got much choice. We'll sort it out when you get back."

"Thanks."

We were silent for a couple of seconds, and something I couldn't identify started nagging at the back of my mind. Without knowing exactly why, I said, "Jane, listen, I want to thank you. We were friends before—" I hesitated. "Before this happened to me. And you're still there. I appreciate that. I wish I could remember." I gave a stupid laugh and said,

"There must be some nice memories there I'm missing out on."

"Yeah." It was hard to read her tone of voice. It was somewhere between sad and pissed. "There are some good memories. Keep me posted."

"Jane—"

"What?"

"I think I remember your name."

"You remember *my name*? Jane Harrison? It's not an unusual name. It's like John Smith."

"Yeah, but I..." I trailed off. "It's nagging at me. Where do you live?"

She was silent for a long time. Then she said, "West 127th, just off Lenox Avenue. Why?"

I gave my head a small shake. "I don't know. I had the Bronx in my mind. Haight Avenue?"

Again she was quiet for a long while. "I used to live in Haight Avenue. But I moved to my parents' apartment on 127th. They died."

"I'm sorry."

"It was a few years ago. You were at the funeral."

"Oh."

"I gotta go. Keep me posted."

"Yeah, you too."

I sat for a long time, staring at nothing in particular, thinking about Jane Harrison and Haight Avenue in the Bronx. Eventually the waiter showed up and asked if I wanted more coffee. I told him I did and called Caroline Gordon.

"Good morning, Mr. Rogue. Aren't you supposed to leave it thirty-six hours, so as not to appear needy?"

"You know how I feel about rules. And by the way, Rogue is not my surname. It's my name. Rogue. Just like that."

"I do apologize. Look, thank you for a lovely meal last night."

"It was my pleasure. Did you talk to Adrian yet?"

She hesitated. "No, not yet. He left me a string of very apologetic messages."

I allowed the humor to show in my voice. "So you are going to forgive him and give him another chance so he can stand you up again for his boss."

"You really are appalling, aren't you?"

"That's what my mother said as the midwife handed me over. Listen, as I can't date you, I want to ask you a favor."

She laughed for a long time. It was like the tinkling of lots of silver bells.

"I am remembering why I decided you were a cad. What favor?"

"Are you aware that Oscar Guzman is on the island? I say on the island, I mean his yacht is anchored a mile off shore."

"And who is Oscar Guzman when he's at home?"

"One of the richest men in the world. His empire is worth billions. And he is a man who is very, very keen to find legitimate investment opportunities. And we are talking about a lot more then ten million dollars."

"That is—" she said and paused. There was a frown of curiosity in her voice. "That is interesting, but I don't see what favor you want from me."

"I need an introduction."

She laughed again. "Well, so do I!"

"That's great," I said. "I'll get you one."

EIGHTEEN

Not much happened that day except that I swam a lot and bought myself some first class binoculars which I used to lie on the sand by the sea and watch the three super yachts. It wasn't hard to make out Ochoa's one. On the starboard spreader, he had the Red Ensign flapping with the coat of arms of Bermuda in the lower right hand side. That was the courtesy flag. But at the stern, his ensign was the vertical red, white, and green tricolor of Mexico.

Of the other two yachts, one was flying the British Red Ensign, which I figured was Hans Fischer's yacht, and the other had the Saudi green flag with the white inscription in Arabic, *There is no god but Allah, Mohammed is the Messenger of Allah*. That yacht, I noticed, looked more like a spaceship than a boat, and it was substantially bigger than the other two. I guess that's what you get when you control almost twenty percent of the energy source of an entire planet.

Oil.

At six o'clock, I saw two boats launch from the *Dama de Blanco*, the Lady in White, Oscar Guzman's boat. I picked up my cell, made a quick search, and called the Bermuda 24 Hour Luxury Car Rental Agency. A man answered and told me who I had phoned.

"I need a chauffeur driven Rolls Royce for tonight. There should be room for six women and me in back. I don't care how much it costs, but I need to pay cash in advance because I was mugged and my wallet was stolen."

He was quiet while he processed this information, but he was smiling when he answered. Cash in advance will do that. "Of course sir. Where would you like the car delivered and at what time?"

I gave him the address of the hotel and told him ten p.m. was a good time. He told me how much that would cost, I said the cash would be ready, and I hung up. Then I made another search and dialed.

"Select Escorts of King Street, how may I help you today?"

"Good evening. I will need six escorts for this evening. We will be spending the evening with a yacht full of billionaires, and I want to make a very good impression. Elegant but friendly. I will have my Rolls collect them at ten-thirty p.m."

"Yes sir, that will be fine."

"I don't care how much this costs, but I was mugged on arrival, and my wallet was stolen, so I need to pay cash in advance. Tell me how much and I'll have my chauffeur deliver an envelope to you. I'll make sure and tip the girls later anyway."

The temperature of her voice rose from agreeable to very warm. "Oh, that will be just fine, sir."

I went and had a shower and dressed. Then I prepared two fat envelopes full of cash and stuffed some more in my wallet. At ten o'clock precisely, the Rolls arrived with a taxicab right behind it. There was a chauffeur in a gray uniform at the wheel of the Rolls, and a man with a thin face and permed gray hair swept back from his forehead in the back. He got out and smiled a lot like he didn't mean it.

"I have the rental papers," he said and shrugged. "But as this is a cash transaction, I don't, perhaps..."

I gave him his envelope and told him, "A gentleman's word will do me fine. You'll have your car back in the morning."

He told me he hoped I had a wonderful evening. I told him I was pretty sure I would, and he went away in the taxi. I approached the chauffeur and gave him five hundred bucks.

"What's your name?"

"Chas, sir."

"OK, Chas, do you know the Select Escorts of King Street?"

There was the hint of an arch to his eyebrow. "Not personally, but I have collected clients from there."

"That is exactly what I want you to do. At half past ten you will pick up six ladies from the escort service offices. Then you will come and collect me from the bar here, at the hotel, and we'll go to the Dharma Night Club on Front Street." I offered him a smile that was a little ironic. "I am guessing the people you've collected from King Street in the past you've delivered to the Dharma Night Club on Front Street."

HELL'S FURY | 177

"Once or twice, sir."

"Good, so you know where it is. Go for it. Come and fetch me when you get back with the girls." I pointed. "I'll be on the terrace."

I watched him drive away and went to sit in the candlelight, enjoying the sea breeze and the smell of brazed fish. I ordered a vodka martini and called Caroline.

"Hello, Mr. Cad. I had a feeling you might call."

"Are you free this evening? Adrian need not worry. I have decided to pursue a platonic relationship with you."

"I feel almost insulted."

"Don't be. You have no idea the things Plato got up to with his friends. Besides, you belong to that exquisite class of women who are drawn to weak, ineffectual men because you feel sorry for them. I only wish I could be weak and ineffectual so you would at least notice me. But I can't, so I have to settle for a platonic friendship."

"I feel, 'You really are appalling' is getting overused. What can I say?"

"You can say thank you, because I am going to introduce you to a man who will make you very rich if you invest his billions."

A long silence. "Come again?"

"I'll pick you up around midnight. Wear something sexy and elegant, aside from your smile, that is."

"You absolute bastard!" She was laughing. "Are you serious?"

"Always, deadly. Where do you live so I can tell my chauffeur."

She hesitated again, like she felt she was losing control of events, but finally gave me a number on Rosemont

Avenue. "It's the pink house with the rubber plant over the gate."

"Gotcha. Be ready. This could be the night that changes your life."

THE DRIVE to the Dharma Club was entertaining. It started out with the six charming, elegant, and very beautiful women fussing over me in the back of the Rolls while I dished out champagne. They asked me all about myself, like they were really interested, and I pretended I believed them and told them lies that made them gasp and laugh. I enjoyed playing the game for a while, then decided it was time to get down to business.

"Ladies," I said, "you are all beautiful, charming, and elegant. I couldn't have hoped for more. Now we are on a mission tonight, and there are bonuses for all of you if we pull it off." There was some cute giggling here. "At the Dharma Club, I am pretty sure there will be a Mexican guy with his retinue of faithful groupies. He is a man who appreciates beauty and elegance, so he is going to notice you—how could he not?—and I am hoping we will all get into conversation and become friends. All I want from you is that you be what you are: beautiful, smart, elegant, and very sexy. And if you get into conversation with his group, mention that the guy you are with has made a fortune investing other people's money." They didn't say anything, so I added, "If any one of you is uncomfortable with the mission, or you are worried about Mexican billionaires, that is not a problem. I am aware it's a big ask. You just walk away. You get paid, but you get no bonus. Are we in?"

They all said they were in and giggled a lot, like I had said something funny.

He wasn't at the Dharma Club when we arrived, but that didn't worry me because he and his entourage were having a big slap-up meal at the bistro right next door. There were tables under the arches out on the sidewalk, and the big plate glass windows were open. So everybody saw the big Rolls Royce arrive and the six gorgeous girls assisted out by the uniformed chauffeur. That gave me time to scan the long table where Guzman was seated at the head, with his faithful gathered all around him.

They were noisy and laughing, and there was an air of happy abundance at the table, like they all felt they owned the world. The girls all looked freshly minted out of plastic molds, the guys were all draped in Armani, and the table looked like it was creaking under the weight of the plates and the bottles. Guzman was easy to identify because he was presiding, but I could see no sign of Yahya Sanjar or Hans Fischer. This was just Guzman having dinner with his tribe and probably discussing the negotiations that had been going on aboard Fischer's yacht.

I climbed out, gathered the girls up in both arms, and had the chauffeur take a photograph of us right where Guzman could get a good eyeful. He'd be mildly pissed that here was a guy not only stealing the limelight but showing off six beautiful women all on his own. That was fine. What I wanted was his attention, hostile or otherwise.

I made a point of ignoring him, and we went down the little alley to the club entrance. There a guy the size of two guys wearing an elegant black evening suit smiled at us, accepted a hundred bucks discreetly slipped to him, and ushered us in. There was a small foyer where the girls left their shawls, and we went through red leather padded doors with heavy brass and mahogany handles, into a sprawling, darkened club that was throbbing with music and colored lights. There was a blond kid behind the mahogany bar. He was wearing a violet waistcoat and a black bowtie. I approached him with my girls in tow, all laughing.

"Give me a couple bottles of Krug, brut." I slipped him a couple of hundred bucks and said, "That's for you. My friends here are really keen to meet a billionaire tonight. I know you have one coming in later, and I'd love a table close to his. Can you accommodate me?"

He laughed as he pocketed the cash and pointed to a dark recess at the back of the club. He had the Australian habit of making statements like they were questions. "He usually sits in there? I'll bring your champagne over in an ice bucket to the table next to it. No worries, mate. That'll be two thousand five hundred bucks? Have to ask you to pay now, I'm afraid."

I handed over the cash. He looked mildly astonished, and we made our way to the table. There we talked toot and shot the breeze for half an hour while we worked our way through the first twelve hundred and fifty Bermudan dollars' worth of champagne.

Then Oscar Guzman came in with his retinue. He stopped and scanned the club, and I knew he was looking for me. That was fine. I'd make sure he found me.

I said to the girls, "That right there is your target."

There was a lot of giggling and chattering while they eyed up the prospect. He was approaching, watching me. I laughed and said, "Eyes on me, girls!" They all turned to me and toasted, and as Guzman and his guys passed within a foot of us I grabbed the girl on my left, buried my face in her neck, and muttered something outrageous that made her squeal.

From that moment on, it would be eating him that he had noticed me, and I had been too busy with my six girls to notice him.

We played around for about ten or fifteen minutes. Then the girl on my right, who might have been called Xena, or Zeena, or Zeta, whispered in my ear that she was going to make a move.

She stood, which of itself was pretty spectacular, and eased her way around the table. While she did it, I saw her glance at Guzman, smile demurely, and walk away to the ladies'. While she was gone, we did some more playful rollicking, and before long, we were getting looks from Guzman's table. Some were curious, others were laughing openly.

Xena returned and, as she was about to slide in to her seat, another one of the girls, who might have been called Kitty or Cocoa, stood to move out. They both collided beside the table, almost fell, and hugged each other as they laughed. In doing so, they bumped into the guy sitting nearest to us. There was a lot of laughing and apologizing. I gave them a moment, then stood, put my arm around each of the girls, and smiled at the guy, who had got to his feet, laughing.

"I am so sorry," I said, trying to talk above the music. "I hope we didn't spill your drink." He was shaking his head and dismissing the whole thing like it was nothing, but he was telling it to the girls, not me. I said, "Please, let me invite you to some champagne as an apology. It's the least I can do."

The guy's eyes shifted to Guzman, who was watching me the way a panther watches a lame deer while he decides if he can be bothered to kill it. I let my face show I had registered he was the host. I smiled urbanely at him and raised my voice again.

"Please forgive me, sir. We did not mean to invade your space. May I please invite the table?"

He spread his hands wide and smiled. "You are very generous. It was a simple collision. No problem. But thank you." He shrugged and grinned around the table. "We never say no to a drink, eh?"

We all laughed, and I left the girls chatting with their new friends. I returned to the bar, and the kid in the violet waistcoat smiled at me. "Don't waste time, do you, mate?"

"If I had more of it, I might be tempted to waste some. Send over a couple of bottles of Krug for my new friends, will you? You'd better make it four." I paid him with a wad of cash. He raised an eyebrow at me, and I shrugged. "I got mugged. What can I do till I get the new cards?"

"Right. Four bottles coming up."

I gave them a while. When I saw Xena, or it may have been Kitty, calling over the other four girls to introduce them and the Latina girls jumping up and hugging them and kissing them on the cheeks, I returned with the waiter and the champagne in tow behind me. As he set the large ice bucket down, I leaned over toward Guzman.

"Will you please excuse me? I just had a call. I have to go and get my investment advisor. She's my better half! Please enjoy the drinks." To the girls, I said, "I'll be fifteen minutes.

I have to go get Caroline. Don't make a nuisance of yourselves!"

They all waved and grinned and told me not to be too long, though I didn't get the feeling I'd be missed much. I told them I'd be as quick as I could and left the club. Chas was parked outside reading the *Iliad* and smoking a cigarette. He looked up as I leaned in the window. He registered the fact that the girls weren't with me and made a question with his face.

I said, "We have quite a party building up in there, Chas. There is just one thing missing—my key guest, Caroline Gordon of Rosemont Avenue. You know where it is?"

"I know where it is."

"Then let's go get our key guest, Chas: Caroline, of Rosemont Avenue."

He closed the book and tossed it on the seat beside him. Then he flicked the butt out the window and fired up the big beast.

"Whatever you say, sir."

NINETEEN

By the time we got back to the Dharma Club, the six girls had worked their magic and had joined Guzman and his retinue. They'd even pulled over our table and chairs so they were all sitting together. There was a lot of laughter and merriment going on, though some of the Latina girls looked less than happy. I glanced at Caroline as we approached the table. Her eyes were wide, and her mouth was slightly open in what could easily have become a gape.

She stopped, looked up at me, and frowned. "What the hell, Rogue?"

I put my hand on the small of her back and leaned into her ear. "This guy owns one of those three superyachts anchored off the coast here. If you can invest his money, he will love you forever."

I eased her forward, and when we arrived at the table, I stood over Xena or Kitty and spread my hands with a big stupid grin on my face, looking down at Guzman.

"We have completely invaded your party!" I looked

around at my escorts. "Girls! Tonight was on me." I allowed a hint of reproach into my voice and looked at Guzman. The expression he offered me in return was smug. "You are all more than welcome at my table tonight. A party is a party, the bigger the better!" His eyes shifted to Caroline. "And who is your beautiful companion? I cannot believe she is an investment consultant. God would not be so unfair to bestow such beauty and elegance on a woman who is also so intelligent."

He stood and waved the girl who was sitting next to him away. He reached out his hand and gestured to the vacated place on the sofa beside him. "Please, my dear, come. Sit with me and tell me about yourself. What is your name? I am Oscar Guzman, and"—they sat, he holding her hand—"I have a problem. You know what is my problem?" He looked around, letting us all know we were going to have to laugh. "I have much too much money!"

We all laughed as we were expected to. Caroline's laugh was perhaps a little shrill. I spoke loudly, addressing the group and pointing at Guzman. "His problem is he is too attractive to women! This guy is a magnet! I came here with seven women, and I have none left!"

We all laughed again, but Guzman's eyes were not laughing. When it had died down, I said, "But seriously. If you have money that you want to invest creatively, Caroline is a genius. We work together on some projects, and she is like the bane of the taxman. The Inland Revenue Service have a contract out on her. Ain't that right, honey?"

She giggled. "It certainly is! And if they haven't, they should have!"

I raised a finger and laughed, driving home the fact that I had no idea who he was. "But she has one rule!"

Guzman arched an eyebrow. "A rule?" He said it like he wasn't sure what rules were, but he knew he didn't like them.

"One rule," I repeated and made my face serious. "She will not invest less than ten million bucks. That's right, isn't it, honey?"

She made an apologetic face and showed it to Guzman. "It's just that less than ten million really isn't worth it, and the kind of investments I go for..."

She trailed off because he was laughing and patting her hand on her knee. "How about—" he said with that smugness that flowed from the very core of his being. "How about five hundred million, and we see what kind of results you get? If you do better than my current advisor, we can talk about serious money."

Caroline was looking at him like she'd just seen the Virgin of Fatima climb out of his eyeball. I had a similar expression on my face. She said, "*Serious* money..."

I echoed her and said, "Five hundred million is pretty serious money."

He shrugged. "Perhaps you need to open your mind and broaden your expectations. I paid more than half that for my yacht. My car collection is worth more than double your minimum investment limit."

She put her hands to her cheeks and managed to blush. "I feel I have made a fool of myself. Perhaps..."

She glanced at me like she thought we should leave, but Guzman was patting her knee again.

"Nonsense, my dear. I know that less than one percent

HELL'S FURY | 187

of people in the world can think about money the way I do. You have just been fortunate enough that your partner's friends bumped into my nephew when they were going to the toilet." He threw back his head and laughed out loud. Caroline laughed with him gratefully.

I turned to Kitty, or it might have been Xena. "Did you make it to the can in the end?"

She gave me an interesting grin. "It would have been a bit of a giveaway if I hadn't."

"Good girl. That's your bonus right there."

"You want to get aboard that yacht, don't you?"

I frowned at her and noticed for the first time that she had intelligent eyes and was actually quite beautiful. "Kitty, right?"

"Emma."

"Emma, forgive me, my bad. Yes, I do."

She leaned forward toward Guzman and spoke above the noise. She managed to sound like Marylyn Monroe after a lobotomy. "I just did the sums. Is your yacht really worth more than two hundred and fifty million dollars?"

He smiled indulgently. "Yes, my dear, two hundred and seventy."

She gasped and made it look pretty. "My goodness!" She put her fingertips to her lips and hunched her shoulders. "Just the extra twenty would be enough to see me for the rest of my life! Is it here in Bermuda? Can we see it?"

He spread his arms wide to include us all in his abundant, poisonous generosity. "Of course! Come, tomorrow we have a barbeque on my yacht, in the evening. I introduce you to some friends, we eat Mexican meat, the best in the world! We drink, we have fun." He turned to Caroline. "And you and I, my dear, can discuss your future career. Maybe I can make you a very, very rich woman."

We all cheered. Maybe I cheered the loudest. I couldn't have scripted it better if I had written the scene. It had been easy. A small voice inside my head said it had been too easy. I told that voice to shut its trap. We had played skillfully on his hubris, his arrogance, and his vanity, and he had done exactly as he was supposed to do. That, I told myself, was skill.

The party broke up at three a.m., and my only worry then was whether Guzman and his boys would insist on taking Caroline and the girls with them back to the yacht. If that happened, and the girls didn't want to go, it was going to be a problem. But as it was, the party broke up peacefully, and I had Chas drive the girls back to King Street before he delivered Caroline to her large, pink house on Rosemont Avenue.

As we arrived, she leaned forward and said, "You can park outside the gate, Chas." Then she turned to me and smiled. "Walk me to the door?"

He pulled up at her gate and muttered to me, "I'll go find somewhere to turn around."

I told him that was a plan and walked Caroline down her drive to her large, white front door. There she fished her keys out of her purse before placing both palms on my chest and pressing close to me.

"I'd invite you in for a nightcap, but will you forgive me? Everything is moving so fast. I am utterly bewildered, and I really need to think about Mr. Guzman's offer. It sounds as if I would be sailing very close to the wind, legally."

"I have no doubt about that. Sleep on it, and we'll talk in the morning."

She frowned into my eyes, like she was inspecting each, one after the other. "You are such a strange man," she said. Then she smiled with pleasure. "I hope you'll be around for a while. When all this madness settles, I'd love to have you over for dinner."

I smiled and leaned down to kiss her cheek. Before withdrawing, I whispered, "I think I'd like to have you for dinner too."

She laughed and slapped my arm, then let herself into the house. She blew me a kiss and closed the door.

I went back to the Rolls, climbed in, and leaned back with my eyes closed. I smiled and said, "Home, Chas."

I heard him chuckle, and we moved off.

On the way there, my phone rang, and I half expected it to be Caroline, but it wasn't. It was Emma. That made me frown.

"Hey, what's up?"

"I just wondered what your plans were for the rest of the evening."

"I think most places are closed by now. I'll probably have a nightcap in my cabin and hit the sack."

"Sounds like a plan."

"Feel like joining me?"

"Well, that *is* why I phoned."

"Are you still at Kings Street?"

I saw Chas glance in the mirror. The car slowed. She said, "I am."

"I'm on my way." I nodded at the mirror. He gave a weary smile, and instead of turning up toward the coast, he turned right along Elliot Street toward Kings Street.

"I guess *everything* is goin' your way tonight, sir," he muttered.

"I guess it is, Chas. I guess it is at that."

WE ROSE LATE, and I made breakfast in my small kitchen while she showered. I called her when it was ready, and she came out in my bathrobe, which was six sizes too big for her. She also had a towel wrapped around her head like a turban. At first she did a lot of smiling while she sipped her coffee and nibbled at her pancakes. But when I told her, "I don't want you and the girls to go to the yacht today," she stopped dead with a piece of pancake halfway to her mouth.

"Why the hell not? You're not going to turn all jealous and possessive on me, are you? This is my job."

I shook my head. "I'm not jealous, and I don't own you, so I can't be possessive. That's not the reason. Guzman is a Mexican cartel boss, and there is some very heavy negotiating going on between those three yachts. I have it on reliable authority that there will be serious trouble there tonight. I don't want anything to happen to you or any of your friends."

She frowned. "Are you serious? Are you a cop? I don't need some paternal asshole looking out for me."

I sipped my coffee and wondered how much to tell her. In the end, I opted for a veiled lie.

"Thanks for the compliment. I love you too. Am I a cop? Not exactly. And the less you know, the better, the safer you'll be."

"Not exactly? So you're some kind of undercover agent."

"Believe me, you really don't want to know. I don't want

to see you or the girls on that yacht this evening. You think I'm an asshole because of it, fine, I can live with that. Just make sure you're not there. Things are going to turn ugly."

Her face went hard. "That was going to be a really good gig for us."

"Yeah? I don't call getting shot a good gig. And just so you know, aside from trafficking in cocaine, these guys traffic in heroin and all its ugliest variations. They also traffic in slaves—women and children—and use heroin addiction to force them into prostitution. These are very ugly, evil people. Believe me, that was not going to be a good gig."

She didn't say anything. She got up and went to get dressed, and I called her a cab. She reappeared five minutes later looking beautiful but mad.

"I called you a cab."

"I heard."

"I'll walk you to—"

"You don't need to walk me anywhere. You've done quite enough as it is."

"You're mad at me."

"You abused our trust, and now you have cost us what might have amounted to thousands of pounds for each girl."

I nodded and allowed the irony to show in my voice. "Yeah, that's rough. Keep a low profile for the next couple of days and stay away from Guzman and his friends."

"Goodbye, Mr. Rogue." She strode out, muttering, "Stupid name!"

I watched her leave and wondered about going after her. I really didn't need her and her friends showing up at the yacht that night. But in the end I decided if there was one thing those six girls were not, it was stupid. They had their heads screwed on, and they would not put themselves in harm's way.

So I called Caroline Gordon instead.

"Good morning, Rogue." She said it like my head was on the pillow next to hers.

"I didn't get to have you for dinner," I told her, "And it's too late to have you for breakfast. How are you today? You up for our meeting tonight with Guzman?"

"You bet. That man is the goose that lays golden eggs. I am forever indebted to you."

"Nice to know. I might call in that debt one of these days."

"I really need to be careful with you, don't I?"

"Probably. By the way, I told the girls not to come along. We want to talk business tonight, not play around with a bunch of beautiful airheads."

She snorted. "If there is one thing those girls are not, it's airheads."

"Agreed, but when they're working, they behave like airheads because that's what those bastards want."

"That's a change of tune. I thought they were your new best friends."

"No. Business is business. But those guys are very dangerous men who think nothing of killing or torturing, and you'd be wise to keep that in mind."

"Now you tell me! I don't know whether to thank you or shoot you!"

I laughed. "Seriously? The man has a superyacht, a Mexican surname, and is looking to launder hundreds of millions of dollars, and you didn't join the dots? I'm not sure I believe you."

"Well, OK, yes, I joined the dots. But you put it in such a stark way, 'very dangerous men who think nothing of killing or torturing,' and I'd be wise to keep that in mind. It kind of brings it home a bit."

"Well, Caroline, I guess it matters to me what happens to you. You need to be aware who these guys are."

She was quiet for a bit. "Really, it matters to you what happens to me? We've only just met. It's a bit soon to start caring, isn't it?"

"Not at all. It takes seven seconds, when people meet for the first time, it takes just seven seconds for your unconscious mind to decide if it wants to have sex with that person or not."

"And you know this because…?"

It's the kind of thing a fourteen-year-old boy finds useful and never really forgets."

"Of course. Where did you pick up this gem?"

"*Reader's Digest*, where else? It was in an article called 'How I Spied on the Communists for the CIA, Found God, and Became a Preacher.'"

"And knowing you, it's probably true."

"Sure it is. So are we on for tonight, or do you want out?"

"No, I don't want out. But you'll be there and keep me safe, won't you?"

"I'll take care of you, Caroline. Don't worry. I'll be there."

"Thanks. It's funny, I barely know you, but I trust you."

"There you go, you see? Seven seconds it took you to reach that decision."

She was quiet, and when she spoke again, there was a warm smile in her voice.

"It's not the only decision I came to in seven seconds."

"Well, you can tell me all about the other one when we come back from dinner with Guzman."

"I might just do that, though I am not sure yet who is the more dangerous, you or him."

I let the smile show in my voice. "Me."

TWENTY

Special Agent Jane Harrison sat in a booth in the Irish New York Tavern on Reade Street less than three hundred yards from Federal Plaza. Across the table from her was Special Agent Cathy Newton. She was small and very pale, with platinum hair and blue eyes that seemed to scan your soul when she looked at you.

Approaching from the bar was Special Agent Elroy Jones, carrying three beers. As he sat, Newton said, "Agent Harrison, we are really grateful to you for spending some time with us. This is such a complex case. I mean, really, it's just plain *weird*."

Jane nodded once at her drink and said, "It's not a case. I think that's what Director Levi was trying to underline for you. There is no case here."

Newton spread her hands. "Yup. That is absolutely right, and we both agree, right, Elroy?" He didn't say anything. He just sipped his beer. "There is no official investigation into any part of this, but having said that, there are things that just don't add up. They don't make much sense." She laughed. "Actually they don't make any sense at all!"

Jane was about to ask what things but instead gave her head a small shake. "I guess there are things we'll never be able to explain."

"I don't know that I'd go that far, Agent Harrison. I mean, the explanations are *there*. It's just that we are not allowed access to them."

Jane spread her hands just a couple of inches and gave a small shrug. Jones said, "We ran this guy's prints and his DNA through the FBI's databanks and drew a blank. Now, according to Director Levi, the guy *is* in the system, but his file is sealed, classified. Why? I'd like to know why. Then Director Levi tells us that this man is, officially, dead. I've just been talking to him at the house on West 81st. I spoke to him on the Mexican border. Mike Marshall gave him coffee, and that's how we got his DNA and his prints. But forget all that because this guy is dead."

Jane Harrison sighed. "I don't really know what you want from me, Agent Jones, or how you think I can help you. The Susan Hanson case was officially closed with the murder of Ochoa, Gavilan, Peralta, and Borja at Long Beach. You claim that this Rogue character's DNA and prints showed up in a sealed, classified file—"

"It's not a claim." It was Jones. "Director Levi told us that."

"But that man is not just officially dead, multiple witnesses saw him shot repeatedly and then incinerated in his car, after which there was a funeral where he was incinerated again." She gave a small laugh. "It's actually on video. There is no way that man is alive."

HELL'S FURY | 197

Jones sat back, hunched, and gave his head a little shake. "Then how do you explain the hit? Director Levi admitted there was a hit, but that the filed DNA and prints belonged to a dead man. How do you explain that?"

Harrison looked him in the eye and held it for a moment before answering.

"Agent Jones, I don't need to explain it. There is no onus on me to explain anything. All I can do is speculate that it was a glitch in the system or that somebody, somewhere along the line, made a mistake. It happens. And you can browbeat me till the cows come home, that ain't going to change. The sealed, classified file relates to a man who is dead. And I have no idea who your Rogue is."

They were both silent for a moment. Jones studied his glass, and Newton studied Harrison's face. Jane held her eye but barely managed to hide her discomfort under the other's scrutiny. Finally, Newton said, "He is living in Susan Hanson's house. Did you know that?"

Harrison narrowed her eyes and gave her head a little twitch. "Let's get something straight, Agent Newton. Are you interrogating me? Are you questioning me or investigating me?"

"No, of course not—"

"Because I would like to examine the syntax of your question for a moment."

"I'm—"

"'He is living in Susan Hanson's house.' That is a statement. It is not a question. The question you're asking me is, 'Did you know that?' Now what I would like to know, Special Agent Newton, is what possible interest it could have for you whether I knew that he was living there or not.

What point were you trying to make with that question, and more precisely, what information did you hope to glean?"

"It was a manner of speech."

Harrison leaned forward. "Well let me acquaint you with another manner of speech. If you are trying to show professional negligence, conspiracy to conceal evidence or any other kind of professional impropriety or felony, you had better get your facts real straight, because I'll tell you what it looks like to me. This looks to me like a personal crusade that has not been sanctioned by the LA Field Office. We have certainly not received any notification of it, and considering it involves multiple murders within New York, that would be at the very least a courtesy. So if you"—she pointed at Jones and at Newton—"are on a private crusade and are aiming to implicate agents from Federal Plaza in some kind of crazy conspiracy, you had better think again. We run a tight ship, and if that man's file is confidential and sealed, somebody on the top floor has good reason for sealing it and classifying it."

"Agent Harrison, I apologize unreservedly." It was Newton. "It was not my intention in any way to cast doubt on the integrity of yourself or any other agent. It really was just a manner of speech. I guess I was inviting you to share what you knew or your views. I did not mean to cause offense."

Harrison gave a brief nod. "Apology accepted. But you got your answer from Director Levi, and I can't add anything to that. The case is closed, and the man you think is Rogue is dead. Maybe he has a twin brother with amnesia. I can't help you."

She went to stand, but Jones asked her, "Do you know where he is now?"

She sighed. "You said he was in Susan Hanson's house."

He smiled. "Well, that wasn't my question, Agent Harrison."

"I don't know where he is now, no."

"Are you investigating him?"

Harrison laid both hands on the table and fought to control a growing wave of irritation.

"Special Agent Jones, I suggest you make a formal request for that information through your office in Los Angeles, but before you do, I would suggest you ask yourself what possible reason we could have for opening an investigation on a closed case."

Newton answered. "He claims to be Susan Hanson's husband."

"So what?"

"He is suspected of committing multiple murders in Los Angeles connected with drug trafficking and slavery."

"In that case, Special Agent Newton, I suggest you get your office in Wilshire Boulevard to open an investigation and make an official request for information. Now I think we have stretched the bounds of courtesy well beyond the call of duty. I am going to go back to my job, and I suggest you both do the same."

She stood, and they watched her silhouette warp darkly and exit through the door into the sunshine.

"She was really mad," said Newton.

"We were treading on corns we didn't know she had."

Newton stared at him a moment, then nodded. "Yup. There is something there. Is she protective?"

"She knows him. She's in love with him." Jones took a pull on his beer. "Let's go out on a limb and put together everything we know, or we think we know. He's a New York Fed. He's gone rogue, and he's on a crusade to finish Sinaloa and all who sail in her. He and Harrison and Levi were pals, and they are trying to protect him. He was shot and killed—do we know that? They say there's a video. Maybe there is, but I haven't seen it. Maybe he was injured, maybe that's what caused his amnesia. I don't know. But he's alive, and he is on a very dangerous killing spree."

"So what now?"

He raised two fingers. "One, I want to know who Susan Hanson was married to and if he was a Fed. Two, we take what we've got and we do exactly what Agent Harrison suggested. We propose an official investigation."

She hooded her eyes and shook her head. "No way, Jones. They killed it at the border, and they'll kill it again now. You heard the man: The file is sealed and classified. He is officially dead. You can't investigate the activities of a dead man because he ain't got none. He's dead."

"We are not going to investigate that man. We are going to investigate a man falsely representing himself as Susan Hanson's husband."

"That's a matter for the NYPD, Jones, not for the FBI."

"Unless it ties in with international drug trafficking. Hear me out. Here are the bare bones of a theory. Susan Hanson was researching her next novel, and her research was getting too close to the truth. Jesus Sanchez, the then leader in waiting of Sinaloa, has her executed along with her kids. Her husband is also killed in the attack. Now this guy, some kind of ex-special ops crazy, is on a crusade to eliminate Sinaloa. Maybe he was stalking her. She was very popular among the Second Amendment brigade. So he gets amnesia, or says he has, and convinces himself he is her husband."

She shook her head. "Jones, that is the craziest theory I ever heard. And I am being polite because you're a nice guy. But that is *way* out there." She shook her head some more. "Besides, it does not address the issue of the sealed, classified file."

He shrugged. "Yeah, it's deliberately meant not to. It just allows us to get an investigation officially opened and go after this guy."

She gave a soft grunt. "I hope you're not becoming obsessed. I gotta tell you, the Second Amendment is in our Constitution for a reason, Jones, and I have not got a huge problem with Rogue. OK, he's breaking the law, but so are the people he's taking out, and they are doing a lot more harm than he is."

"We've already had this conversation, Newton. Let's at least go and get his marriage certificate and see if it is him."

"OK." She stood, a little reluctantly, and sighed. "I can't help wondering why he hasn't done that himself."

He stood too, with a grunt and a sigh. "That's not as strange as you might think, Cathy."

"Cathy? Are we on first name terms now?"

He ignored her as they crossed the bar toward the door.

"Often people don't look into the obvious because they know what they are going to find. If he investigates too deeply, he is going to prove to himself that he was not her husband."

He opened the door and stepped out after her into the

sunshine. She stopped and turned to face him. "You're awful sure of that, Jones."

He opened the door of their rental car, climbed in, and slammed the door. She watched him do it, then climbed in beside him and stared at him, waiting for a reply as he fired up the engine. He said nothing, and she shook her head again.

"And I'm going to say it again: the crazy stalker with amnesia who believes he's her husband. Man, that is *way* out there."

"When you have a theory that covers all the facts, let me know. Meantime, quit griping and call the City Clerk Marriage Bureau, will you?"

She pulled out her cell, muttering, "Jeez, Elroy, I knew you cared, but this is all moving a bit fast."

"Funny."

She spoke on the phone, and while she spoke, he drove without thinking through Tribeca, down Chambers Street, and then right onto West Street, running parallel to the Hudson River Greenway, going north.

Newton hung up. She stared at him a moment and said, "She'll have it for us in an hour. We can go pick it up. Where are you going?"

"Just drivin', baby," he said facetiously. "Drivin' and chillin' in New York."

"You just happen to be drivin' and chillin' toward the Upper West Side."

"Izat so?"

"You want him to sue us for harassment? You need to cool off, Jones."

"Relax, I just want to drive past. He won't even see us."

"What do you hope to see, a reception committee from the Federation of Obsessed Amnesiac Assassins?"

"Get off my back, Newton. You signed up for this, remember?" He was eying the houses as he drove. He slowed, staring at the house. When he spoke, it was almost a whisper. "He's not there."

"Come on, Jones! How can you tell? That's his Jeep."

"Son of a bitch. He's not there."

He pulled in to a space just beyond the house and killed the engine. Newton covered her face and groaned. "Jones, you are going to get us into serious trouble!"

"Just chill. I want to talk to the neighbor. Relax, he's not here. I can tell."

"*How? How can you tell?*"

He ignored her and climbed out of the car. After rolling her eyes, Newton pushed open her door and followed. There was an elderly lady with a small shopping bag and an even smaller dog on a leash. She was standing at the door to the house next to Rogue's and watching them with no discernable expression.

Elroy produced a charming smile that Newton had never seen before and said, "Good afternoon, madam. I have been trying to talk to the gentleman next door. I've tried a couple of times—"

"They ain't there."

"You wouldn't happen to know—"

"They took a plane. There was people in and out all day. Then she come and they went out and came back. Then she went out again, and when she come back another time he come out with a travelin' bag."

Newton said, "A traveling bag? Like a carry-on?"

"That's what I said. I think that's what I said unless I'm getting stupid in my old age. They're gone."

Jones kept his charming smile on his face. "They didn't happen to mention—"

"They got in her car. Coz that's his car." She pointed to the Jeep. "But they got in her car, and I heard them talking about Teterboro, which is an airfield in Jersey. And he was goin' to Bermuda. You can rent your own air taxi at Teterboro. If yer rich. He was goin' to Bermuda coz she told him to call her when he got there and keep her in the loop."

Newton said, "The woman—"

"I'm not nosy. I just happened to be at the door."

"Of course. What was the woman like?"

"She was awful pretty. Dark hair but pale skin—not as pale as yours—and pretty blue eyes. She was in a business suit. She smiled at me. I don't know if they'll come back. You never know if people are going to come back. But she was real smart."

It was as Jones was thanking her that Newton's phone rang.

She walked away with the phone at her ear. Jones thanked the woman and followed Newton. She put the phone away without saying anything and got behind the wheel. There she sat staring down the road. After a moment, Jones got in, slammed the door, and said, "God dammit! Bermuda? Seriously?"

She seemed not to hear him and spoke staring up the street. "That was the city clerk."

"Yeah?" He glanced at her. "They have the certificate?"

HELL'S FURY | 205

She nodded. "Susan Hanson was married to one Ted Hanson." She turned to face him. "Ted Hanson died seven years ago, and Susan never remarried."

TWENTY-ONE

Carmen Mendoza sat on the upper deck of the *Eden Dawn* in the shade of an awning and played with the small remains of a freshly baked croissant. Hans Fischer sat opposite her but would not look at her. His eyes were hidden behind his heavy black Wayfarers, and he stared fixedly at the *Dama de Blanco*.

"Hans, we need to talk."

"No, Carmen, you need to talk. I do not *need* to do anything—at least where you are concerned."

For a moment, she went very still, then raised her eyes to study his profile.

"That is not a smart attitude, Hans."

"And that, Carmen, sounds like a threat. Considering that you are alone on this yacht where I have half a dozen armed men plus Aleki and Kong, that is probably not very smart either."

"Bring it down a notch, Fischer. Aside from the fact that I am more use to you alive than dead, do you think I am that stupid that I did not take out insurance against you and Vogel?" He turned and regarded her for the first time. She smirked at him. "I work for the CIA, Hans, remember? This shit is second nature to us, and we are the best. So let's just stay friends, shall we?"

His mouth smiled under his black lenses. "You are my dear and beloved Carmen. What would you like to talk about?"

"I can't go back. I'm finished."

He gave a small shrug. "I would have to agree with you." He didn't say, "So what?" but it was implicit in his tone.

"So I need a solution. I have to retire after this job, and I need a place to retire to and a retirement fund."

Somehow he managed to communicate the glazing of his eyes through the black lenses of his shades. "How do you figure on doing that?"

"You have to help me."

"I do?"

"Yeah, Hans, you do. Let me explain so that you understand. You don't want me dead, and you sure as hell don't want me arrested. No. Let me rephrase that. You don't want me arrested, and you sure as hell don't want me dead. Actually, you know what? It works both ways. But let's not go there because the witness protection program is something I just don't want to think about, and I'm guessing you feel the same. So let's stay with the fact that I am your beloved Carmen and you are my beloved Hans. So we need to work something into this deal with Sanjar and Guzman so I can retire when it's done."

"You are overlooking something. You are overlooking the very reason you are here. Vogel is dead, and I need a CIA representative. If we are speaking of need, I *need* you *in* the CIA."

"I can be part of the deal, then I can hand it over. I know at least two guys who'd be willing to step in. I can make the transition smooth. But you have to set me up with a new ID and a place to live."

"That's a big ask."

She sighed. "Hans, let's not take this conversation where neither of us want it to go. You have to help me, and you know it."

He took a deep breath and gazed again at the *Dama de Blanco* anchored a quarter of a mile away.

"Let me think about it, Carmen. I will find a solution. Meantime, there is a favor you can do for both of us."

"What's that?"

"Oscar Guzman."

"What about him?"

"He is playing hardball while pretending to play softball. He is everyone's friend, he just wants to party, and in the end manages to communicate the idea that he doesn't give a damn about the deal. It is a very Spanish way of negotiating. He is your friend, your brother, he will spend five thousand dollars on champagne for you, and all the while he denies you what you most want: a deal. Until finally you negotiate on his terms out of desperation, just to get the damned deal done."

"What do you want me to do?"

"You saw he went ashore last night."

"So?"

"He went to a nightclub."

She repressed a small sigh and sipped her coffee. As she set down the cup, she asked him, "How do you know that?"

"I guessed it was likely. There is only one nightclub here that he would go to, the Dharma Club. I called them this morning, and they confirmed that he had been there with a large party. Apparently another table joined them, seven women and one man."

She went very quiet. He turned to examine her face.

"Oscar Guzman has one major weakness. He does not consider it a weakness. He considers it a strength."

"Women."

"Beautiful women and intelligent women. He needs to own them and control them." He pointed at Guzman's yacht and wagged his finger, like he was telling it off. "I have been watching them today. He is ignoring us. I have spoken on the telephone to Sanjar, and I have called Guzman. I wanted this afternoon to have a meeting to start tying things up." He spread his hands. "We are talking about hundreds of millions of dollars. But Guzman is occupied, busy, asleep, in the can..." He pointed again, this time like he was taking a shot. "But I can see the preparations for a party." He looked at her again. "Have we been invited? Have you been invited?"

Mendoza was frowning. "What the hell is he playing at?"

"It's what I told you. He wants to give me and Sanjar the impression that he is so rich, that he wields so much power, that this negotiation is not really that important for him."

"You want me to go and talk to him?"

He seemed not to hear her. "I know one other man who negotiates in this way, clowning to make you think he is not really interested. It is very effective."

"Yeah? Who?"

"Donald," he said absently. "I want you to get yourself invited to this party. I want you to take Guzman aside and tell him Yahya Sanjar is sailing in the morning because he has had enough, and he does not believe Guzman is serious. Make him understand that Arabs don't work this way and that he risks jeopardizing the whole deal."

"Who's this guy with the seven dames?"

He shrugged. "Some playboy in a rented Rolls Royce. He does not concern us. Call Guzman. He likes you."

"That's because I am beautiful and intelligent."

"No doubt. Take care of this and we'll deal with your problem."

She nodded at him a few times with her eyes narrowed. "Our problem, Hans. Let's not kid ourselves. You're a powerful, useful man, and we all like having you around. But believe me, you do not want the Company getting pissed at you. They are above the law, and they count their budget in trillions. And they understand that in the long run it pays to protect your own." She shook her head and leaned across the table. "Don't fuck with me, Hans, or I swear I will crucify you. This is the third and last time I am going to tell you. We need to be friends."

She stood and walked away with the phone to her ear. Oscar Guzman answered after the fifth ring. She told him who she was, and he said, "Carmen Mendoza." He said it stressing the Mexican pronunciation. "This is a Spanish name."

"My grandfather was Mexican."

"This is why you have the black eyes and the black hair."

HELL'S FURY | 211

"Yeah, it's also why I have the smarts to stay away from Mexican men."

He laughed. "Oh, you will break my heart, Carmen."

She put a smile in her voice. "I didn't become an operations officer in Central Intelligence by having a soft heart, Mr. Guzman. I have two very special organs in my body. Did you know that?"

He almost growled. "I can imagine."

"I don't think you can. I have a brain that is pure gold and a heart that is pure granite. We need to talk."

"Talk what about?"

"Guns, drugs, sex, and money."

"My four favorite subjects. But Hans has sent you to talk to me, verdad?"

"You've lived too long in Mexico, Mr. Guzman. American women don't get told what to do. I keep telling you I am an operations officer for the CIA. You don't get there by being passive and obedient. Now listen to me. I do not like the way this negotiation is going. I can see it falling apart, and Hans is losing control. He doesn't understand Arabs, and neither do you."

He grunted. "What is happening that makes you unhappy? I have been distracted yesterday…"

"Yeah, well you need to stop thinking about skirts for a while and start thinking about business. Because we are talking about hundreds of millions of dollars just being flushed down the can. You need to get serious, Guzman." She paused. "Are you having a party tonight?"

"Yes, sure. I am always having a party. I met some nice girls last night. They comin' over for some food, some dancin'."

"Make room for me. I'm coming over, and we're going to talk. Just you and me, OK? Hans doesn't need to know about this."

He chuckled. "You sure he didn't tell you to call me?"

"I don't work for Hans, Mr. Guzman. Like I told you twice already, I'm a CIA officer, and it's in our DNA to make business deals with men like you. Do I need to paint you a picture?"

He was quiet for a while. Then he chuckled again. "OK, Carmen. You come over at seven-thirty and we have a drink and a talk. Then you stay for the party, OK?"

"You're on. Listen, I have to hang up. I have company."

She hung up and stood leaning on the gunwale staring at her phone. She had lied out of habit and because she knew instinctively that it was often the small lies that sold the big lies. If she had to hang up because she had company, that sold the idea to Guzman that she didn't want Hans listening to their conversation, which sold the lie that she was going behind Hans' back.

She walked back to the table. Hans was still there, reading the *Financial Times*. He looked up at her.

"He's having a party tonight with a bunch of girls he met last night. I flirted with him and told him to invite me. I'm going over at seven-thirty to talk business and then join the party."

"Good. I want him and Yahya Sanjar on my yacht tomorrow at ten a.m. shaking hands. Make him understand that. If he doesn't show, I'm going with the Gulf Cartel, but I want him to understand that he is damaging my reputation, and that has a price to pay."

"I'm not going to threaten him, Hans. He's a psychopath. He's perfectly capable of killing me."

"You don't have to threaten him, Carmen. Just make him aware."

"Make him aware, right."

He smiled, and she thought that his mouth was like a worm curling through slime. "Don't forget," he said through thin lips, "I am also a psychopath, Carmen."

She shook her head. "No, you're not. You're just evil."

She went down to her cabin and lay on her bed for a while, thinking about seven girls and a single guy. Then she showered and dressed for the evening.

Oscar Guzman met her at the aft platform as though she were his long-lost lover. He spread his arms wide, embraced her rather more closely than was necessary, and kissed her four times, twice on each cheek. Then he led her up a short flight of steps to the aft lounge, where he gestured her to a sofa.

"What will you drink, Carmen? Tequila?"

"Vodka martini, shaken, not stirred. And put a damn olive in it."

As she spoke, she sat in a leather armchair beside the sofa Guzman had gestured at. She had a deep aversion to doing as she was told. He chuckled again, and Mendoza decided she would like to shoot him in the head, preferably while he was chuckling. He turned to the barman and told him, "Vodka martini, shaken not stirred, with an olive. Give me a bourbon on the rocks."

He went and sat on the sofa and patted the seat next to him. "Come, sit next to me, Carmen."

He watched her face turn hard and her eyes bright with suppressed anger.

"What do you want, Guzman? Let me see if I can make you understand. Do you want all-out war with Central Intelligence? Mitch Vogel is dead. I watched him die. I am now taking his place. Keep making me mad, get me real pissed, and I will walk away and go have a talk with Rafael Gonzalez in the Gulf. We have invested time and money to get this meeting together. It has taken a lot of work and effort to bring Mr. Sanjar to the table to talk to us, and I will be *damned* if I am going to allow you to screw that up with your stupid games. You pat the sofa for me, you pat the sofa for the Company. You make a move on me, you make a move on the Company.

"And let's be clear about something else, Guzman: The next time you touch me in an inappropriate way, I am going to break each and every one of your *fucking* fingers. You disrespect me and you disrespect the CIA, pal. And don't you run away with the idea that we need you. We can have you annihilated tomorrow and happily do business with the Gulf. Am I getting through to you? You want to tell your boy behind the bar to pull a gun and shoot me? What do you want, Guzman? You want a visit from Delta? It can be arranged."

She watched him, waiting for an answer. Eventually he offered her a smile that wasn't so much thin as anorexic. "I am sorry," he said, "if you misunderstood my gestures of hospitality, Miss Mendoza."

"Yeah? I don't give a damn what I misunderstood, Guzman. I just want to be sure that *you* understood *me*. Are we clear and on the same damned page?"

"Of course."

"Good." She sat back, crossed her legs, and sipped her martini. "Good. So let's talk about the meeting tomorrow at ten on our yacht. This is how it works. You are there at ten a.m. and we agree on a deal with Mr. Sanjar. If at ten-thirty you are still fucking around and playing games with your girls instead of talking business, we sail, with Mr. Sanjar, down to the Bahamas. Is there anything in this that is too complicated for you to understand?"

"It is perfectly clear. Tomorrow at ten on your yacht, no putas, no more games." He gave a small shrug. "Simple."

"Who are your guests tonight?"

"Come, Carmen, relax. They are just some high-class escorts. Very charming, very pretty."

"Who's the guy?"

"Oh, him and his partner. She is very lovely. Caroline Gordon, she is an investments expert. Maybe she is going to help me invest some of my money."

"The guy."

"I don't know his name. Mark? I was not very interested in him. It was his woman, his partner, Caroline, who I was most interested in. You will meet them all tonight. They were very excited about seeing the yacht."

"I bet they were," she said. "I am pretty excited about seeing them."

TWENTY-TWO

BEAUTY DOES NOT ELIMINATE OR CANCEL OUT ugliness. It just hides it. Now the rising moon and the sparkling lights from the yachts created an illusion of luminous beauty over the cold, black depths of the North Atlantic. They carried the promise of elegance, exquisite food, and a warm, welcoming reception. What they concealed was a darkness of soul, a dispassionate ruthlessness, and a willingness to destroy lives and cause pain and suffering on a global scale—not because it was necessary but because it was rewarding. It was rewarding financially to the tune of billions of dollars every year, but it was rewarding psychically too, because it made these men powerful beyond imagining. It gave them the power of gods, the power to mete out death at will.

For Guzman, his dream was to rule like an emperor over a broken people who both feared and adored him. For Yahya Sanjar, it was the dream of exterminating an entire nation for the crazed, insane glory of his own people and for a god who demanded absolute subjugation; and for Hans Fischer, it was the power of being himself the god of gods and enabling these men to fulfill their dreams. The darkness these sparkling, twinkling lights concealed was the cold, dead darkness of true evil, as cold and deep and black as the ocean on which they drifted.

We were delivered in a launch to the platform at the rear of the yacht. Guzman was there to great us and made a big fuss of Caroline while he carefully ignored me until he asked, "And the girls? You did not bring them?"

I raised my eyebrows high. "Aren't they here? They said they'd make their own way. They were so excited I thought they'd be here ahead of us."

He shrugged and held Caroline's shoulders. "Well, my new favorite investment expert is here. I need nothing more." He turned to me with that smugness I had noticed in the Dharma Club. "You, my friend, I have some beautiful ladies to entertain you while Caroline and I talk business."

We all laughed like he was the wittiest guy in town and made our way into the sparkling elegance of his lounge. Sometimes you hear a yacht described as a floating palace. In this case, it was no exaggeration at all. It was exactly that. In the rooms and cabins we passed, there were oak paneled walls, vast chandeliers, genuine Picassos, Matisses, and even a Monet hanging above genuine Rococo, Queen Anne, and Art Deco furnishings.

We sat in the lounge, and a guy in a white tux and a black bowtie brought a bucket of ice with two bottles of Dom Pérignon in it and three chilled flutes. While the guy unwound the wire and popped the cork, Guzman spoke, first to Caroline and then to me.

"Caroline, I will be very honest with you. I make more money than you can imagine, billions of dollars, and I pay no tax. I make this money from crime." He spread his hands in a *What can I do?* gesture. "Is the truth. I make and sell drugs, I take young women and introduce them into prostitution." He laughed and pointed at me, like I'd understand. "Most of them are very happy. If they stay at home, they marry some lazy bastard, have seven children, and spend the rest of their life working like a slave for this hijo de puta. But they work for me and they make lots of money! They make movies, visit the world, travel first class, and when they are thirty or forty, too old to work, they retire. They have made a lot of money. Or they marry with some millionaire and live in the luxury." He hunched his shoulders while the waiter poured our drinks and distributed them. "But is a crime. Is a crime to give people freedom and opportunity in this world. What can I do? So if you will work with me, you must know this is the kind of money you will be managing."

He grinned at me. "She must make bad money disappear and good money appear—*puff!* Like alquimia."

I shifted my gaze to her and smiled. "Do I get a finder's fee?" To him I said, "I'm just joking."

He wagged a finger at me. "You are joking, but I have questions. Caroline, I can understand why she has manipulated to meet me. I am her dream client. But you, why you set up one complicated, expensive situation to arrange this meeting with me?"

I didn't bat an eyelid. I kept the smile on my face and

HELL'S FURY | 219

said, "She's sitting right next to you. She's beautiful, she's intelligent, and I am crazy about her." I sipped my champagne. "I am staying at the Sandyman, and I saw the yachts and I thought, 'Man, that is billions of dollars sitting right there.' Then I thought whoever owned one of those yachts could use Caroline's services." I allowed my face to become serious. "If I have overstepped the mark, I apologize."

He shook his head and waved a hand at me, and I knew he had decided to kill me. "Please, don't worry." Then he spread his hands and frowned. "I don't remember if you told me your name...?"

I was going to tell him it was Mark Connors, but my mouth had other ideas. "Rogue," I said. "John Rogue."

"John Rogue. I will remember this name now. You are a resourceful man, and you are not afraid to take action."

I allowed my smile to broaden and gestured around me. "Coming from a man who has achieved all this, I call that praise indeed, and I am flattered."

It was like I hadn't spoken. He said, "Enjoy the champagne. My girls will come and keep you company. Caroline and I must go and talk business."

"Of course."

I went to stand but realized I might as well remain seated. I had passed from their consciousness into oblivion. They crossed the parquet floor to what looked like an original 1930s Art Deco elevator and rose to some upper floor.

I sipped my champagne. I figured he would not waste time. If he felt Caroline could help him, he'd make her watch while they killed me, tell her she was technically an accomplice, then pack her off home with a bag full of money to seal her loyalty. It was what they called the two types of motivation in NLP, away from and toward. She would be motivated away from getting butchered the way they were going to butcher me and toward all the money she could make out of being loyal.

I grunted and rose. The waiter watched me.

"Can I help you, sir?"

I moved over and leaned on the bar. "Yeah, Mr. Guzman has gone up to his office, and I forgot to give him some important information."

He was already smiling and shaking his head as he polished a glass.

"He cannot be disturbed, señor. He will be down in a while—"

He stopped talking because I had jabbed him in the throat, just below his windpipe. It's not lethal, but for a while, you think you're going to die. I walked behind the bar, kicked him in the back of the knee, and lowered him to the floor.

"Take it easy," I told him. "Your breath will come back faster if you just relax. I am not going to hurt you. Just relax and take it easy."

He made a couple of retching, wheezing noises in his throat, and I wondered where Guzman's retinue were. I reached up and took the knife he'd been using to cut lemons. I locked on to his eyes and said, "Where is everybody? All Guzman's friends, where are they?"

"There is pool party on top deck," he croaked. "They up there. They come down later for dinner."

"OK." I nodded. "Now it's up to you. I am going to ask you where Guzman's office is, where he took Caroline. You are going to say you can't tell me, and I am going to cut off one of your fingers to prove to you that I am serious. So do I need to start by cutting something off just to save time?"

He was shaking his head and sweating badly. I put my right knee on his solar plexus and the left on his right elbow and seized his wrist. I jammed the small knife against his knuckle joint and pressed. He was panicking badly, clenching his teeth and screaming in his throat.

I said, "Where?"

His eyes locked on mine. He was hyperventilating through clenched teeth and spraying spit from his lower lip. I began to press. "Where?"

"The elevator to the top deck. It is the only door. Señor, he gonna kill me. He gonna torture me and kill me."

I nodded. I knew he was right. I said, "People make really bad choices. Kid like you could have worked for anybody, made a life for himself anywhere. Why Oscar Guzman?"

I leaned forward, covered his mouth with my left hand, and drove the blade deep into the side of his neck, severing the carotid artery and the jugular vein. He thrashed violently for two or three seconds. By then, the massive hemorrhage had drained his brain of blood and he died. I left the blade in place and felt under his jacket. As I had suspected, he had a Glock under his arm. I took it and slipped it in my belt behind my back, under my jacket, and made for the elevator.

The concertina door opened, and I climbed in. I pressed button four, and it began to rise but stopped at three and the door opened. It was the pool party. There were maybe two dozen people. Most of them were dancing. The reggaeton was thumping in the loud speakers, there was shouting and squealing and laughter. A guy and a girl stood in the doorway blinking at me. I pointed at the ceiling and said, "Going up," then stepped forward and pressed button four again. The door closed, and I began to rise.

It was like the kid had said. The elevator stopped on a small, wooden deck. There was a door eight or ten feet in front of me and, aside from the railings from the door to the elevator, that was it.

I had three options: assume it was locked and blow out the lock, knock, or just turn the handle and walk in. Logic dictated that as this yacht was his private kingdom and everybody was terrified of him, he had not bothered to lock the door. On the other hand, logic also dictated that the man was a paranoid schizophrenic and always locked every door all the time. Ultimately, where trying to walk in and failing because the door was in fact locked alerted him, blowing the lock alerted everybody. So I had nothing to lose by simply turning the handle.

I stepped forward, turned the handle, and the door opened easily inward. They were sitting at a coffee table. He was holding her hand in both of his, and she had been smiling over the rim of a gin and tonic at him. Now she was looking at me in surprise. His expression was more the expression of a man whose version of reality has ceased to work.

He said, "What the—" and stood.

I stepped inside and closed the door. "If you sound the alarm, by the time they get here, you will be dead." I saw his eyes flit to his desk and shook my head. "Don't do that. It would be a big mistake." I pulled the Glock from my belt and showed him the muzzle.

He looked at Caroline. "You knew!"

She shook her head. I said, "She was the hook, the girls

were the bait, and you are the fish. Get on your knees, Mr. Trout, or I'll blow them right out of your legs." He hesitated. "I am serious, Guzman. Get on your knees, put your hands on your head, and lace your fingers."

He did as I told him, talking all the while.

"You are out of your mind. Do you know what they will do to you? They will make an example of you! Do you know what that means?"

I sat opposite him. "I'm trying to help you, Guzman. Every time you are evasive, I will shoot you somewhere nonlethal, like a knee or an elbow, every time you hesitate too long, every time you lie. Now think about that, Guzman. You don't know who I am or how much I know. I knew you were here, didn't I? I knew enough to hook you with Caroline. So if I plant a question and catch you in a lie, I will blow out your ankle or your wrist. You understand that, right?

"Now, first I am going to ask you what I asked the kid in the bar—he's dead now—do I need to prove to you that I am serious? Do I need to remove a toe or a finger?"

He had gone very waxy and pale and he was sweating profusely. His pupils were pinpricks, and he was shaking his head. "No, no, no," he said. "No need to prove nothin'. Look, amigo, I can make you very rich man. Anything you want—"

"I want—" I said, and he stopped dead, and there was a trace of hope in his eyes. "I want to know two things. First I want to know why you killed my wife."

His face creased into disbelief. He managed to shrug, keeping his hands on his head. "Who is your wife, for Chrissakes?"

I turned to Caroline, who was staring at me fixedly with no expression at all on her face.

"He kills people," I said, "and he doesn't even know who they are." I turned back to him. "She was a famous novelist, a *New York Times* bestseller. Her name was Susan Hanson. You had her killed, and her two children."

He shook his head. "That wasn't me. Uh-uh." Then he frowned. "She was your *wife?* You were *married?*"

"She was my wife and we were married, and we had two kids together. You sent Ochoa, Gavilan, Peralta and Borja to do the job, and they almost killed me too."

"It wasn't me, pendejo. I wasn't even jefe back then. That was Jesus. He organize that. She was too smart, man. She was doin' her investigation and she was learnin' too much! She was—sorry—but man, she was askin' for trouble."

"Who were the people involved? I want every name, every CIA officer, every FBI special agent, every judge, every congressman, every mayor and police officer—"

"You out of your mind, pendejo! It can't be done. You want to list every fokin' piece of hay in a haystack? There are too many, pendejo! It cannot be done!"

The crazy fear in his eyes said he was telling the truth, plus it made sense. I said, "OK, Guzman. This is your chance to live. You are going to write me a list of the congressmen and women, of the government officials, the CIA officers and the FBI special agents. You are going to sign it and you are going to come with me to New York, where you are going to be debriefed by the FBI."

"You crazy. You outta your *fokin'* mind!"

I took aim at his knee. He waved his hands at me like he

HELL'S FURY | 225

could stop the bullet with his palms. Then I heard the door click behind me.

"I had a hunch it was you. You are a real pain in the ass, Rogue. You're like an indestructible rat. What am I going to do about you?"

I turned and looked at her. "Mendoza."

TWENTY-THREE

"*Kill him! Shoot him! Kill him now! What are you waiting for?*"

She watched him with hooded eyes.

"Keep your panties on, Guzman. I know this guy. We have business to settle." To me she said, "You keep your panties on too, Rogue. I don't aim to kill you—not yet—but I have no problem spoiling your friend's good looks. So let's just keep it cool so nobody gets hurt."

I shook my head. "She's not my friend. She works for Guzman. Leave her out of this."

Guzman was on his feet, backing away from me and Caroline and shaking his finger so hard at Mendoza he was shaking his whole hand. "No! No! No! She is no workin' for me! She is a plant! He bring her here—"

I snapped, "Take it easy, Guzman! I used her. I'd never met her before yesterday. She's exactly who she said she is!"

His voice was shrill. "You think I am gonna believe you? Hijo de puta!"

I looked at Caroline, whose eyes were huge and bright with fear. I shrugged. "I'm sorry."

"How could you do this to me?"

"I told you it would be risky working with this guy."

"But this, you didn't tell me…"

She trailed off, and Mendoza cut in. "OK, enough soap opera. Guzman, get a couple of your boys up here. We're going to visit Hans."

She pulled her cell from her pocket and dialed while Guzman went to his desk and made a call. He snapped something in Spanish, and Mendoza said, "Hans, I have a surprise for you." She listened and rolled her eyes. "Yeah, OK, OK, enough with the borderline autism. Turns out Guzman's dinner guests were a looker from the island and Mr. Rogue himself. Guzman wants to kill him. I don't, not yet. I think we need to know what this guy's story is."

The statement made me frown. Suddenly everything that had happened to me since I had arrived in New York flashed through my mind. It was too fast for me to follow it consciously, but suddenly I knew something was wrong. The shooting, that truck in flames with the open door, the fifth gunman, Jane telling me, "You have to remember for yourself," Mendoza and Vogel.

It was all wrong.

Mendoza was saying, "OK, we'll bring them over." She smiled at me. It was the kind of smile that can curdle milk and make poisonous cheese. "Let's see if we can cure Mr. Rogue's amnesia."

Caroline turned to Guzman. "I am not a part of this. Mr. Rogue simply offered to help me get a job. I had no idea—"

"*Silence!*" His voice was shrill, almost a scream. He turned his twisted, hateful face on Mendoza. "You bring all this to me—"

Her voice cut across his, quiet and lethal. "Go ahead, punk," she said. "Make my day." He fell silent, though the rage was still turning his face red. She went on, "If you'd kept your dick in your pants and done business like a grownup, none of this would have happened. What went down here was that this damned Rogue was smart and you were stupid, and he read you like a book." She took a step forward and pointed at Guzman with her left hand. Her right hand never wavered from Caroline. "And let me point something out to you, asshole. Rogue and his bitch are on your boat. They are not on Hans' yacht, and they are not on Yahya Sanjar's. They are on *yours!* Why do *you* think that is?"

Before he could answer, there was a knock at the door, and two of his thugs, dressed in double-breasted shiny Armani suits came in. I saw their brows twitch as they took in the scene. Guzman screamed at them and waved his hands around. One of them had a pencil moustache and gummed, vertical hair. He took out a Taurus semi and didn't seem to know who to point it at. So in the end he pointed it at me.

The other one left in a hurry. I figured he was going to arrange a launch to take us over to Hans Fischer's yacht. I smiled a friendly smile at Mendoza and gave my head a small twitch.

"Sometimes things just work out the way you want them to all on their own."

She narrowed her eyes a sixteenth of an inch, then sighed and shook her head like I was a lost cause.

Fifteen minutes later, we were seated in a large launch

HELL'S FURY | 229

smacking across the small, dark waves under moonlight and starlight, toward the *Eden Dawn* anchored a quarter of a mile from Guzman's *Dama de Blanco*. I sat in front beside the Armani guy with the pencil moustache. Mendoza sat behind me with her Glock 19 pointing into my kidneys. Guzman was beside her with his arm around Caroline, not in a nice way, and Armani Two, who had no moustache but did have an earring, sat in back with his Taurus pointing into Caroline's kidneys. If things went bad, they were going to make a mess of his leather upholstery.

As we pulled up at the boarding platform at the stern of Hans Fischer's yacht, we could still just about hear the throb of music from the *Dama de Blanco*. I glanced back and saw all the lights on the upper deck flashing red and blue, reflecting on the ocean. It looked beautiful, but I reminded myself, as I had thought earlier, beauty does not cancel out ugliness. It just hides it.

There were half a dozen guys with assault rifles waiting to greet us when we arrived. Armani Moustache docked the launch in the docking bay, and we climbed out. As they shoved us toward a bank of elevators at the back of the bay, Mendoza sneered at me and punched me playfully on the shoulder.

"Hey, Rogue, you got ten weapons trained on you. You feeling lucky? This should be a walk in the park for you." She laughed out loud. I smiled at her.

The elevators were large and chromed with mirrors inside. We got in one with four guys, and Mendoza pressed up hard against me. I could feel the muzzle of her Glock pressed hard into my lower belly. Her face was barely an inch from mine, looking up into my eyes.

"Want to have a go, Rogue? What a way to go, huh? It would be a good way for you. Appropriate." She grinned. "Better than lying in bed remembering the good days, huh?"

I gave my head a barely perceptible shake. "I don't approve of violence against the weaker sex."

Her eyes narrowed. "You son of a bitch. You were about to throw me out of the window."

"Maybe I'd make an exception with you. I'll think about it. Come and see me in my cabin after I've killed Guzman and Fischer."

She smiled, then laughed again, but with less conviction. As the elevator came to a halt, she shook her head, still grinning. "You are such an asshole. I could almost grow to like you."

We came out onto a deck, high above the water. The moon was clear in the sky, touching the small waves below with liquid amber. Hans Fischer was sitting in a large, whicker armchair at a low table. Around the table were a couch and two more chairs of the same design. He had in front of him a tall, frosted drink with lots of ice. He was watching us emerge from the elevators with his chin in his hand and his fingers crooked over his mouth. It made him look mad. Everything about him said his patience was worn thin and about to snap.

We all remained standing in front of him, like naughty kids in the director's office, except Guzman, who strutted to the sofa and sat heavily. He spoke in a shrill rattle to one of his Armanis, and they went off to get him a drink.

Fischer's eyes dropped to stare at his drink while Guzman finished. By the time Armani Earring had placed Guzman's drink in front of him, Fischer's silent immobility had become a menacing physical presence. Everybody became still and silent. Finally Fischer spoke to his glass.

"Mr. Rogue, is that your name? The last time we met, you killed my bodyguard, Jonah." He raised his eyes. "How many people have you killed since then? You are relentless, and you are becoming a problem. Do I kill you and dispose of the problem, or do I interrogate you and then kill you? Carmen Mendoza tells me there are things about you she does not understand and which worry her."

"Are you asking for my advice?"

He looked slightly surprised. "No, I am thinking aloud."

"I'm going to give it to you anyway. Either kill me right now or go and find the most remote corner of the planet and hide there. Because I am going to kill you, and I am going to destroy your organization—and Fischer? There is nothing you can do to stop me."

There was laughter in his face, but it wasn't so much amusement as amazement. He looked at Mendoza and gestured at me. The gesture was a question along the lines of, *What the hell?* Mendoza said, "I want to know what he's about. He says he was Susan Hanson's husband. He's on some kind of crusade for vengeance. And before you ask, I believe the amnesia is genuine."

His eyes flicked over me and then back at Mendoza a few times. "Does it matter? We are working a billion dollar deal. What do we care about this guy? Why are you focusing on this?"

Guzman shouted suddenly, waving his hand in the air. "*Kill the bastard! I kill him myself!*" He reached under his arm for his piece and found six assault rifles pointing at him.

Fischer waved them down and leaned toward Guzman. "I decide who lives and who dies, Oscar. Forgive them, but my boys are trained to react instinctively when someone pulls a gun." He turned back to Mendoza and spread his hands. "Why are you focusing on this man?"

"Because he doesn't make sense. Because I don't know where he came from, and if he dies, will there be another one to take his place? We have a trillion dollar black budget at the Company, Hans. We do a lot of weird shit..."

She left the words hanging, and I suppressed a smile. "I am not the product of the CIA's black budget, Carmen. I am a man who is driven to avenge his wife and his kids. I am a man who wants to rid the world of scum like you. And above all, I am a man who has nothing left to lose."

Fischer sighed loudly and ran his fingers through his hair. "I say we kill him and throw him overboard for the sharks. I just haven't time for this."

Mendoza's response was instant. "I have. And I am speaking for Central Intelligence here. I want to know what's in this guy's unconscious memory."

"And how do you plan to find out?"

"Give me a cabin. I want him cuffed to the bed and I want the woman in there with him."

He glanced at Caroline. She shook her head and said, "No!" She stared at me like I could do something about it, then back at Fischer. "No!"

He gave his head a microscopic shake. "No, Mendoza. Acute stress will only aggravate the amnesia. We'll lock him up. I need time to think." He looked at one of the guys with rifles. "Cuff him."

Then he narrowed his eyes and seemed to take Caroline in for the first time. "How did you get into this? You are a professional? How can you be involved in this mess?"

I felt the cuffs bite into my wrists. Caroline was trying to talk, but her lower lip kept trembling, curling in.

"I didn't know. I had no idea. Mr. Rogue approached me in a restaurant. He offered to get me a job with Mr. Guzman. I had no idea. It all just got out of control. Mr. Rogue is such an unpredictable, impetuous man. I didn't know what was happening."

He spread his hands. "Everything you have seen. Everything you have heard…"

She was shaking her head hard. "No!" She said, "I am an investment specialist. I specialize in laundering money. This is Bermuda! Millions of pounds come through my office for laundering every month. I will not talk to anyone about what I have seen and heard. I have seen and heard nothing! You must see, the risk to me is huge. I can work for you instead! Just give me the chance!"

He turned to Guzman and pointed at him. "This is your fault. I knew your reputation. I should never have worked with you."

Guzman flushed, but there was nothing he could do. He had to sit and take it. Fischer turned to the guard who had cuffed me. "Take him to the Majestic Room. Take the woman too. Cuff him to the bed. She does not need to be cuffed." He turned to Caroline. "I have not decided. But be clear. If you live, you work for me."

She nodded. "OK, yes, sure. I work for you. Thank you."

"I told you I am undecided. I need to think." He flapped his hand at his men. "Go. Take them." To Mendoza he said, "You stay here. And you." He pointed savagely at Guzman.

We were led back to the elevator and rode down into the bowels of the yacht. When we stepped out, we were led along a narrow corridor to a door that must have been just above the engines. They shoved us inside. Two of them stood by the door while the third one cuffed one of my wrists to the bedstead. Caroline sat in an armchair staring at me with tears in her eyes, and the three guards left without a word. The door closed, and I heard the lock.

She stared at the door for a moment then looked back at me.

"This is madness. I feel I've slipped into a nightmare. This can't be real. This can't really be happening."

"It's happening, Caroline. It's real. And the last thing you should do is work for that guy. Do that and it will never end."

"I don't want to. I really don't. But why did you drag me into this? How could you do that to me?"

"We'll have plenty of time for that when we get out of here. But right now we need to focus on exactly how we are going to do that."

She looked at me like I was crazy. "Get *out* of here? That's impossible!"

"I know, Caroline, but the great thing about impossible actions is that nobody expects you to do them."

She frowned, giving her head lots of little shakes like I didn't make sense. It was something I was getting used to. She said, "But what *can* we do?"

"Caroline, I need you to listen very carefully. This is not going to be easy, but you have to understand that our lives depend on you getting this right. OK? So you have to get it right. Are you with me?"

She whimpered and bit her lip. "I'll do my best. Tell me what I have to do."

I drew breath, but before I could answer her, the latch clicked and the door opened. And for the second time that evening, I sighed and said, "Mendoza."

TWENTY-FOUR

She closed the door and regarded me for a moment.

"I have said it before and I will say it again: You are some kind of asshole. Why can't you just stay out of things and let the professionals do their job?" She smiled, and it was oddly pleasant. "I like to think that if you'd done that, we could have been friends. You're quite a guy."

"Let the professionals do their job?" I arched an eyebrow at her. "Like helping out an international criminal in organizing a deal between Sinaloa and Hamas? That's the job I am supposed to let the professionals get on with?"

"You don't get it, do you? You don't think. You just feel and act. Bam! Bam! 'This guy sells drugs, I'm going to kill him.' 'That guy sells drugs so I'm going to kill him and all his pals too.' You act, but you never stop to think, 'Hey, if I watch that guy for six months or a year, I can identify all of his associates, and when they do their next big deal I can get him, his pals, the guy he's dealing with, and all *his* pals too. All in one go.'"

She turned to Caroline and pointed at her. "You. Shut up and sit down."

Caroline sat. "I wasn't going to say anything."

"Then don't."

She turned back to me. I said, "You're wrong."

"Not often."

"Well, you're wrong this time on three scores. First, I think and I plan ahead plenty." I allowed a leer to twist my mouth. "And I think if you look at the body count, you'll agree it works for me. But the second way you're wrong is that the way you do it—or claim you do it—means thousands of victims go down and thousands of lives get destroyed while you sit around playing spooks and making friends with the enemy, drinking and snorting with the devil. And the third and most important way you are wrong, Mendoza, is that the longer you take to cut out the cancer, the deeper it goes and the more it metastasizes. Look at you. You yourself have become a tumor.

"If you shot every son of a bitch who sells dope on the streets, within a month, there would be no one on the streets selling dope, and that would mean bastards like Guzman would have no one to supply. But that wouldn't benefit you or the Company at all, would it? It would decimate your trillion dollar black budget and cripple you. Because over half your money comes from trafficking drugs and arms that kill millions of weak and vulnerable people all over the planet. You are wrong on more levels than you can even dream of, Mendoza."

Her expression was a mask of disgust. "Christ!" she said.

"A lethal, amnesiac goody-two-shoes. It's like a nightmare come to life."

I sighed. "What do you want, Mendoza? I'm pretty sure you didn't come here to tell me if I was just a little bit badder things would go a little bit better for me."

"No." She shook her head. "The fact is I came on a forlorn hope. You're a pain in the ass, Rogue, and when I put that cord around your neck in the car, I didn't know what the hell I was going to do. I was playing it by ear, and I guess my plan was to stop when you went unconscious, pretend to take your vitals, and claim you were dead."

I nodded. "Sure. Hey and let's play I'm stupid and I believe you."

"I said it was forlorn, and there is no reason why you should believe me, but the fact is I was investigating Vogel because we knew he had turned bad. Whatever you may think, the CIA today is not the same organization it was in the '60s. Sure we break rules and sometimes we have to be ruthless, but you don't seem to me to be the right guy to lecture us on that score. The fact is I was not going to kill you. But I did need to get you out of the way and into the hands of officers that could help you."

"You're full of bullshit, Mendoza."

"Yeah, you want to tell me why I am talking to you, then?"

"Because you think I have some big secret locked in my unconscious, and you want to find out what it is."

"Uh-uh, smartass. That, what you just said, is the reason you are not dead right now. Engage that brain you say you use so well and ask yourself, who was the last person to save your life? You have been putting my cover at risk from the moment you walked into Susan Hanson's house. And you are alive right now because I have convinced Fischer and Guzman that we need to look inside your head."

Caroline Gordon spoke half in a whisper, as though she were talking to herself. She said, "My God, I think she's telling the truth."

Mendoza turned on her. "I told you to shut up!"

She turned back to me. "And now you have a real problem, buster. Because now he wants to send you to a clinic he owns in Poland. It's a psychiatric institution where problem people get sent from Russia and China to be readjusted. They are outside the law and ignored by the European Union because a good number of their most problematic opponents end up there. They conduct experiments in consciousness and autonomic responses that would be illegal anywhere else. He wants to send you there so they can open your head and look inside. And I can't say no without blowing my cover."

I narrowed my eyes at her, trying to see inside her mind. "What reason did you give for coming down here?"

She pointed at Caroline without looking at her. "Her."

"What are you talking about?"

"I'm telling Fischer that I agree with him, we need some kind of program of treatment to get inside your head: drugs and hypnosis. Guzman is insisting that if we start taking bits off her, your memory will start working again out of imperative need."

"Jesus, it's not his damned week with the family neuron, is it? That guy couldn't be more stupid if they removed his brain. Doesn't he get that it was violent trauma that caused the amnesia in the first place?"

"Yeah, well, he's got it in his head that another violent trauma will cure it."

I shook my head and sighed. "If all this is true, why the hell didn't you tell me from the start?"

"It's called deep cover and professionalism. It is also complicated. I know what you're like. You're a loose cannon, and a loose cannon with this kind of information is a liability."

Caroline was looking from one to the other of us with panic writ large on her face. She blurted out suddenly, "Please don't let them kill me! I have tried to be brave, but I don't want to die! Please!"

Mendoza swiveled and pointed at her. "*Shut up!*"

I said, "I am very far from believing you, Mendoza, but if what you're saying is true, what are we going to do? Have you got a plan?"

Caroline had got to her feet with her hands clenched in front of her. "Please..."

I said, "Relax, nobody's going to hurt you."

"*Sit down! Goddammit! Sit!*"

I frowned at Mendoza. "Take it easy, will you? What are we going to do?"

"There is only one thing we can do. You probably think you can shoot your way out of here. But you can't. There must be fifteen armed men up there plus Fischer and Guzman, and Yahya Sanjar is just a phone call away. There is only one way out of this." She pulled her Glock from her pancake and pointed it at Caroline's legs. "You start talking or I blow her knees off."

"Are you serious?"

It was hard to tell from the expression on her face. And

HELL'S FURY | 241

the expression didn't change. She fixed my eyes with her own and said, "Talk."

Caroline whimpered, "Rogue...?"

"Talk! Who are you? What's your relationship to Susan Hanson? Why are you obsessed with Sinaloa? *Talk, goddammit!*"

"Mendoza, will you calm down? I don't know who I am! Will you bring it down a notch? I think I am Ted Hanson. You know that—"

"You don't get it, Rogue! They don't believe that, and they won't believe it! Ted Hanson is dead! I have to give them something to justify taking you back to Langley or you die, she dies, and I probably die too. Give me something! Who *the hell* are you?"

I tried to stand, but the cuff holding me to the bed would not let me.

"For crying out loud, Mendoza! I have flashes of memory! I remember being with her!"

"False memories. Implanted memories."

"That is stupid! Science fiction!"

"Is it? We do it all the time."

"You saw the photograph on her desk, Mendoza! What is your problem?"

"You cannot be Ted Hanson! They won't buy it! *I* won't buy it! *You are not Ted Hanson!*"

I tried to stand again. Rage was welling up in my belly. "Why the hell not?"

"Ted Hanson is dead!"

"The truck door was open. I rolled out somehow before it exploded. I know Susan was my wife. I *know* that photograph is real! The kids..."

I trailed off. She was scowling at me. "You *have to remember!* Give me something I can tell them!"

"I am Ted Hanson, Mendoza. I could lie, I could invent something, but this is where your story falls down. If I give you something you can tell them, instead of sending me to Fischer's clinic, what will they do to me? Shoot me in the head and throw me to the sharks."

"No, it buys us time. It postpones the moment of your death and could justify my taking you to Langley. But you have to listen to me. You are not Ted Hanson. You *can't* be Ted Hanson. Because Ted Hanson—"

There was a scuttle and a small rush, and Caroline was clinging to her, shouting, "*You're crazy! You're all crazy! You're talking all this crazy stuff, but they want to torture me and kill me! Don't you understand? You can't let them!*"

I saw Mendoza frown. She grunted softly, and her frown deepened. The hand holding the Glock moved a couple of times like she was trying to get purchase on Caroline's arm. Then she dropped the gun and gripped Caroline's arm with her fingers before very slowly sinking to the floor. As she lay down, I saw a huge pool of dense, red blood spreading underneath her, from where the handle of a pair of scissors protruded from her kidneys. Her face had gone waxy. She made an ugly rasp as her lungs emptied and everything that was Carmen Mendoza ceased to exist. Had she been for real? Had she been in Hans Fischer's pay? Had she been after all that quintessential CIA creature of eternal moral ambiguity? Now I would never know.

Carmen was staring at me, transfixed. I said, "What have you done?"

"She was going to let them torture me and kill me."

HELL'S FURY | 243

My head was spinning. "There is no time. Check her pockets. See if she has a key for the cuffs."

Her eyes went wide. "*Her pockets?* But she's dead..."

"Caroline, you just killed her. Get a grip. Look in her pockets!"

She hunkered down and went through her pockets like they were infected with the plague, making small, squealing noises as she went. Finally she said, "Yes! Yes! Is this it?"

She held up a small key, stepped over Mendoza's dead body, and unlocked the cuffs from my wrist. I reached down and took Mendoza's Glock, then searched her for other weapons. I found a razor sharp needle-like stiletto concealed in her belt. There were a few other things that I thought might be useful, including her wallet and a couple of card-keys.

Caroline was watching me and looked like she might be going into shock. "What are you going to do?"

I frowned at her. "Kill everyone." I had no time for catering to shock.

I weighed up the possibility of there being a couple of guards outside the door and decided it was high. I pointed and said, "Open the door and tell the guards Mendoza needs them. Be convincing."

She didn't pause. She trotted to the door, opened it, and leaned out. "Excuse me! Hello! Can you come? Miss Mendoza needs your help."

By the time they arrived, I had positioned myself behind the door. They came in, and it took them all of three seconds to process what they were seeing: Mendoza dead on the floor in a pool of blood with a pair of scissors protruding from her back. Of the two guys, the second one to come in never got to finish processing. I drove the stiletto right through the vertebrae at the base of his skull. His pal heard him hit the floor and turned to look down the barrel of Mendoza's Glock.

"Put down your weapon and lace your fingers on your head. Believe me. This is not worth dying for. How do I get to the engine room?"

He told me where the door was, then added, "Listen, I'm just security."

"I know, I get it. Do as you're told and you get to go home. Now Fischer's office. Where is it? How do I get there?"

"Oh, man..."

"Don't sweat it. They all die tonight. Your best chance is talking to me. But make it fast. I am running out of time and patience."

He told me, started shaking his head, and asked me, "Mister, can I go? I won't talk."

"Sure, let me fast track you out." I said it and shot him through the middle of his forehead. I heard Caroline gasp but ignored her. "You carry a gun for Hans Fischer, you've spent any credit you had with me for compassion."

I now had two assault rifles, three semi-automatics, and two fewer guys to get rid of. I turned to her. "Plus," I said, "I have the element of surprise, and I know where their lithium batteries are." I gave my head a small shake. "Don't talk. Follow me in silence."

"Rogue, I am terrified. This is unreal."

"Save it for when it's all over. We'll get drunk. Be very quiet now."

I opened the door and stepped into the narrow corridor.

I gestured her to follow, and we moved silently along the route the guard had told us. Right and right again brought us to a short staircase that descended to a steel door. I went down and pushed the door open, and we were in a cavernous, echoing engine room. It was quiet and still. Caroline came in behind me, and I heard the door close softly.

I moved silently among the exposed tubes and machine housings and soon began to hear the echoing murmur of voices. Another few steps brought me to a gap in the machinery through which I could see a small office. Two men sat there. One was reading a book, the other was watching a small TV. Beyond him, I could see a small propane stove with a coffee pot on it. I turned to Caroline and mouthed to her, *Stay here.*

She nodded, and I walked over to the small cubicle. They both frowned up at me. Their expressions said it wasn't their job to know who I was, but they didn't know who I was, and that wasn't good. They were right.

I shot the guy with the book through the head so the other guy would know I was serious. He staggered back, raising his hands, and fell over his chair onto the floor.

I shook my head. "It's OK. I won't hurt you. I need to know where the lithium-ion batteries are. Show me."

"I'll show you, man. Don't shoot me. I'll show you."

He got to his feet, and I followed him down another narrow passage among pipes and housings to a huge bank of batteries. Caroline had ignored my instructions and followed. I turned to her. "Go to the office. Bring the propane stove and a box of matches."

His face had gone pale. "What are you going to do?"

"Don't worry. You'll have time to escape. Where are the fuel tanks?"

He pointed either side of where we stood. "There and there. But you can't. The whole yacht..."

I had seen the bulge under his jacket, and now he reached for it. I shot him through the heart, and all his worries about what I could and couldn't do were over.

TWENTY-FIVE

Lithium-ion batteries are subject to a phenomenon called thermal runaway. This was a fact my unconscious clearly didn't feel the need to suppress. Thermal runaway is a chain reaction which occurs when the battery increases rapidly in temperature. This leads to an intense release in energy resulting in catastrophic failure, causing them to burst into flames and explode. My idea was that the chain reaction would expand exponentially because of the large bank of batteries, each setting off the next.

I took the small propane heater from Caroline, lit it, set it under the nearest battery, and smiled at her.

"We need to leave very fast."

I took her hand, and we ran. We retraced the steps we had taken when we were locked up, which brought us to the elevator. We rode that up to the lower deck, and from there we crossed the saloon and came to the docking area. I figured everyone was upstairs having a crisis meeting, because we hadn't come across anyone up to that point. But now I saw two armed guards standing beside the launch that had brought us over from Guzman's yacht. They scowled at us as we approached, the way simple minds scowl when proper routine is broken. I gripped Caroline's wrist, returned the scowl, and made no move to grab a weapon as I marched toward them, gesturing for them to approach because I wanted to talk to them. It was like pressing a pause button. They waited to see what would happen next.

What happened next was that, as we drew level with them, I looked the nearest guy in the eye and said, "You want to explain something to me?"

Then I kicked him hard in the groin with my instep, and as he sank to his knees I shot the guy behind him in the heart. I stepped behind the guy I'd castrated and said, "You want to explain to me why you didn't shoot me?" and I broke his neck.

I pointed to the launch. "You know how to use one of these?"

She gave a small, frightened frown. "I'm a native Bermudan. I grew up on boats."

"Good. Get in and get the hell out of here. Go to the most remote beach you can find and make your way home, and tell no one about any of this. You understand? No one!"

She nodded, and I grabbed her shoulders. "I will make it worth your while, I promise!"

I turned and ran. I ran with one of the assault rifles at my shoulder, sighting down the barrel as I went. When I came to the elevator that went to the top floor, there were two guards standing at the door. I guess, as far as everyone was concerned, the only threat they had was cuffed to a bed below the waterline. So security was not that tight.

On the other hand, they weren't working for Guzman. They were working for Hans Fischer, who knew that chance was a fickle lover who would kiss you on the mouth and stab you in the back while stealing your iPhone with the other hand. Chance was his disinherited mistress, and he left nothing to her. His view would be that they had a threat onboard, so there were guards at the elevator door.

I double-tapped twice, high in the middle of their chests. When they tried to scream or shout, all they managed was red bubbles from their sternum. I hunkered down and removed the mic and earphone from the nearest punk. I put the piece in my ear and made my way to Fischer's office. It was all dark wood and a deep blue carpet with a vast sweep of glass showing the moonlit ocean and the sparkling lights of Bermuda. I closed the door and went and put my ass on his desk while I mapped out my next moves.

Then something weird happened. The ship began to move. Slowly the prow started to heave away from the coast toward Guzman's yacht. It made me frown, but I had no time to try and work it out. I spoke into the mic.

"Can you hear me?"

The voice that answered had a frown of its own. "Who is this?"

"I'm your worst nightmare. Tell Fischer the lithium-ion batteries are about to explode."

"*What?* Holy shit!"

"Stay with me. They're going to blow the fuel tanks, and the whole ship is going to go up. You need to start evacuating. You have very little time."

He had started shouting before I had finished. Now there was absolute chaos on the upper deck, and his men were divided among the short-termers who didn't want to be vaporized in a fireball and the long-termers who didn't want to be in Hans Fischer's bad books if he managed to survive the explosion. I figured there would be a steady osmosis from camp B into camp A.

Fischer himself was a cool customer, and what he would do now would be to take his two or three most loyal lieutenants and come storming up to his office to collect essential papers and drives before fleeing the sinking yacht.

Right on cue, there was a dull thud that shook the ship.

Through the earpiece, I heard a storm of shouts and screams. I rose off his desk and went to lean on the far wall, about six feet from the door. It took them all of three minutes to get there. The door burst open, and Fischer strode in, making for his desk, followed by three guys with rifles.

Four is difficult. Three can be done if you stay cool and go for the outside guys first. The guy in the middle is going to find it hard to turn with dead guys falling either side of him. I shot the guy on his right in the head, shifted a couple of inches and took the guy on the left through the heart. The guy in the middle took two in the chest as he was struggling to turn, and I was left with the gun trained on Fischer, who was standing with his back to me, frozen. That was when the other cells blew. There was a massive rumble and a blast that split the glass in the windows and sent flames licking out across the water.

He steadied himself on the desk and turned to stare at me with savage eyes. "Who *the hell* are you? Why aren't you *dead?*"

I shrugged. "I don't know, Fischer. Maybe I am. Now I'll

tell you what I am going to do. I am going to shoot you in the knees and the elbows and leave you either to burn to death or drown, depending on how the gods feel about you. Then I am going to take whatever I can grab and hope for the best when I hand it over to the Feds. Or you can help me to collect relevant information, I take you ashore with me, and you explain to me in detail, crossing the Ts and dotting the Is, exactly why you killed my wife and everybody else who was involved."

The boat was making ugly noises, and the abundant fiberglass that made up much of the structure was beginning to burn with a furious heat. I could see in his face that he was beginning to panic. He was flushed, and his neck became corded. The billowing flames outside reflected off the water and off his face.

"We have to get off!"

"I'm not stopping you. I'm trying to help you."

Then another voice spoke. "Quit stalling, Fischer. You're out of options." The voice was a woman's. He stared hard at the door and hissed, "You?"

Caroline was there holding a gun and pointing it at his chest. "Get your shit and make it fast. This boat is going to collide with the *Dama de Blanco* in about two minutes if it doesn't explode first."

I screwed up my brow. "That was you? Starting the engines?"

She glanced at me. "It didn't seem much use blowing this ship and leaving the other two. I thought we may as well take out two of the three."

Fischer was scrabbling in his desk. He grabbed two attaché cases, opened one of them, and threw in handfuls of junk from the drawers. It was beginning to get hot, and the boat was creaking and groaning badly. He got on his knees and opened a safe with fumbling fingers. He pulled out handfuls of junk and a heavy sports bag. He closed the open attaché case and made for the door. Caroline stepped in front of him.

"On a ship like this, Mr. Fischer, you have your own emergency launch. That's the one we are taking."

"I should kill you here and now!"

"Not a good idea. I go first, you tell me the way, and if you do anything stupid, my friend Rogue here breaks your neck. I've seen him do it. He's good at it."

There was a lot of smoke, but fortunately our route took us along the decks and down external stairs, so we avoided most of it, but the stern and center of the yacht were engulfed in huge flames, billowing black smoke up into the sky. And ahead of us, the *Dama de Blanco* was looming fast. I could make out frantic activity aboard with people swarming on the decks and leaping into the water.

On the forward deck of the *Eden Dawn*, Fischer heaved open a hatch, and Caroline went down the steps ahead of him. He followed, and I went after him, keeping close in case he was moved by last-minute desperation. We came very quickly to an enclosed docking bay with a power launch in it. Caroline turned to him and snapped, "You in the front passenger seat. Are there remote controls for the hatch in the launch?"

"Yes, of course."

He said it as he scrambled in. Caroline got behind the yoke, and I jumped in back. I leaned forward and spoke to him. "The Glock is loaded and cocked and pointed right at your spine. Stay cool and maybe we can all get out of this alive."

The bay door creaked open, and the bay flooded with flame-flecked water. Next thing we surged out into the burning waves and described a wide, speeding arc spraying foam high into the night around the burning yacht. Fifteen seconds later, the bows of the *Eden Dawn* plowed into the starboard side of the *Dama de Blanco*, caving it in, ripping through the decks and the cabins and tearing open her fuel tanks. A couple of seconds after that, the fuel ignited, and a huge explosion ripped the night apart, sending a vast, churning fireball up into the sky, showering orange light and burning debris down on the black waters.

Caroline did whatever the marine equivalent of burning rubber is for about eight or ten miles until we reached the northernmost tip of the islands, off Fort St. Catherine. Nowhere is really remote on Bermuda, it's too small, but this was about as remote as it gets. Caroline killed the engine. There was a moment of rocking and sloshing as our backwash caught up with us, and then we settled into a drift.

I sat back, feeling the cold sea air on my face with the Glock leveled at Fischer's back, and observed Caroline with interest.

She had her hands on the wheel and seemed to think for a moment, biting her lip.

"This has been a strange couple of days for me. I have had to do a lot of growing up, very fast. My whole life has been turned upside-down in just a few hours. If the cops associate me with this, what has happened here tonight, I have no idea what conclusion they'll come to or what will happen to me. The fact is I could go to prison for the rest of my life."

Fischer started to talk. "You, neither of you, have the faintest idea of the trouble you are in—"

"Shut up, Fischer." It was Caroline. "Aside from the fact that I am *telling you* the trouble I'm in, the unarmed guy sitting in a boat by a shark-infested reef with two armed people who don't like him very much is you. So the guy who is in real trouble, right here and right now, is you."

I smiled. "I think she's right, Hans. I think she is trying to tell you something."

She nodded. "Right. Here's the deal. I have a couple of numbered accounts here and there around the world which I use for various transactions. Now what we are going to do is this: You, with your laptop which you have sitting at your feet in that attaché case, are going to make two significant transfers, one for me and one for Mr. Rogue. After that, you will surrender your two attaché cases and that big, fat bag to Mr. Rogue. And if you do that nicely, we won't cut you into pieces and *feed you to the goddamn sharks!*"

To say I was surprised would be to understate it. I had known from the start that there was more to Caroline than met the eye, but this was a revelation. I waited to see Fischer's response. All he did was stare at the sea, shake his head, and hug his attaché case.

"You can't do this. I will hunt you down wherever you go—"

I leaned forward and placed the muzzle of the weapon against the back of his neck.

"You're not strengthening the case for leaving you alive, Fischer. I want to talk to you. I want information you have and I need. Those are reasons to keep you alive. But my friend Caroline, she is really mad at you—"

She burst in, and her voice was becoming shrill. "He wanted to cut bits off me to make you talk! *Cut bits off me!*"

"And if it was up to her, she'd just throw you overboard right now." I turned to her. "Could you hack in to his account? Maybe make the transfers yourself?"

"Maybe. Not here, but at my office I might."

"OK, wait! Wait! Wait!" He held up both hands. "How much? How much do you want?"

I watched her. She glanced at me and saw I wasn't going to say anything. So she said, "One hundred million pounds sterling." She glanced at me. "Fifty million each."

He almost shrieked, "*Are you out of your mind?*"

She raised her weapon and placed it an inch from his head. "I fire on three, two—"

"*Wait!*" He scrabbled at the attaché case. "For Christ's sake! You are out of your mind! You are not thinking about the consequences! You can't do this! *You can't do this!*"

"Say that one more time, Hans Fischer, and I will put a bullet through your knee. Set up the payments. I'll type in the account numbers. And then we'll take it from there."

He was typing frantically. "You'll kill me!"

"Not if I don't have to. Rogue needs you alive. But you can be damned sure if you keep stalling, I will blow your damned head off!"

He kept rattling with the occasional whimper, then handed her the laptop. She read the screen, took a photograph of it with her cell phone, and said, "I press send?"

He stared at her for a long moment, then nodded. "Yes."

She pressed send, threw back her head, and laughed like

a crazy woman. When she was done, she said, "Hand him all your stuff."

He shook his head. "No."

She looked him level in the eye. "Do you know what will happen to your leg if I put two 9mm rounds through your knee at point blank range? Do you know what will happen to you if I do that and then get this beast to throw you overboard? You need to rethink your decision in—" She placed the muzzle on his knee and said, "three, two—"

He let out a horrible, inarticulate scream and threw the laptop at me, then the second attaché case and the bag. He was weeping as he did it. She said, "Stand up, Hans."

"Don't kill me. Please, I can do a lot more for you. A hundred million more. You will live like a queen. Please—"

"I am not going to kill you. Stand up or you'll never stand again, you son of a bitch."

I said, "What are you doing?"

He stood, with his hands raised. "I said, "I need to talk to this guy, Caroline."

It was like I wasn't there. She was staring into his face. "You were going to destroy *me*, bit by *bit*? You were going to take *me* apart to make this man talk?"

She put a round through his right shoulder. His face creased in pain, and his mouth sagged open. I shouted "*No!*"

But she put another round through his left shoulder, screaming at him, "*You were going to cut me to pieces? You son of a bitch. You were going to chop me up?*" And as she screamed, she put a round through his belly, another through his thigh, and another through his chest as he fell over backward into the sea. Then she stood and emptied the magazine into the black water.

I stood, wondering if she was going to try and kill me now. But she just stood frozen. I stepped over the seat into the front section, put my arms around her, and took the gun from her hand. After a while, I sat her down where Hans Fischer had been sitting a while earlier. She curled in on herself, covered her face, and started to weep and convulse. I started the launch and took it toward the northeast coast of the island and Drew's Bay.

TWENTY-SIX

We sat for a long time on the sand, letting the dark water lap at our feet and the sea breeze cool us and ease away some of the stress. After a while, she leaned against me. I put my arm around her, and we watched the launch drift slowly out into the black ocean. I had wiped off all our prints and any trace of our having been in it, then shoved it out for the Canary Currents to take it away into the Sargasso Sea.

Eventually I turned to her and took hold of her face in my hands.

"Caroline, I need you to listen to me and believe me. We are going to pull through this. We are going to get out of this hole and prosper. You are in shock right now, but what you have done tonight took real courage and strength, and intelligence. But we are not out of the woods yet. We still need to make one last effort. We need to get back to my hotel, have dinner, get up for breakfast, and convince everyone that we were together in my apartment all last night. Are you ready?"

She nodded. "How?"

It was a good question. We were five or six miles' walk from the hotel. Getting a taxi would not be easy, and the driver would be sure to remember us. I thought a moment.

"This is what we are going to do, but I need you to engage. When we are alone, you can crack up and let it all out, but till then I need you to keep it together. OK?"

She nodded. "I won't let you down."

"Good. When we stopped by Fort St. Catherine, I noticed there was a kind of holiday resort beside the fort."

"The St. Regis."

"OK, so we are going to go there, to the hotel, and we are going to call a taxi to take us to the airport. We are going to carry an attaché each, and I'll carry the bag, like we were guests and now we are leaving."

She frowned. "To the airport?"

I nodded once. "At the airport, we will call another taxi to take us to my hotel. If anybody ever asks them, those drivers will never connect us with the yachts that burned and sank off the Naval Dockyards."

She kept frowning but said, "One will think we were leaving, the other will think we'd just arrived."

"Right."

"And at your hotel?"

"We'll cross that bridge when we get to it, but the paths to the cabins are barely lit. I doubt anyone will see us. For now, let's just get to the hotel."

I stood and held out my hand. She took it.

It took no more than an hour to get to my cabin, though it felt like a long, weary exhausting odyssey. Caroline started to strip as I closed the door. She made her way to the bathroom, dropping bits of clothing as she went. I looked at the time and saw it was just after ten p.m. I picked up the phone and called room service. When the receptionist answered, I told him, "Listen, I think my guest ordered a meal for our room about an hour ago, but we are still waiting."

He sounded scandalized. "My goodness! I am so sorry! I have been here for the last four hours. Do you know who she spoke to?"

I called out, "Darling, who did you speak to in room service?" I paused like I was listening, though all I heard was the slosh of water and Caroline's weary, "*What?*"

I waited a moment longer and said, "No, it's me who should apologize. We have been so involved, she went to have a bath and forgot to call. Is it too late?"

"Oh, I quite understand, Mr. Connors. It's not too late at all. What would you like?"

"Give me two dozen oysters and a very cold bottle of Krug. Then we'll have two flame grilled sirloin and a bottle of *Muga Reserva*."

"Of course, coming right up. Shall we do the oysters first, and you give us a call when you are ready for the steaks?"

"Sounds like a plan."

I leaned in the bathroom door and was struck, seeing her lying in the bath with her eyes closed, by how attractive she was. When she opened her eyes, I said, "We have two dozen oysters and a bottle of champagne on their way. I'm going to set the table on the terrace. I want you out of that bath and earning yourself the Oscar for best actress in ten minutes."

Her expression didn't change, but she nodded. I went to set the table.

She came out as I was lighting the candle, in a giant bathrobe with a towel wrapped around her head like a turban.

"I had nothing to put on. I couldn't put on what I was wearing. I tried, but I couldn't."

"You look beautiful, relaxed, at ease."

Her smile was ironic, with a bitter twist, like an especially sophisticated cocktail.

"Are you being kind or just dishonest?"

I was saved from having to answer by an electric golf cart that rolled up with two waiters in it. They set out the silver dish with the oysters, popped the champagne cork, and poured it into two very frosted glasses.

Caroline smiled and clapped, and as they were gathering to leave, she told one of the waiters, "I have been here all my life and never visited this hotel. But I have spent the most wonderful day and night here. It is so *peaceful!*"

They bowed and smiled and said they did their best. I slipped them a hundred bucks and figured we probably had that base covered.

She sat. I sat opposite, and we raised our glasses. For a moment, we were silent. Then I said, "To new beginnings."

She nodded. "Yes, to that."

We worked our way through the oysters in relative silence. I refilled her glass twice, and as she put down the last shell and picked up her champagne, she spoke, looking out at the sea.

"You wanted very badly for Hans to tell you who you were. I am sorry."

I gave a small shrug. "I guess, when all is said and done, I am I. When the end comes, the body decays, our personality decays with it, perhaps even our mind and soul. What is left, in the end? I. I am."

"That doesn't seem to be enough."

"I'll never know. I think Mendoza and Fischer were the last people left who might actually have known who I was."

She frowned. "You talked about a wife, Susan Hanson, and a photograph."

"Yeah." I gazed at her a moment, thinking, then out at the ocean where the moon's light seemed to rain soft from the midheaven. "I seemed to remember the house. I had memories of her. She had a photograph of us on her desk." I spread my hands. "But Mendoza was so adamant I could not be Ted Hanson. She said it was impossible. I don't know. I don't remember. And in any case—" I reached over and emptied the bottle into our glasses. "In the end, you stop trusting your memory. Remembering is a creative process, isn't it?"

She frowned. "It is?"

"Sure. It's not like your memories are filed away in an album somewhere in your brain. Your brain recreates those images and sounds and smells, tastes, feelings, every time you remember. Who knows in the end what is real and what is imagined?"

She said softly, "They robbed you of your memories, and they robbed you of who you are."

I gave my head a twitch. "Or did they reveal who I really was?"

She studied me for a long time, like she was thinking about what I'd said. When she spoke, her voice was almost a whisper. "You are brutal, bestial, and ruthless. But somehow there is a humanity to you, even compassion. I don't understand it."

I picked up the phone and told them we were ready for the meat and the red wine. When I'd hung up, I stood and went to lean on one of the wooden columns by the steps down from the veranda to the path that now seemed to lead a luminous way to the sea.

"I guess there is a ruthlessness in all of us, Caroline. We are driven by the need to survive." I paused, not looking at her, then, "You, faced this evening with the sudden and total collapse of your life, played a very clever and subtle game with Hans Fischer."

I turned to face her, leaning my back against the column and folding my arms over my chest.

"I don't mind telling you I was very impressed. In some bizarre way, it was quite a turn-on. You took a situation that was totally out of control, you made use of the primary source of the chaos—the destruction I had caused and the threat I posed—and you used it to make yourself a very, very rich woman."

"I made us both very rich people."

"Not yet. As of right now, that money is all in your possession. But what I am talking about is that most of us don't actually know who we are until we look into the maw of oblivion." I gestured at her. "Did you know you had it in you to do what you did in the face of such danger?"

She thought about it. "No, I didn't." She took a deep breath, avoiding my eyes. "It just welled up inside me. It was almost as though it was somebody else, somebody I don't even recognize, working through me."

"Are you going to keep the money?"

Now she met my eye. She looked surprised. "Of course. I mean—" She frowned and gave her head a quick shake. "I don't know what you mean."

"The full hundred million, are you going to hang on to it?"

"I said it was fifty-fifty. I am not dishonest, Rogue. Do you want me to make the transfer now?"

I smiled on the ironic side of my face. "Sure, why not? Then I can really enjoy the steak and the *Muga*, and we can have another bottle of champagne to celebrate."

She looked wounded. I went and got the attaché case with the laptop in it and placed it on the table in front of her.

"I have a reason," I told her. "I have no identity, so I have no bank account, no passport, no driver's license—at least that I know of. But if you set me up with a numbered account in Belize, for example, or Panama, you can get me a credit card and some kind of identity, right?"

"Not exactly, but partly, kind of."

"So you would be doing me a real big favor."

She gave a smile that was on the sad side of happy and nodded. She typed for a while and said, "I have requested your documents and credit cards to be Fedexed to the hotel. They'll arrive tomorrow. Meanwhile, I can email you your account details so you have a record."

"Sounds good."

When she'd finished, she sighed and closed the attaché case.

"What must it be like being married to you?"

"I have no idea."

"You must be impossible to live with."

"I find it quite easy."

"Will we sleep together tonight?"

"I hope so."

"I need..." She trailed off. "I can't be alone, not tonight."

I said quietly, "I don't want you to be."

The golf card rattled to a stop, and the same two waiters delivered the steaks, sautéed vegetables, and potatoes. They poured the wine and told us to enjoy. Their buggy whined into the darkness along the winding path, and I cut into my steak.

"What will you do?" I asked her, leaning back in my chair as I chewed.

"I don't know," she said. "I'm not well. I'm confused. I need help, Rogue."

"I can recommend a therapist. She helped me."

Her eyes searched my face a moment, and she said, "Yeah," but it didn't really mean anything. Then she asked, "What will *you* do? What are your plans?"

I shrugged and cut into the steak again. "I guess I'll keep doing what I'm doing. Searching for myself, trying to find out who I am, and doing what I do."

"What?" she asked her steak. "What do you do?"

I gave a small shrug. "Leave the world a slightly better place than I found it."

She gave a shrill laugh. "By killing all the bad guys? A one-man slaughterhouse on wheels!"

She laughed out loud for a moment with her fingers over her mouth, but within seconds, the laughter had collapsed into sobbing.

"I'm sorry." She said it two or three times. "I'm sorry, I'm sorry..."

Slowly she steadied her breathing and started drying her eyes with her napkin. "I'm sorry," she said again.

"You don't need to apologize, Caroline. You've been through hell, and you're coping surprisingly well. By tomorrow, this will be all over, and we can start to rebuild our lives, largely thanks to your foresight and quick thinking. You don't need to apologize. Believe me."

"Thank you. You are so strangely kind." I smiled, and she gave another laugh. "Rogue, can we go to bed now? I need to lie in the dark and hold you and believe everything is going to be all right. Can we do that, please?"

"Of course." I stood and took her hand. We switched off all the lights and moved into the bedroom. There she removed her turban and shook out her hair, then let her robe drop to the floor. Her pale skin seemed luminous in the moonlight that insinuated in from the open terrace doors.

She sat on the bed with one leg bent under her. "Do you mind if we don't...if you just hold me? I need to feel safe. Is that very selfish of me?"

"No."

I pulled off my boots and my jacket, and she lay back, reaching up for me. I lay next to her and held her. She ran her fingers through my hair and stroked my face and whispered in my ear, "You are so strong, like a man of iron. I feel so frightened and weak. I need to feel you, feel your strength. Hold me, Rogue. Hold me tight to you. Squeeze me."

I knew it was coming. I had known it was coming from the beginning, when I had asked her to join me at dinner. It had never been a question of if. It had only ever been a question of when. She had my right arm trapped under her body and both her arms around my neck. I waited till I felt her hand slip under the pillow, then heaved myself up, landed with my elbow on her forearm, and seized her throat with my left hand. Another shift, and I had my knee on her arm and she was struggling for breath. I flipped on the bedside lamp and tossed the pillow on the floor. There was the stiletto Mendoza had had in her belt and which Caroline had pulled out of the guard's neck when we'd left the cabin.

"You killed Mendoza, you killed Fischer, and you killed Guzman, not to mention a hundred people who went down on the two yachts. And you call me a one-man slaughterhouse. And now you want to kill me. Who the hell do you work for? The IRS?"

Her face flushed, and her neck was corded as she struggled to get her arm out from under my knee. "*I will never tell you! Never!*"

"Why? You're done, Caroline! It's over! From here you go to jail! Who do you work for? Who the hell wanted *all* of us dead?"

She relaxed suddenly and smiled at me. "All right, Rogue. I'll tell you. Hans Fischer hired me to kill you."

"But then why—"

"And somebody at Central Intelligence whom you have probably seen being interviewed on TV more than a dozen times contracted me to kill Mendoza, who had become a liability, *and* Hans Fischer, who had also become a liability after you showed up and killed Vogel. You see, you go around making the most awful mess wherever you go. This should have been three simple, discreet deaths. But you come along with your lithium-ion batteries and exploding gas tanks. What could I do? I had to ride the tsunami."

I picked up the stiletto. "Do you know who ordered Susan Hanson's death?"

"Yes."

"Was it the CIA?"

"No."

She moved her right hand, and suddenly there was a small Smith and Wesson in it pointing right at my belly. "The man who briefs me is *way* above the CIA," she said and pulled the trigger.

TWENTY-SEVEN

It didn't kill me because I knew it was coming. It didn't kill her because she was using a small .22 and I couldn't get a good grip on the barrel. As she uttered the words "...*way* above the CIA," I twisted my body to the left and slammed my left hand down onto the minute barrel of the gun. It discharged into the mattress and scorched my thumb. Automatically, I backhanded her and sent her tumbling off the bed. She struggled to her feet, staggered back, dizzy, and fell across the armchair and lamp table, sending them crashing to the floor. I was off the bed and going after her.

She screamed, "*Leave me alone!*" but I gripped her arm and dragged her to her feet. I shook her hard and shouted into her face, "*Who do you work for? Who is way above the CIA? Answer me!*"

Her answer was to grit her teeth, claw at my face with both hands, and ram her knee where no man should ever have a knee rammed. I managed to deflect the blow, but the pain in my face was excruciating. I tried to fight off her hands as she went for my eyes. She wriggled free of my grip and ran.

I turned and went after her, but she surprised me again by stopping, spinning to face me, and delivering a powerful roundhouse kick to my thigh. Three inches lower and it would have broken my knee. She didn't pause. Her naked body glowing surreally in the moonlight, she cocked her hip and delivered an exquisite roundhouse with the same leg and smashed her instep into the side of my head. If I had not reacted instinctively by leaning away and raising both arms, she would have killed me. As it was, she stunned me, and I staggered back. By the time the room had stopped spinning and rocking, she was a faint, luminous figure running among the trees toward the beach. Again I went after her.

She was running with difficulty, with her bare feet on the dirt track that wound among the dense trees and the cottages. Though the small stones and grit hurt my feet too, I managed to ignore the pain and began closing on her.

Suddenly she darted to the left and went in among a clump of palm trees. I went after her, keeping her pale, glowing body in sight, aware that she could ambush me at any moment from behind a tree and finish me.

She darted down the narrow track, her golden hair dancing out behind her. She was now just fifteen or twenty feet ahead of me, and the ground was turning to soft sand, making it harder to run.

We came out of the trees into a sandy cove with low rock cliffs on either side. She seemed to stumble, almost went down on her knees, and I closed the gap to just seven or eight feet. Then she exploded to her feet and hurled two handfuls of sand in my face, lunged at me and kicked me twice in the thigh, where she had kicked me before. I was really close to death right then. The next blow or two could kill me, and I knew it. With searing pain in my eyes, half blind, I lashed out at her with three kicks that, if they had caught her, would have finished the fight and the chase. She must have seen that because she turned and ran for the sea.

I went after her, not so much now to catch her as to wipe the agonizing grains from my eyes. And she knew that. She was cunning, smart, cold, and calculating, and very, very dangerous. I was trapped and had no options but to plunge in the water and for long seconds render myself totally blind, vulnerable, and defenseless while I splashed water in my eyes to wash away the sand that was tearing at my eyeballs.

I heard her coming, running, plowing through the water as the waves sighed and thudded around us under the moon. I heard her coming but I could see nothing until I raised my head, with the saltwater blurring my vision, and saw the long, evil blade of the stiletto glinting in her hand, just a few inches from my belly.

I felt the blade pierce my side as I gripped her wrist with my right hand and forced it back. With my left hand, I grabbed her hair and plunged her under the water. She wriggled and thrashed and kicked, and I knew that with that kind of exertion, and her heart racing, she could last only seconds without breathing. I pulled her up, and she gasped and dragged in air. I growled in her ear, "Who do you work for? Who is way above the CIA?"

Before she could answer, I plunged her under again and held her until her thrashing and kicking screamed of panic, then pulled her up again. She erupted from the water gasping, half screaming, and I snarled at her, "Who do you work for? Who is above the CIA? Who killed Susan and the kids?"

She had dropped the stiletto and clawed at my arm with both hands, "*Wait! Wait! Wait!*"

"*Talk!*"

"*Don't kill me!*"

"*Talk!*"

"*Kristos!*"

"*What?*"

"*Christopher—*"

There was a strange spitting noise, like a piece of fat dropping on a hot griddle, an almost inaudible zip, and the ocean side of her head exploded in a shower of dark gore which sprayed across the small, dark waves. I stared into her dead eyes, which stared back at me, seeing nothing. It was a fraction of a second, but it lasted an eternity before I plunged below the surface, leaving her body to float grotesquely above me.

High velocity rounds smacked the water over my head. But high velocity rounds will not penetrate water more than an inch or two. They disintegrate on contact. So I swam down to the bottom and, with my lungs screaming for air, I made for the rocks.

When I got there and quietly pulled myself out of the sea, I could just make out the fang shaped fins of the sharks circling and devouring Caroline's body. I lay flat and peered at the beach. There was no one there. At least, there was no one visible.

I took another five minutes to crawl back to the beach, making sure I made no silhouette against the moonlit sky. Once there, I lay immobile for another five minutes scanning the dark undergrowth for movement. There was nothing, so I made a sprint for the darkened, winding paths and made it back to my cabin at a run.

It was as I arrived at the steps to the veranda that I saw the light in the living room was on. When I had gone after Caroline it had been off. A sudden weariness came over me, an exhaustion born of fighting, struggling, killing and seeing nothing but death. Susan had been all about life, about love and righteousness. And what I was doing in her name was all about death. Yet no matter how many of them I killed, it changed nothing. She was dead. Gone. Extinguished.

She had ceased to exist.

And I climbed the wooden steps to the veranda, ready to take whatever was coming, and die.

I recognized him, his platinum hair and his pale blue eyes, the easy smile that just managed to avoid being a smirk. He had a rifle with a scope lying on the floor beside him and a Sig Sauer P365 held loosely in his lap. In his left hand, he had a glass of whiskey.

"You've come a long way for a political survey."

He didn't smile. He just observed me a moment and said, "Not many men can say that the North Atlantic has saved their lives. If I had shot with the Sig, I might have hit you. Low velocity to shoot into water, right?"

"I'm right here and I'm unarmed. What do you plan to do, bore me to death?"

Now he smiled and raised his glass. "I helped myself. I don't plan to kill you."

I frowned. "Why not?"

"I just got a call. You killed my employer. I won't get

paid. I don't get paid I don't work. That's fair enough, isn't it?"

"I'm not complaining." I trailed water to the kitchen and poured myself a shot. As I sipped, I said, "So what are you doing here?"

"To be honest, I was curious. You are not the only person going crazy trying to find out who you are. How much research have you done?"

"Not much." I moved over and sat opposite him. "I've been kind of busy."

"Yes." He sipped. As he lowered the glass, he frowned at it a moment. "I am one of the best, one of the highest paid assassins on the market. My victims' deaths don't get investigated by the police—"

"Were you the fifth gunman when my wife and kids were killed?"

He paused. "No. As I was trying to tell you, my victims' deaths do not attract official attention. They are accidents, suicides, even illness. Or the body is never found."

"Why are you telling me this?"

"I have killed a lot of people. But you..." He gestured at me and snorted a short laugh. "You are the Reaper! How many people did you kill tonight?"

"I had some help."

"Caroline Gordon. Kristos will be sorry to have lost her. She was an artist. Really very good."

"Kristos?"

"She was going to tell you. I had to kill her."

"Who is he? Did he order the assassination of my wife and children?"

He sat and watched me for a long while with the hint of

a smile playing at the corner of his mouth. Finally he said, "No. Rogue, Kristos does not exist. He is like you, a ghost. Like you, he can do what he likes, kill whom he pleases, take what he likes, because he does not exist. If they search for him in their databanks, they will not find him. Like you, because you are both dead."

He drained his glass and stood. "I am glad I did not have to kill you. Kristos wants you alive. You have strong protection, Rogue. For now."

He walked out, and after a moment, he had vanished into the dark.

I took my whiskey out to the terrace and sat on the steps looking out at the beauty of the moon reflected on the ocean. Underneath that beauty, what little was left of Caroline Gordon was being devoured by the fish. A mile or two out, Hans Fischer, Oscar Guzman, and Carmen Mendoza were drifting, dead and bloated on the ocean floor, among their crews and men, and the girls who had just wanted to have fun.

Carmen Mendoza. Had she told the truth? Had she truly tried to save me? Or had it just been an attempt to find out who I was? What it came down to in the end was, which one of her lies was the real lie, and which had traces of truth? She had seemed so sure, so emphatic, that I was not Ted Hanson. More lies? I had seen the photo on the desk.

But so had she.

When the sun eventually stained the eastern horizon with blue-gray, I was still sitting on the step with my third glass of whiskey. A little ways up the path, I could see one of the guys from reception in his golf cart heading my way. On the seat beside him was a large manilla envelope.

TWENTY-EIGHT

I RETURNED THE WAY I HAD COME, IN A HIRED Gulfstream from LF Wade International to Teterboro in New Jersey. I hadn't called Jane because I didn't feel able to talk, but I sent her a message telling her I was on my way. It was a short flight, a little over an hour, and as when I had left, all my baggage was hand baggage.

It was a pleasant surprise as I came through arrivals to see her standing waiting for me. She wasn't in her blue business suit. She was in Levis and a Snoopy sweatshirt, and she was smiling. The sight of her made me feel strange, but I decided it was strange in a good way.

She watched me approach and when I dropped my bag and the attaché case beside her she put her arms around me and gave me a hug, which I found myself returning.

When she let go, she said, "Have you been keeping up with the news?"

I shook my head. "Not really. Just chillin' on the beach. You know how it is."

"Two yachts collided off Bermuda, no more than a mile from your hotel. I'm surprised you didn't see it. Apparently they both burst into flames."

"Huh!" I gave my head another shake. "I guess I must have been on the other side of the island at the time."

"Go figure. My car is outside." I followed her out. As she pressed the fob and the lights bleeped, she said, "One of the yachts belonged to Hans Fischer, the other belonged to Oscar Guzman." She leaned on the roof and looked at me as I opened the door. "So far no survivors have been found, but Guzman and Fischer are confirmed dead."

I gave my head a little twitch. "It'll be a busy day in hell."

I dumped my stuff on the back seat, and we pulled out onto Industrial Avenue. We drove in silence for a moment, then I pointed at the back seat with my thumb.

"I need to see Director Levi. What I have back there is two of Hans Fischer's laptops, several flash drives, a stash of documents I haven't looked at yet, and two million bucks in cash which I am going to keep as the spoils of war. The rest of it is for him." I studied her profile for a moment. There was no reaction except that her cheeks had colored slightly. I went on, "I don't remember anything about him, but I do remember that I trust him, and I trust you."

Again there was no reaction.

"I'm going to tell you everything that happened, and I want to tell Levi too. When you know, then you can take whatever action you think is right."

Now she turned and looked at me, but she didn't say anything.

I told her everything that happened from the moment of my arrival until the Arian assassin left.

I paused as we crossed the Hudson and began to move south down Broadway.

"I don't know if Mendoza was on the level or not. I'm not sure even she knew anymore. The fact that Caroline Gordon killed her makes me think she might have been. We'll probably never know. But she was adamant that I could not be Ted Hanson."

She didn't say anything.

"Jane, we were friends, we worked together, you knew Susan. I'm asking you please, as a friend, am I Ted Hanson?"

She took a deep breath and pointed to the glove compartment.

"Open that. There's a manilla envelope in there. I want you to open it and read it, but before you do, let me tell you something. Special Agents Cathy Newton and Elroy Jones did some digging and managed to swing a meeting with Director Levi. He has asked me to tell you in broad terms what went down."

"Why can't he tell me?"

"I'll come to that. When Jones ran your DNA and your prints in LA, he drew a blank."

"I know that."

"He drew a blank not because you weren't in the system but because the file relating to those prints and that DNA is sealed and classified."

"*What?* Why?"

She sighed. "I don't know, Rogue. It's sealed and classified."

"That doesn't make any sense!"

"Does any of it?" I couldn't answer, so she went on. "So I had a meeting with them and I told them to butt out, drop the two-man crusade and go back to work. They didn't. What they did was what you should have done from the beginning, which was dig out Susan Hanson's marriage certificate. It is the most logical starting place for your research, right? Agent Newton seems to have a soft spot for you. She brought that envelope and asked me to give it to you. I looked at what's inside."

I had a hot, nauseous burn in my belly. I pulled out several sheets of paper that had been clipped together. One was a marriage certificate between Susan Hanson and Terrence Hanson. The other was Terrence Hanson's death certificate, dated 2017.

Agent Newton's note told me Susan Hanson had never remarried.

"I am not Ted Hanson."

"No."

"You knew."

"Yes."

"You could have told me. You should have told me."

"No." She looked at me as we cruised slowly down Broadway. "I couldn't tell you. I told you, you had to remember for yourself."

"And this?" I held up the documents.

"That is not from me. That's from Agent Newton."

"Sweet Jesus, this is *stupid!* Just tell me who I am, goddammit!"

Her face flushed and she stabbed a finger at me. "This! This is why! This is why you have to come to it yourself! Because you will not be told! You are *always* right! When you *know* something, that is the holy *truth!* And there are no two ways about it. But sometimes you are *wrong*, Rogue. W-

R-O-N-G *wrong!* You are *not* Ted Hanson, and *you were not married to Susan Hanson!*"

I sat staring at her in silence. Suddenly she erupted again, stabbing her whole arm forward with her hand like a blade. "You obsess about things! You get tunnel vision! You can only see what you want to see. You don't see what's going on around you. And all you could see was..." She stabbed her hand forward again, three times, "Susan, Susan, Susan! You became obsessed with her."

We pulled in to West 81st Street and she stopped outside Susan Hanson's house. I sat staring at it, trying to absorb the fact that it was not my house, not my home, and never had been.

"You should have told me."

"I couldn't. It wasn't my place, and besides, would you have believed me?"

I stared at her. "No."

"You need to collect your stuff. Levi wants to meet with you in a couple of days. Meantime you can stay at"—she hesitated a moment—"at my place in the Bronx."

I said automatically, "Forty-two Haight Avenue."

"Yeah, that place."

She handed me the key. I climbed out of the car and went to cross the sidewalk toward the door, and a man I hadn't seen collided with me. I stepped back, apologizing, but he was looking at me and smiling. He was small and had on a shabby old coat and a worn off-the-peg suit. His pale eyes were like two lasers piercing my mind.

"Oh," he said, "We meet again." I frowned and he laughed. "We were at the Gates of Hell." He pointed at me. "You noticed me and I noticed you. You stayed but I left."

More quietly he said, "Shame about Hans. A hard man to replace." Then he held out his hand. "Christopher." I took it without thinking. He said, "Your name?" with a strange, knowing smile.

"I don't know."

"Well." He was still smiling and shrugged. "What's in a name? A Rogue by any other name would be as wild. No doubt we'll meet again."

He hurried down the road and at the corner a silver Rolls Royce pulled up. He opened the rear door himself and climbed in, and the car took off.

I stood staring, and after a moment I noticed Jane by my side. "Are you OK?"

I shook my head. "No."

She sighed. "Come on, let's get your stuff, and I'll take you home. Then we'll go and see Director Levi tomorrow or the day after."

"Jane, does the name Kristos mean anything to you?"

"No." She gave her head a shake. "Why?"

"It's come up a couple of times. Jane, will you stay over? I mean, you know, in your own bed like, but, kind of, be there?"

She smiled on one side of her face, and the look in her eyes confused me. "You don't want to sleep with me? Is that it? I repulse you now?"

"No! No..."

She laughed. "Sure, we'll hang out and talk and get drunk. But I will *not* tell you who you are!"

Don't miss ICE BURN. The riveting sequel in the Rogue Thriller series.

Scan the QR code below to purchase ICE BURN.
Or go to: righthouse.com/ice-burn

DON'T MISS ANYTHING!

If you want to stay up to date on all new releases in this series, with these authors, or with any of our new deals, you can do so by joining our newsletters below.

In addition, you will immediately gain access to our entire *Right House VIP Library,* which currently includes *SIX* riveting mysteries and thrillers.

righthouse.com/email

(Easy to unsubscribe. No spam. Ever.)

ALSO BY DAVID ARCHER

Up to date books can be found at:
www.righthouse.com/david-archer

ROGUE THRILLERS
Gates of Hell (Book 1)
Hell's Fury (Book 2)
Ice Burn (Book 3)

PETER BLACK THRILLERS
Burden of the Assassin (Book 1)
The Man Without A Face (Book 2)
Unpunished Deeds (Book 3)
Hunter Killer (Book 4)
Silent Shadows (Book 5)
The Last Run (Book 6)
Dark Corners (Book 7)
Ghost Operative (Book 8)
A Fire Burning (Book 9)

ALEX MASON THRILLERS
Odin (Book 1)
Ice Cold Spy (Book 2)

Mason's Law (Book 3)

Assets and Liabilities (Book 4)

Russian Roulette (Book 5)

Executive Order (Book 6)

Dead Man Talking (Book 7)

All The King's Men (Book 8)

Flashpoint (Book 9)

Brotherhood of the Goat (Book 10)

Dead Hot (Book 11)

Blood on Megiddo (Book 12)

Son of Hell (Book 13)

Merchant of Death (Book 14)

NOAH WOLF THRILLERS

Code Name Camelot (Book 1)

Lone Wolf (Book 2)

In Sheep's Clothing (Book 3)

Hit for Hire (Book 4)

The Wolf's Bite (Book 5)

Black Sheep (Book 6)

Balance of Power (Book 7)

Time to Hunt (Book 8)

Red Square (Book 9)

Highest Order (Book 10)

Edge of Anarchy (Book 11)

Unknown Evil (Book 12)

Black Harvest (Book 13)

World Order (Book 14)

Caged Animal (Book 15)

Deep Allegiance (Book 16)

Pack Leader (Book 17)

High Treason (Book 18)

A Wolf Among Men (Book 19)

Rogue Intelligence (Book 20)

Alpha (Book 21)

Rogue Wolf (Book 22)

Shadows of Allegiance (Book 23)

In the Grip of Darkness (Book 24)

Wolves in the Dark Book (Book 25)

SAM PRICHARD MYSTERIES

The Grave Man (Book 1)

Death Sung Softly (Book 2)

Love and War (Book 3)

Framed (Book 4)

The Kill List (Book 5)

Drifter: Part One (Book 6)

Drifter: Part Two (Book 7)

Drifter: Part Three (Book 8)

The Last Song (Book 9)

Ghost (Book 10)

Hidden Agenda (Book 11)

SAM AND INDIE MYSTERIES

Aces and Eights (Book 1)

Fact or Fiction (Book 2)

Close to Home (Book 3)

Brave New World (Book 4)

Innocent Conspiracy (Book 5)

Unfinished Business (Book 6)

Live Bait (Book 7)

Alter Ego (Book 8)

More Than It Seems (Book 9)

Moving On (Book 10)

Worst Nightmare (Book 11)

Chasing Ghosts (Book 12)

Serial Superstition (Book 13)

CHANCE REDDICK THRILLERS

Innocent Injustice (Book 1)

Angel of Justice (Book 2)

High Stakes Hunting (Book 3)

Personal Asset (Book 4)

CASSIE MCGRAW MYSTERIES
What Lies Beneath (Book 1)
Can't Fight Fate (Book 2)
One Last Game (Book 3)
Never Really Gone (Book 4)

ALSO BY BLAKE BANNER

ALSO BY BLAKE BANNER
Up to date books can be found at:
www.righthouse.com/blake-banner

ROGUE THRILLERS
Gates of Hell (Book 1)
Hell's Fury (Book 2)
Ice Burn (Book 3)

ALEX MASON THRILLERS
Odin (Book 1)
Ice Cold Spy (Book 2)
Mason's Law (Book 3)
Assets and Liabilities (Book 4)
Russian Roulette (Book 5)
Executive Order (Book 6)
Dead Man Talking (Book 7)
All The King's Men (Book 8)
Flashpoint (Book 9)
Brotherhood of the Goat (Book 10)
Dead Hot (Book 11)
Blood on Megiddo (Book 12)

Son of Hell (Book 13)

Merchant of Death (Book 14)

HARRY BAUER THRILLER SERIES

Dead of Night (Book 1)

Dying Breath (Book 2)

The Einstaat Brief (Book 3)

Quantum Kill (Book 4)

Immortal Hate (Book 5)

The Silent Blade (Book 6)

LA: Wild Justice (Book 7)

Breath of Hell (Book 8)

Invisible Evil (Book 9)

The Shadow of Ukupacha (Book 10)

Sweet Razor Cut (Book 11)

Blood of the Innocent (Book 12)

Blood on Balthazar (Book 13)

Simple Kill (Book 14)

Riding The Devil (Book 15)

The Unavenged (Book 16)

The Devil's Vengeance (Book 17)

Bloody Retribution (Book 18)

Rogue Kill (Book 19)

Blood for Blood (Book 20)

The Cell (Book 21)

DEAD COLD MYSTERY SERIES

An Ace and a Pair (Book 1)

Two Bare Arms (Book 2)

Garden of the Damned (Book 3)

Let Us Prey (Book 4)

The Sins of the Father (Book 5)

Strange and Sinister Path (Book 6)

The Heart to Kill (Book 7)

Unnatural Murder (Book 8)

Fire from Heaven (Book 9)

To Kill Upon A Kiss (Book 10)

Murder Most Scottish (Book 11)

The Butcher of Whitechapel (Book 12)

Little Dead Riding Hood (Book 13)

Trick or Treat (Book 14)

Blood Into Win (Book 15)

Jack In The Box (Book 16)

The Fall Moon (Book 17)

Blood In Babylon (Book 18)

Death In Dexter (Book 19)

Mustang Sally (Book 20)

A Christmas Killing (Book 21)

Mommy's Little Killer (Book 22)

Bleed Out (Book 23)

Dead and Buried (Book 24)

In Hot Blood (Book 25)

Fallen Angels (Book 26)

Knife Edge (Book 27)

Along Came A Spider (Book 28)

Cold Blood (Book 29)

Curtain Call (Book 30)

THE OMEGA SERIES

Dawn of the Hunter (Book 1)

Double Edged Blade (Book 2)

The Storm (Book 3)

The Hand of War (Book 4)

A Harvest of Blood (Book 5)

To Rule in Hell (Book 6)

Kill: One (Book 7)

Powder Burn (Book 8)

Kill: Two (Book 9)

Unleashed (Book 10)

The Omicron Kill (Book 11)

9mm Justice (Book 12)

Kill: Four (Book 13)

Death In Freedom (Book 14)

Endgame (Book 15)

ABOUT US

Right House is an independent publisher created by authors for readers. We specialize in Action, Thriller, Mystery, and Crime novels.

If you enjoyed this novel, then there is a good chance you will like what else we have to offer! Please stay up to date by using any of the links below.

Join our mailing lists to stay up to date --> righthouse.com/email
Visit our website --> righthouse.com
Contact us --> contact@righthouse.com

facebook.com/righthousebooks
x.com/righthousebooks
instagram.com/righthousebooks

Made in the USA
Middletown, DE
08 January 2025